Tied Together

BALEIGH JAYNE

Playlist

Feather - Sabrina Carpenter
Sway - Kacey Musgraves
The Prophecy - Taylor Swift
Suddenly I See - KT Tunstall
Suite from The Devil Wears Prada - Theodore Shapiro
Paris - Taylor Swift
Jade Green - Kacey Musgraves
Tres Tres Chic - Mocean Worker
Emily in Paris Main Title Theme - James Newton Howard
Mon Soleil - Ashley Park
Begin Again (Taylor's Version) - Taylor Swift
Falling Slowly - Ashley Park, Kevin Dias
The Alchemy - Taylor Swift
You Are in Love (Taylor's Version) - Taylor Swift
Dinner With Friends - Kacey Musgraves
La Vie En Rose - Ashley Park
Glittery - Kacey Musgraves, Troye Sivan
Feels Like - Gracie Abrams
Heaven Is - Kacey Musgraves

For the girls who relate a little too much to "The Prophecy" by Taylor Swift, this one's for you.

Author's Note

Tied Together is a story full of swoony and sweet moments that I hope will tug on your heart strings and allow you to escape the world for a few hours. That being said, there are some topics that might be upsetting for some readers. Don't worry, there is a happy ending, but there are some things along the way that you might want to be aware of.

Some elements of this story might be triggering to some readers, such as: body shaming, comments on eating choices, panic attacks, and parental neglect in childhood and adulthood.

If any of the above are triggering for you, please read with caution. Your mental health comes first.

I hope you love Alex and Alana just as much as I do. Their story is one of kindness, care, and ultimately finding the person that you feel safest with.

With the most love,
Baleigh

Prologue

ALANA

"Are you really planning on eating all of that?"

I pause, my fork suspended in midair, a single piece of fettuccine Alfredo swirled around it and on its way to my mouth. After hesitating, I slowly lower my hand and place my fork back on my plate.

The words snap me out of the trance I had floated into while my boyfriend of three years, Brad, was droning on and on about something a coworker did to *disrespect* him today at work.

He's sitting across the table from me at the intimate Italian restaurant he chose for our anniversary. I've been working overtime these last few months trying to convince myself that I hadn't wasted the last three years of my life on someone, but tonight is proving that my denial is extensive.

Brad is a jerk. He is the kind of guy who makes coffee and leaves the pod in the machine for someone else to clean up. The kind who doesn't say hello in an elevator or when passing someone in the hallway. He's the kind of guy who listens to his phone on full volume in an airport with no headphones. The kind who doesn't use his blinker before he changes lanes.

The kind of guy who asks a woman if she's sure she should eat "all of that", *whatever that means.*

He is a good looking guy, in a traditional sort of way. He's around six feet tall, has blond hair and blue eyes and wears decent clothes. He always smells nice and has good hygiene. That used to be enough, but now I'm realizing that maybe it isn't.

I've also noticed he tends to not only be annoying, but also extremely disrespectful. He didn't show it much in the beginning of our relationship, but within the last year he seems to have gotten comfortable and is now showing his true colors.

We're at a small table for two, tucked away in the corner. The candlelight flickers on his face as he stares at me, his brows furrowed in irritation as he waits for my response.

I shake my head to bring myself back to the present. "What was that?" I ask, giving him the opportunity to realize his mistake and take it back. "I zoned out there for a second."

"Seriously, Alana? Have you heard anything I've said to you in the last hour?"

He knows I hate it when he uses my full name. My family and friends all call me Lana or Lan, but Brad says nicknames aren't becoming, and it makes me seem *immature.*

"I'm sorry. What were you saying?"

I need to get us back on track and hide the annoyance in my voice, or this is going to turn into an all out war about my inability to pay attention when he speaks. He hates it when I space out.

"I said, are you really planning on eating all of that?" He gestures to the plate in front of me that was just delivered to the table. I tried to give him an out, but I guess he isn't taking it. This restaurant has pretty big portion sizes, but I haven't had much to eat today, so I am fully prepared to enjoy this entire meal.

Even if I *had* had plenty to eat today, I can still enjoy this entire meal. Not that I need to explain that to him, or anyone else for that matter.

"Um...yeah, I had planned on it."

Brad has made comments like this before, but it's hitting me a bit differently tonight. My ability to put up with him is probably something that should be studied at universities, because I don't fully understand how I've done it for so long.

Unease and contempt begin to build in my stomach as the reality of this situation becomes clear to me. I've been tolerating an egotistical jerk for three years, and I don't think I can do it anymore. Not only is it extremely frustrating, but I deserve so much more.

"I told you last week that you really need to watch what you eat. You're always snacking, eating huge portions, and you've been getting takeout way too often. I have the company Christmas party in about two months, don't you want to look your best?" He rattles this off like he's had this speech prepared for a while now.

"Why do you feel like it's your job to pay attention to my eating habits?" I snap.

Go me. I've never stood up to him like this before.

"Don't be dramatic," he says with an eye roll. He pulls out a black gift bag and places it in front of me. "I got you a gift."

I shift a little in my seat, shaking off the bad feeling that was building and trying to calm myself down enough to get through this dinner.

I slowly pull away the paper and take out an emerald green dress. It's a beautiful silk material and it feels smooth and cold against my hand.

I look a bit closer at the dress and notice it's two sizes too small. I've been with the man for three years and he can't even get my dress size correct.

I want nothing more than to start an argument right now, but we're in the middle of a small restaurant and I don't want to cause a scene. Plus if I decide to leave, which I'm pretty sure that's where this conversation is headed, I don't want to agitate him more than necessary. If I do, I know he'll follow me out and that will just make it more difficult to go get my things from our apartment and get out.

"The gift is lovely, but I'm a size twelve, not an eight. Where did you get it? I'm sure we could exchange it," I say, trying to keep the peace.

"Oh, come on, Alana. Of course, I've realized the weight you've put on in the past few months. Like I said, the firm's Christmas party is coming up and I'm going to need you to lose at least ten pounds before then," he says nonchalantly as he stabs his grilled chicken with a fork.

I'd like to stab him with that fork.

Who eats grilled chicken at an Italian restaurant?

"This dress is a great goal to work towards. If you can fit into it by then, there might even be a ring in it for you."

The intense revulsion that I feel towards receiving a ring from this man is more than enough proof that I cannot continue in this relationship. I'm not even sure why I let it go on this long.

I guess the security of it and the constant companion was enough of a pull. At the beginning of our relationship, Brad had been kind. We met through mutual friends and he won me over with his humor and charm. We moved in together after dating for just a few months and it was a sweep-you-off-your-feet romance. As time went on, though, things changed and he got a new job in a big corporate office. The men there were brutal and cutthroat and he soon took on those qualities as well, leaving the funny and charming guy I met in the dust.

"Don't start with me. This is supposed to be a nice dinner to celebrate. Let's just focus on that," he says.

Normally, I would let it go. Normally, I would brush it under the rug, eat half of my dinner, and let him lead me out of the restaurant like the good little girlfriend I'm supposed to be. But I am done being his doormat.

"You can't just say something like that and then move on like nothing happened. I will not be spoken to that way, and to be honest, I am not okay with the way you've been speaking to me at all recently."

Well, there goes keeping the peace. I take a deep breath and wait for his response. He stares at me like he has no idea who I am.

"I'm only trying to better you. You will be more respected if you look a certain way. I'm just looking out for you."

Alright, I'm out.

I stand, and push away from the table abruptly. I calmly set my napkin down next to my plate and look into his eyes as I speak.

"Brad, we're done."

I turn to grab my purse from the small stand that sits by the table and when I glance back at him, he's staring at me blankly. It seems I've shocked the man speechless. *A miracle.*

The sound of the chair's legs scraping against the mahogany flooring must fix his momentary silence, such a shame, because he speaks as I get ready to leave.

"Absolutely not. Sit down right this minute."

"You aren't my father. You're extremely disrespectful, you're rude to others and to me, you make comments and say things that have absolutely no business coming out of your mouth, and I am done. I can't do it anymore. You've changed and I don't like who you've become." I start to leave, but turn back before stepping away.

"Oh, and another thing, I lied. You can absolutely tell your hair is thinning. It looks ridiculous."

I pass a table of women as I walk out with my head held high and they give me a small thumbs up, clearly having heard the whole thing go down. I take a deep breath and continue walking, but just before I reach the door I hear Brad shout from the table, "This isn't over, Alana. I'll call you." I don't grant him a response.

I step out onto the chilly streets of New York City, then pull my phone out of my purse and block his number. Next, I hit the name of the one person I want to talk to right now. The phone rings twice before she picks up, the sound of our favorite TV show, *Vanderpump Rules*, playing in the background.

"I dumped Brad. Can I stay over?"

Cami cheers so loud, I have to move the phone away from my ear. The heaviness in my chest dissipates the longer I hear her screams of joy, and it makes me thankful to have a best friend I can count on.

I hail a taxi and head back home so I can grab my things before Brad gets back. It's time to stop morphing myself into something I'm not, just to make everyone else happy. I am going to focus on myself and find out what makes *me* happy. That means no more dating, no more men. I've become far too comfortable letting a man tell me what to do and how to feel. I am going to spend some quality time getting to know myself.

CHAPTER 1

Alana

ONE YEAR LATER

"Alana, do you have the presentation ready for the meeting?" the managing editor, Ian, shouts at me as he rushes by my desk.

The office is always insane during the last push before we release the issue. *Impress* is quickly becoming one of the top fashion and lifestyle magazines in the world and with the growing success has come growing pressure. Everyone runs around like the building is on fire.

"Yep," I shout back at him. "I've got everything ready."

I know Ian is particularly stressed about his meeting with our editor-in-chief, Heather, at the end of the week. The meeting we are having today is to discuss topics and spreads for the next couple of issues.

Typically, the editors meet with Ian before each issue and hammer out ideas, but it's never been this formal before. Normally, I jot my ideas down on a post-it note and call it a day. The real brainstorming happens in the meeting with everyone.

I groan when my phone chirps with a notification for the third time today. I pick it up, having a good idea of who it is, and slam it face down on the desk when my suspicions are confirmed.

"Brad again?" my best friend Cami asks as she slides her chair back to look into my cubicle.

A year ago, I walked out of the Italian restaurant and left him behind. I hadn't spoken to him since. Unfortunately, as I was walking to work yesterday, I bumped into a wall of muscle and looked up to find his baby blues looking right at me.

We exchanged a moment of weighted silence, and once I gained the ability to move again, I pushed past him and continued toward the office.

He has since sent me two text messages, and it seems like he isn't done. I guess he got a new phone number, because the block I put on it a year ago isn't in place today.

UNKNOWN

It was nice to see you, Alana.

UNKNOWN

Im sorry for the way things ended.

UNKNOWN

It really would be polite of you to at least respond.

Hah. It took three unanswered text messages for him to slip back into the worst version of himself.

I hit the block button after I read the third message, cringing a little as I do it.

The truth is, the night I broke it off with him, I had a rare moment of boldness. I had been pushed to my limit and I snapped. Normally, I work pretty hard to make sure the people around me are happy, even if that means I'm not. I've gotten better about this since I vowed to work on myself, but I'm certainly not perfect and still struggle with it sometimes.

I close my eyes, take a deep breath, and rub my fingertips in small circles on my temples. I can already feel the stress headache coming on.

"He won't leave me alone, Cam. I didn't even speak to him and now he's texting me like we had some kind of conversation."

After I ended things with Brad, I swore off men altogether. No dates, no dating apps, no hookups. I made a pact with myself that I was going to focus on my career and work hard to climb the ladder and find what made me happy. So far, I have worked my way up to one of the top editors in our group and I'm hoping for a promotion in my near future. I'm not sure that my position at work is contributing much to that goal of happiness, but success and happiness are hard to come by, so I'm thankful I've got at least one of those things in the works.

Alex, another editor at the magazine and one of my work friends, peeks his head around the walls dividing our desks and looks at me with a stern look.

"Are you having trouble with someone, Lan?"

Alex was already working for *Impress* when I started about a year ago. He was warm and welcoming and we quickly became good friends.

On my first day I got lost on the third floor trying to find the copy room and he came across me looking dazed and confused. He showed me to the room I was looking for and offered me a square of chocolate he had in his pocket. He told me it cured first day jitters and he was right, it did the trick.

Ever since then, he brings me a chocolate square each morning. Sometimes he hands it to me, sometimes he puts it on my desk with a little note, but he never fails to bring me one.

He is absolutely someone I would go for if I wasn't on a dating hiatus, but he hasn't shown any interest in me other than friendship. Our relationship is one that lives inside the four walls of this building. We know each other's favorite foods and drinks and he could probably anticipate how I'd react in any given work situation, but beyond that we're pretty surface level.

Despite the fact that he hasn't given me any reason to believe he isn't trustworthy, I can't get myself to move past the basic levels of friendship with him. He's extremely kind and respectful, he makes me laugh and he's absolutely gorgeous, but previous experience tells me that I never really know what hides behind the charm and the looks.

Thanks, Brad.

"Ah, nothing I can't handle," I reply quickly, giving him a smile that I hope is reassuring.

"Well, you'll let me know if someone is bothering you, right?" he replies, eyes not leaving mine despite my effort to break contact. I like Alex and we're good friends, but I haven't shared many personal things with him. He definitely doesn't know about my ex, and he doesn't need to.

"Um...yeah, sure. I'll let you know if I need any help," I respond.

Alex gives me a stiff nod and turns back to his desk.

Cami looks at me with wide eyes and mouths, *What the hell was that about?*

Alex has always been a good friend, but the exchange felt way more protective than I'm used to from him. I shrug and turn back to my desk, focusing on the work in front of me.

I enjoy being an editor. There's something extremely satisfying about looking at a first, second or third draft of something and picking it apart to make it perfect. *Maybe because it reminds you of your parents*, the cynic in my head suggests.

She isn't wrong, that is pretty accurate to what my childhood was like. It's a bit ironic for the people pleasing daughter to be paired with the parents who are impossible to please, but I made peace with the fact that they would never be fully happy with me a long time ago.

I clear my thoughts and take a deep breath, trying to focus on the beauty spread in front of me. Abstract photos of different shades and textures of blush line the top of the page, followed by a detailed guide on finding your perfect shade.

Being a section editor means that I do a lot of different things when it comes to editing. Sometimes I'm arranging photoshoots, rewriting articles or handling logistics for interviews. My favorite part of the job, though, is managing it all.

I love the scheduling and ticking off of to-dos. Marking something out on your to-do list is equivalent to the strongest drug. I will stand by that.

Aside from the management piece, I love the satisfaction I get when I look at a spread that has been carefully crafted and put together by talented photographers, designers and writers. It's like the last pass of the pressure washer on those rug cleaning videos you see at two in the morning when you've been scrolling social media for way too long. It reveals something brand new that looks nothing like it once did.

With that reminder, I turn back to my computer and continue weeding through this spread, making changes and comments.

CHAPTER 2
Alex

I TURN BACK TO MY DESK AND TRY TO BUSY MYSELF WITH work, but I can't help but dwell on the conversation between Alana and Cami.

Alana Cade.

The woman I haven't been able to get out of my head, no matter how hard I try. And believe me, I've tried.

We have worked together for a little over a year now, and she continues to surprise me. I remember the first staff meeting she was in when she got hired. I already noticed her because she was beautiful, but the addiction began when I saw the way she intently listened to everything each person shared.

Our staff meetings were made up of a lot of idea sharing and that can become draining really easily, but the way she paid attention was mind boggling to me. Her clear blue eyes and sweeping lashes held eye contact, she nodded her head at all the right moments and asked all the right follow up questions.

I figured this intense attention to those around her was a one off, something she made special care to do at her first meeting in order to look good, but this continued for all of the meetings after. It endeared me to her more than anything else about her.

I made it a goal of mine to get closer with her and get to know her, and our jobs have made that possible. As two of the section editors, we work closely together daily. Over the last year a humble friendship has blossomed between us.

She is fierce and determined and doesn't let anyone do anything for her, in fact she is almost always off doing something for someone else. She throws herself into her work and is more dedicated than anyone I've met.

She's let me in, but barely. It's a special kind of torture to be friend-zoned as harshly as I've been friend-zoned. I have tried to get to know her deeper, but she's a vault that only opens to her closest people. Cami, her best friend from childhood, and Charlie, her brother.

I have this irritating desire to protect her, which isn't rational, because she has proven time and time again she can take care of herself. She hasn't ever asked for—or quite frankly allowed—my help and rarely does she ever let Cami or Charlie help her either. She's extremely stubborn and fiercely independent. Nevertheless, I find myself wanting to fix her problems.

I draw my attention back to the screen and look closer at the ideas I have brainstormed for the next few issues. I think our ideas are solid. I'm still struggling with the reasoning behind this unusual meeting with Ian, but whatever. He switches things up sometimes just for the hell of it. Keeps us on our toes, I guess.

I'm adjusting the wording on our presentation when I hear Cami whisper to Alana.

"You're not going to meet up with him, are you?" she asks cautiously.

"Cam, you aren't serious? Of course not. I'm done with him," Alana replies in a terse tone.

This is the first I'm hearing of a relationship from Alana. The whole time I've known her, she's never even mentioned a man. They're whispering, clearly trying to keep the conversation private, so I lean a bit more to the right in my chair, attempting to get closer to them and hear through the walls of the cubicle.

"Okay, good. I just wanted to make sure you were still sticking to the b—"

Cami's words are cut off by my desk chair, which betrays me by sliding out from underneath me, throwing it and me down in a loud crash.

I lay still for a few seconds with my eyes closed, silently cursing myself for my amateur eavesdropping capabilities.

I slowly peel open my eyes to find Cami and Alana staring down at me. I focus my gaze on the vintage baseball cards lining the wall above my desktop in an effort to not look too closely at the beautiful woman leaning over me.

"Alex, are you okay?" Alana gasps, bending down and softly touching my arm. "How did you fall like that?"

I hesitate for a moment, the heat of her hand on my arm sending an electric current through me. I look down, my gaze frozen on her small hand against my not so small bicep and realize I've been staring instead of answering.

"You both know how clumsy I am."

Because what else would I say? The truth? *Oh I was just desperate to know any detail about you so I was eavesdropping and my chair decided to give me away.* Yeah, real smooth.

I stand slowly, wincing at the pain in my right leg. "It must have a loose wheel or something, but I'm fine."

Alana looks from me, to the perfectly attached wheels of my chair and back again. She doesn't seem convinced, but thankfully she lets me off the hook.

"Well, good. Wouldn't want to have to complete any extra paperwork, Ashford," she says with a giggle. "I also would hate to do this presentation alone. Grab your stuff and let's go set up. We only have like twenty minutes before Heather and Ian show up."

I grab my laptop, notebook, and pen and we head to the conference room. I veer off to the break room as we walk and grab a Diet Coke for Alana and a sparkling water for me. She doesn't ask where I'm going or wait for me, because this is part of our routine. We meet each morning in this conference room to go over our day and start it the same way each time.

Diet Coke.

Sparkling water.

Chocolate.

I catch myself daydreaming about a future of starting our mornings like this in my apartment after spending the night together, but quickly remind myself of reality.

Alana Cade is not available.

I meet her back in the conference room and crack open her soda with a satisfying pop. I place it at her spot, then I reach into my pocket and pull out today's chocolate—dark chocolate caramel and sea salt.

I hand it to her and she reads the label before tearing the packaging and placing it between her soft pink lips and taking a bite.

A satisfied hum lets me know that she likes it and I turn, smiling to myself for a job well done. Anything with caramel seems to be her favorite, so I try to bring those more often.

If you saw the stash of various chocolates strewn around my apartment you would probably think I'm addicted, and I am, just not to the chocolates but to the girl who consumes them. I have tried many different brands and flavors, taking notes of the ones she loves and throwing out the ones she hates.

At this point I should be buying stock in Ghirardelli and HERSHEY.

Alana floats around the room setting things up and pulling documents up on her computer. Neither of us really know what this meeting is for, and I think it has us both feeling a bit off kilter.

We are section editors within the fashion and beauty sections of the magazine. There are a few other editors that are in charge of other sections like lifestyle and health, but after observing the two of us working together Ian has shared many times that he thinks we're two of the best the magazine has.

We normally present our ideas to Ian and he takes them to Heather, but it's very informal. Alana and I sync up briefly each week before we meet with Ian and pinpoint a few thoughts. After that, we share them with him and then take them to our team once we've nailed them down. Today, however, he's asked us to come up with more formal proposals on a few ideas for the next couple of months. We have been working on trying to nail down the best ideas for a few weeks now.

Ian walks in about ten minutes later and addresses us with a nod.

"Alana, Alex, good to see you both. Thank you for brainstorming several concepts for us to review. I know this differed from our normal routine, but there's a reason for that."

His words cause a storm of nausea to build inside of me. Even though I know Ian likes us, my brain automatically goes to the worst case scenario.

Are they firing us? Do they want a batch of ideas so they have something to work through while they hire to backfill our spots?

"Heather will explain more when she gets here. For now, just settle in. We will begin shortly."

I can feel the nervous energy radiating off of Alana and everything within me desires to soothe it. I wish I could reach over and take her hand, but I can't. We aren't *that* good of friends.

Instead, I do what I always do.

I lean over and whisper in her ear, "Want another chocolate?"

She shivers and I ignore it, but I can't ignore the gorgeous smile she sends my way.

"Two in one day? Ashford, you're breaking the rules." Her eyes are teasing and the uncertainty of moments ago is gone. Mission accomplished.

"There are no rules when it comes to chocolate."

"Well, if you insist." She puts her hand out and I reach into my pocket and hand her the wrapped square. Sparks ignite where our skin brushes, but I ignore it.

She opens it and takes a bite, then holds the other half out to me.

"I think we could both use something to take the edge off."

I take the chocolate from her fingers and pop it into my mouth. At least if I get fired I can say I had a good last day. Any day spent with Alana is a good day.

Alana

HEATHER WALTZES INTO THE ROOM WITH INCREDIBLE grace. She's wearing a white pantsuit and her silver hair is curled and gathered atop her head. Gold teardrops hang from her ears and glitter in the fluorescent lighting of the conference room.

"Hi Alex, Alana," Heather greets us both.

She isn't cold, but she certainly isn't warm. She has this air about her that demands attention and respect, but I know she genuinely cares about each and every member on the *Impress* staff, and that's hard to find in this industry.

"Good morning," we say in unison, before glancing at each other with a quick grin.

The bittersweet taste of the chocolate he brought me today lingers in my mouth like a reminder of his care. He is always trying to take care of me, but I rarely let him. The chocolates and Diet Coke each morning are just about the only way I've felt comfortable allowing him to do anything for me.

Yes, Diet Coke in the morning. Sue me.

Since breaking up with Brad and deciding to learn what makes *me* happy, I have become extremely independent and focused on work. To a fault, my therapist would argue, but that's a problem for another day.

I moved into my own apartment in the same building as Cami and have learned how to take care of myself and do it well. Despite Dr. Rodriguez's encouragement to allow others in, I've decided I'm happy and safe in my little bubble of me. I know I can count on myself to keep my promises and if I don't open up to anyone else, then I can't be let down.

Ian, Heather, Alex and I are all sitting at the large conference table and the view would be comical to an onlooker. This room is made for large meetings, so the four of us are sitting at a table built for twenty. Alex and I sit at one end, down by the large monitor we present on, and Heather and Ian are at the other end.

This all feels very formal, which is common any time Heather joins us, but the ambiguity surrounding this meeting is putting me on edge.

I've done a lot of work in the last year to rebuild my confidence and recognize my worth and value, but even the most secure people have insecure thoughts. Mine tend to creep in more often than not, but progress over perfection, right?

I know the value I bring to this magazine, and yet I can't stop the thoughts from flooding my brain.

Am I even qualified for this job?

Am I getting fired before I can move up in this company?

Am I even worthy of a promotion?

They must think I haven't been performing up to standard.

I doubt anyone here besides Cami even likes me.

Ian announced a few months ago that he would be moving to California because his husband landed his first acting role. We all met Adrian at last year's Christmas party and he pops in every now and again to bring Ian lunch or drop off a treat for the staff. He is one of the nicest people I've ever met, so even though I was sad to lose Ian I was thrilled for Adrian.

Ian leaving means Heather and the CEO will be looking at the section editors and scouting candidates to move up into his role. As the managing director of the magazine, Ian makes sure all of the sections flow together and the overall magazine is cohesive. It's a big promotion, and one that I am working hard towards. They haven't said so, but I have a feeling Alex and I are top contenders.

My parents were never thrilled at the prospect of me working for a fashion magazine. They saw it as *frivolous* and said it wasn't a real career. I don't speak to them often anymore, but the desire to earn their approval still burns deep within me. No matter how much I try to tamp it down, I never can fully douse it.

My older brother Charlie was the golden boy in our household. He grew up playing hockey and our parents gushed to everyone we met about their little hockey star. I was shoved behind their legs while he was pushed forward and presented as their most prized possession. When he landed a position on the New York Rangers as a winger, the comparison game only got more intense.

I'm thankful Charlie and I's relationship was not one of competition, though. He saw through our parents' games and tried his best to get them to notice me and my accomplishments. He was rarely successful, but that's okay. All I needed was him.

Heather's voice snaps me back to the conference room.

"I'm sure you're both wondering why we've called you into a more formal meeting."

Alex

I feel Alana tense beside me.

Before I can think better of it, I absentmindedly reach over and squeeze her hand lightly. The same electric sparks fly through my fingertips at the touch. She quickly glances at me and then down at our joined hands, but she doesn't pull away.

Interesting.

I feel her relax just slightly, so I pull my hand back and wipe my clammy palms on my jeans.

"We have an exciting opportunity for the two of you," Heather says, and her previous stern face slips into a grin.

For a moment, I just stare at her smiling face. I had convinced myself that we were about to be fired and was almost certain I'd be scouring LinkedIn for a new job within the hour.

"Wait, you aren't firing us?" Lana asks in disbelief, stealing the thoughts right out of my brain. We're always on the same wavelength.

"Firing you? No, absolutely not," Heather replies in an incredulous tone. "You two are far too valuable to let go. I apologize for not giving you more information about the purpose of our meeting today. I hate to think you've been worried sick since we scheduled it."

Alana clears her throat. "Well, that's good to hear."

"Yes, I'm sure it is. Now, onto the matter at hand." Always right to business with this one. "You are both aware that *Impress* has a European branch that operates out of Paris, France right?"

We both nod, glancing at each other. It's safe to say, neither of us knows where this is going.

My nerves have faded, replaced with an anxious bubbling excitement. I have to be honest, if this opportunity means more time spent with Alana, I won't *not* be happy. There is an intense connection between the two of us, and I want nothing more than time to convince her that it's worth exploring. Over the last year, we have worked seamlessly with one another—we listen to each other's opinions and talk things out when we disagree. Even though she seems to be on a dating hiatus, for whatever reason, I can't help but be a little bit interested.

"Well, the European branch has just lost all but two of their editors. A competitor apparently offered them a large sum to leave *Impress* and work for them. They reached out and asked if we would send a pair of strong editors to help out." She pauses and we stare at her, waiting for her to continue.

"Ian and I spoke and we agreed that the two of you would be perfect for the job. You would be helping with any tasks that need to be done as far as section editing to help fill the gap, while also helping interview, staff, and train a new team."

Alana looks over at me and then back at Heather and Ian.

"Okay..." she says hesitantly. "So what does this look like for us? Weekly video conferences to consult with them, I assume?"

"Oh, no," Heather replies with a dismissive wave of her hand. "You two will travel to Paris and work in the office there in the city."

There is a moment of silence as we take in what she's just said.

Paris. With Alana. For how long? What will the editors here do? When do we leave?

Questions begin to flood my mind. I'm cautiously excited, but also a bit uneasy. This is a huge project and it says a lot that they are trusting us with it. I haven't heard of *Impress* doing anything like this before now.

"When is this to take place?" Alana asks.

I can tell she's apprehensive. She's talking quieter than usual and with less than her normal amount of flare and sass, although she typically dials it down around Heather.

"If you accept, you're set to leave in three weeks. You'll be staying in a gorgeous little apartment that we've arranged for the month. One of my old colleagues owns it and her family is spending the holiday season in the States, so she needs someone to water the plants and keep up the home. It's right by the Eiffel Tower, just a few steps away. A dream, really."

For the month?

"For the month?" Alana asks, like she's reading my mind. There's a note of panic in her voice, I think, but maybe I'm imagining it.

Personally, I have little ties to New York besides my job. I'm a quiet man with a quiet life, and I like it that way. I grew up in a single parent household, just my mom and I, on a small farm in Texas. Because of this, I've learned to be content with the simple things in life.

I was homeschooled until eighth grade when my mom decided to put me in the small school in our town so I could make friends and be in a better position to get into a good college. I struggled for a long time with the decision to go to college and pursue my career. My dad left when I was ten and when he did, I took over as man of the household. Mom was wrecked for a while in his absence, even though they only ever fought, so I had to take care of her and the house. She came back to herself eventually, after she started going to therapy, but the burning need inside of me to provide and care for her has never gone out.

When it came time to pick a major, I knew I wanted to go to school for journalism. Back when my dad was still around, he always took me to baseball games. It was our thing, how we spent time together. I didn't necessarily love the game of baseball or think it was extremely interesting to spend hours watching, but I loved spending time with my dad and that was how I got it. He used to show me articles that were written about his favorite players and I would study up on them so I'd have something to talk to him about that would interest him. Through reading them, I began to have a strong interest in journalism and writing. I eventually ended up at University of Wisconsin - Madison in their journalism school.

You might be wondering, why Wisconsin? Well, that's a great question. One day, I googled "best colleges for journalism majors" and it was the first school I saw. I applied, got in, and the rest is history.

I spent four years there and after I graduated I packed up my Wisconsin belongings, moved to New York and started at *Impress* right out of college. I worked my way up to section editor and it's been fantastic.

My mom has always been my biggest supporter and never let me feel as though I was lacking in anything, especially love. Now, I do everything I can to care for her even from hundreds of miles away. I send groceries, a cleaning service every now and again, whatever she will allow me to do without sending it back.

Don't get me wrong, she's incredibly self sufficient—but ever since I landed this job, I've tried to pay her back for giving me the life she did despite our circumstances.

"They expect it to take that long to hire new editors. Although I suppose it could be longer depending on how things go. Will that be a problem?" Heather frames this as a question, but it's pretty clear that there is only one acceptable answer.

"I suppose not," Alana answers hesitantly.

"Alex, what do you think about this?" Ian asks. "You've been awfully quiet."

I take a deep breath, trying to figure out what the best response here would be. I obviously am excited to spend time alone with Alana. This is also a great opportunity to expand my resume and portfolio. However, I don't want to seem too excited and make Alana nervous.

"Well, I would need some time to think about it," I say, knowing I'm going to say yes, but trying to give Alana some time without her having to ask for it.

"Oh, of course," Heather replies. "Can you both let me know by the end of the week?"

We both nod at her.

The rest of the meeting is business as usual. We present our ideas; they love them and explain that they wanted a batch of ideas so they could use them in our absence.

Heather leaves us with Ian, who gives us a bit more information on our trip.

"You'll fly out right after Thanksgiving. That gives you about three weeks here to get things in order and prepare the other editors," he explains. "You'll have the weekend to acclimate to the time change, and then you'll start working in the office that next Monday."

So essentially we will be in Paris for the entire duration of the holidays. Awesome.

I usually go visit my mom during the week of Christmas. She doesn't have anyone else to celebrate with her so I try to make it a priority to be there.

I'm not sure what Alana's situation is. We don't discuss family often, but even when we do she never talks about her parents. If she's upset, she doesn't show it.

"Thank you for the opportunity," Alana says in a polite, but tense, tone.

I gather my things, shake Ian's hand and follow Alana into the hallway.

CHAPTER 5
Alana

Paris. For a month. In December.

I walk out of the conference room in a daze, totally in my head. I am so busy obsessing over how this trip is going to derail my life that I don't even realize Alex is talking to me.

"Alana, did you hear me?" he says softly as he dips his head a little so our eyes meet.

"I'm sorry, I was in my own world there for a minute," I reply, snapping my gaze to meet his. His beautiful green eyes hold my attention.

"Don't apologize," he says gently. "A pretty big bomb was just dropped, so it makes sense that you would be lost in your thoughts."

I know it sounds dramatic. I should be over the moon right now. With this opportunity, the promotion I have been dreaming of is likely just around the corner. I know the only correct answer is yes. Plus, my job is paying for an extended trip to one of the most desired vacation spots in the world. You can't get much better than Paris, France.

Despite all of that, the list of reasons why this is going to be a huge problem starts to form in my head involuntarily.

1. I am a planner. I need to have everything in order. From what I'm having for my meals that day to my hair washing schedule for the week. The unknowns in this situation are extremely overwhelming.

2. I have severe flying anxiety, so eight-ish hours in a tiny flying machine sounds like my own personal hell.

3. Christmas is one of my favorite times of the year. Charlie and I have an extensive list of traditions we complete each year and we always spend Christmas Eve and Christmas Day together. The thought of missing that makes me want to cry.

4. A year ago, I recognized how awful my boyfriend was to me and ended a three year relationship, then swore off men for the foreseeable future. I really don't need the *"City of Love"* to remind me left and right how single I am.

So, even though this trip could be really exciting, my brain won't allow me to get there yet. Not until I'm done over thinking every possible thing that could and will happen between now and December 31.

I glance back up at Alex, who is patiently waiting for me to reply to whatever question he asked. He has this steady patience about him that feels like no matter how long I take, he will wait to hear what I have to say. It's that important to him.

His quiet stare is making me want to be honest about where I'm at, even though I've literally never once gotten deep with him about the inner workings of my brain.

"To be honest, I'm kind of freaking out," I say as I look down to avoid his intense stare.

Work gets tough, so naturally Alex has seen me frazzled before, but I don't think I've ever felt this out of control around him. It's been a while since I've felt like this in general.

He says nothing, so I chance a brief look up at him through my lashes. He's looking at me, waiting, and it feels like he is staring into my soul. I feel stripped bare, like he can see every single thought that's in my head.

"I'm...sort of a control freak?" I say it like it's a question. He probably already knows this about me, having worked with me for a year, but I still feel the need to explain. "And I'm feeling extremely out-of-control right now," I whisper as I glance around. My breathing picks up and I feel my heart beginning to race. *Ugh.* I haven't had a panic attack in probably six months and this, of all things, is what's going to bring another one on?

"I just need some air," I say quietly enough that only Alex can hear me. I know my voice has grown shaky, as evidenced by the look on his face when he hears it.

"Hey, hey, Lan. It's alright. Here, let's go." He takes my hand in his and pulls me down the hallway, away from the main office area where everyone else is working. He takes me into the break room that's small enough to feel secure, but not too small that it feels closed in.

He closes the door behind him, leaves the light off and flips the lock, turning to face me. All that lights up the room is the glow of the television in the corner, where Rory and Lorelai Gilmore are drinking coffee at Luke's Diner on mute.

"Here, sit down." He guides me to sit on the couch, then places a hand on my upper back and applies gentle pressure, guiding my head down between my knees in order to help regulate my breathing. I am working so hard to get control of it, one breath at a time, that I barely notice the small circles he's rubbing on my back.

"Breathe in for four counts." I glance up at him with confusion as I pant and try to slow my breathing, but it isn't working.

"Come on, trust me. I'll count, you breathe."

I take a breath slowly as he counts *1-2-3-4.*

"That's my girl, now hold it for seven seconds." He counts again for me. "Now slowly let it out for eight seconds. Okay, good. Let's do it again, breathe in."

We go on like this for a few rounds, his hand never moving

from my back, and after a while I notice my breathing is under control, my heart calm.

"No, don't stop," I practically whine when he pulls his hand away.

"I'm right here, Lanie. I'm not going anywhere. I'm just grabbing you some water," he whispers. "Hang in there for a second."

Alex stands quickly and takes a water bottle out of the fridge. He brings it back to me, twisting off the cap and lifting it to my lips.

"Good girl," he says as I take a small sip.

I look up, barely registering his words, as his gaze sweeps up and down my body checking for signs of distress.

After who knows how long, I start to feel a bit more like my rational self. Heavy exhaustion takes over my body and I yawn. I almost always crash after a panic attack. It really takes it out of you. I lay down on my side, place my head on the armrest, and close my eyes, breathing deep.

"Thank you. You didn't have to do that," I say, eyes still closed. Alex grunts in acknowledgement, muttering something to himself that's too quiet for me to hear. I try not to be embarrassed by the fact that he just witnessed me having a panic attack, but I'm not very successful.

At some point Alex moves to sit next to me and pulls my feet into his lap. His soothing circles have moved to my calf and I feel goosebumps pop up all over my skin. I'm wearing pants today, thankfully, so he can't see them.

As I lay here, my mind snags on something he said mid-attack. Something he called me.

"What did you call me?" I ask him, turning my head so my eyes meet his.

"What do you mean?" he furrows his brow in confusion, cocking his head to the side.

"Did you call me Lanie?"

He hesitates and looks unsure of himself. "Is that okay?"

Was that okay? I mean, obviously it isn't a big deal. It's just no one has ever called me that before.

I hate it when people use my full name, it makes me feel like I'm being scolded by my father, but I've gotten used to it when it comes to professional settings. Alex calls me by nicknames often, Lan or Lana like everyone else, but he hasn't ever used the name Lanie. For some reason, it feels more intimate. Maybe because no one else has ever used it, but I love that it's exclusive to him.

I smile up at him. "Yeah, Ashford. That's okay."

He smiles back at me, a barely there blush creeping up on the apples of his cheeks.

It is at this moment that the mistrusting voice in my head reminds me of why we've sworn off all men.

"It isn't smart to start to depend on him," she whispers to me. *"One day he'll leave and you'll be left to pick up the pieces."*

For the last year I've let my inner voice protect me from heartbreak like I experienced with Brad, because here's the thing...men are honestly the worst. They either decide I'm not enough and treat me like it, or they leave. Eventually everyone leaves.

Alex is likely no different than Brad or any of the other men before him. I'd do well to remember that. Even if he was the exception to the rule, Alex doesn't have feelings for me. He's just been a good friend, and that's it.

"You feeling stable enough to go back out there, or do you want to stay here for a bit longer?" he asks as his thumb continues its ministrations on my leg.

Taking another deep breath, I pull myself to sitting and push up onto my feet. I wobble slightly, still affected by the panic attack, and Alex steadies me with his hand softly under my elbow.

"Can we, like, not talk about this out there? I really don't want the stares and questions."

He nods as we walk through the break room door and leads the way back into the main office area.

Even though it felt like time had paused, the office is moving along with business as usual. The buzz of conversation is like a comforting white noise that brings me even closer back to earth.

I return to my desk and sit in my chair. Cami wheels backwards, away from her desk, so she can look over at me.

"You okay, Lan?" she whispers. "What was that meeting about?"

"I'm okay, I guess," I reply with a shrug. "But your presence is needed at happy hour tonight. The conversation about the meeting is going to need to happen alongside a margarita and guacamole."

"Oh, well, if you insist. Should I call Charlie and ask him to meet us there?"

Charlie has been the third person in our trio ever since his friends did something in high school that caused him to pull away from them. He hasn't ever told anyone what happened, but one day he stopped hanging out with them and his entire personality shifted. What was once the charming and charismatic hockey prodigy became an isolated and secretive young man. His love for me never wavered, he was always adamant about that, but his entire personality changed and that was a hard pill to swallow. Now, he's extremely closed off and keeps to himself, the fact that he even let Cami in was surprising to me, but I'm thankful he did because he needs someone besides just me.

Now, the three of us do pretty much everything together, and he and I are very close. He played in a major junior hockey league back in Florida and went to NYU once he graduated. Cami and I obviously followed him there and he was drafted into the NHL when he was a senior. We both were pursuing journalism, so his draft to the New York Rangers worked out perfectly for all of us.

I give her a quick nod and she wheels back to her area, leaving me alone in my space to process the last two hours of my life.

My ex-boyfriend is contacting me again.

I am going to be living in Paris for a month.

I only have three weeks to get ready for this trip, and I have to reorganize all of my December plans.

I won't be here in the city with Charlie for Christmas.

And, probably the most unnerving of them all, I just had the most embarrassing moment with my new roommate.

I started having panic attacks after I left Brad. They used to be extremely frequent, but since I started seeing Dr. Rodriguez, they've gotten a lot better. Even though leaving Brad was the best thing for me, the unknowns and constant changes were a shock to the nervous system. Any time I have intense feelings of being out of control, there's a possibility of one. That seems to be the trigger.

Dr. Rodriguez has taught me how to spot one coming and has given me tools to help ease them or at least make them a bit more bearable.

This one, though, I didn't see coming at all. Probably because it came on so quickly.

I have been really private about my panic attacks and haven't shared them with anyone. I don't like being seen as weak, especially not at work. I don't let the cracks show. It hasn't been easy to keep them from Charlie and Cami, but using the strategies from my therapist has helped a lot. It's not that I don't trust them to know, but I don't want them to be worried about my problems. It isn't theirs to worry about.

It's been a while since I've had one like I did today, which is frustrating, but even more so because Alex and I aren't close enough to be on trauma sharing level. I don't open up to people easily, so I never planned to get that vulnerable with him, but I don't have a choice now.

I have a suspicion we aren't done with the conversation surrounding my stress regarding our Paris trip, but I'll handle that another day. Right now, I need some tequila and my besties.

CHAPTER 6

Alana

THE REST OF THE AFTERNOON GOES BY IN A BLUR. Everyone around me is moving through their day, getting last minute deadline pieces in and I feel like I'm watching them in a haze. At some point, I look up at the clock on my computer and realize it's 4:45 p.m. A pang of guilt hits me as I realize I accomplished absolutely nothing today. It grows heavier when I think about everything I need to get done before we leave for Paris, but I force the feeling down and roll my chair back. Standing and stretching my legs brings some clarity to the fog I'm in and I give my back a little twist before walking just next door to Cami's cube.

"What are you working on?" I ask, leaning against the side of her desk.

"Hey girl." She smiles up at me. "I haven't heard a peep from your station in a few hours. You okay?" Her concerned eyes find mine and I smile back at her.

"Yeah, I'm good. It's been a long day," I answer, running my hands through my hair and brushing through the tangles.

"Okay good, I haven't left my desk in hours." She stands with a groan and does the same stretching maneuver I just completed.

"I've been trying to get this shoot organized all day and I feel like I am still right where I started."

Cami is one of the beauty assistant editors for *Impress*. She researches trends, comes up with ideas for pieces we can write on makeup and beauty products, and puts together shoots for them. She also gets to go to trainings for brands and the amount of products that get sent to her every week is enough to bring the jealousy out in any person.

"Are you still up for margs?" I ask as she starts to pack up her things.

"How could I say no to quesadillas and tequila? Just give me a few minutes to get everything together and we can head out. Charlie said he would meet us there."

I step back into my cubicle and glance around at the state of disarray. My fingers itch to clean it up, but I don't have the time or energy to do that right now, so I grab my things and turn my back to the mess. I notice Alex moving around at his desk next to me, most likely getting his things together as well. Sometimes he stays late, but he typically leaves right around five like most people in the office. Healthy work/life boundaries and all that good stuff. I usually don't leave before six on a good day, but I can't be in this building for another hour today.

I realize after a few seconds that I'm staring and watching him, but the way his muscles flex and move against his button up make it hard to look away.

I'm not quite sure what is going on with me. I haven't ever looked at Alex like this before, but after his kindness during my freak out earlier, my body seems to be drawn to his. Like it's searching for the comfort he provided only hours ago.

He must feel my stare, because he looks up and meets my eyes, flashing a quick smile in my direction before continuing whatever he is doing. I avert my eyes quickly and resume staring at the mess in front of me.

You know how sometimes when a space gets so untidy, it's

almost impossible to make the first move to begin to clean it up? That is how I feel. It's infuriating, because I cannot function in a mess, but I also can't gather the strength to start to pick it up.

Alex must notice my inner turmoil, because he turns and walks slowly into the disaster zone.

There are papers everywhere from where I've just dropped them after meetings. There is a half eaten banana sitting on the counter, a few water bottles, papers that need filing and various knick knacks that lie around everywhere.

I try to keep my space clean because it keeps my mind clean. I like organization, order and planning. However, the last week before a deadline always gets crazy and things just start to pile up. Typically when it's this bad, I'd spend a day like today getting my life together, but I've been too busy recovering from the panic attack and overthinking.

Alex pulls my attention from the mess when his hand softly lands on my shoulder. He pulls it gently back toward him, spinning me slowly so I'm facing him.

"The mess stressing you out?" he asks with a kind smile in his eyes.

Obviously Alex knows me pretty well after working with me closely for a year, but I'm just now noticing how he seems to be able to read me like a book. During the meeting with Heather and Ian, in the break room, and now this.

My eyelashes flutter as I look up at him, his six-foot-five frame towering over me.

"You know how it is right before a deadline," I reply with a shrug, trying not to focus on his hand that still rests on my shoulder.

He nods slightly and then slowly slides his hand down my arm and places his hand in mine. I know it isn't intended to be romantic, but it sure as hell feels like it is. My skin burns under his touch.

"We're going to get everything sorted, Lanie," he says softly for only my ears. There's that nickname again. "I'm here to help however I can." He squeezes my hand three times, releases it, and turns to go back to his cube.

I am frozen. I'm not sure if it's from his kind words, his hand in mine, the way he looked into my eyes with assurance, or that nickname he's decided belongs to me. Whatever it is, it takes me at least thirty seconds for my brain to come back online.

He must think I am completely unstable after today's events, but I can't bring myself to care. If he's interested in me at all outside of work, the desire will dissipate after he gets what he wants and the chase is no longer as exciting.

That's how people work. I thought it was just my parents that didn't want me, didn't have an interest in my life, but Brad clearly felt the same way. He might not have been the one to physically leave, but he hadn't been present for a long time when I finally pulled the trigger and left. Because of this, I've learned to not grow close to too many people. That way I can control how bad the damage is if they leave.

I start to gather my necessary items, leaving the mess for tomorrow, and make a vow to myself.

I will not fall for Alex Ashford.

CHAPTER 7

Alana

I walk through the door of the restaurant and am assaulted by the smell of Mexican food and the sounds of snapping tortilla chips. The familiar environment of buzzing conversation and the comforting smell of good food immediately lifts my mood and I feel ten times lighter.

The multicolored bulb lights line the ceiling inside and the main lights are dimmed, giving the room a warm, colorful glow. It's dark enough to be relaxing, but not so dark it feels dirty. *Angel's* is one of our favorite restaurants and one we frequent often. The restaurant is just one big open room with booths framing it and tables littered throughout. The bar sits over to the right and is pretty full given it's dinner time.

Soft music plays over the speakers and it gives the space a friendly and inviting feeling.

I immediately spot Charlie in our booth in the back corner of the restaurant.

"Hey ladies, he's already back there," Sierra, the hostess, says in greeting.

We head back towards my brother, who slides out of the booth to give us each a hug. Cami sits on the bench on the left with Charlie and leaves the right one open for me, like she always does.

"Charles, how was your day?" Cami asks as she nudges his shoulder with hers.

Cami has been my best friend since we were awkward high school freshmen stumbling through the halls of Celebration High. I grew up in a small town in Florida and the summer before freshman year of high school, Cami's family moved into the pastel yellow house beside our baby blue one.

We were instant friends and I was happy to have someone to navigate those years with. Charlie never really hung out with us until whatever happened with his friends junior year. Ever since then, the three of us have been inseparable.

We all had big dreams about living in the city, so when Charlie got a full ride to NYU for hockey it just seemed like fate. He started there after he graduated high school and we joined him the very next year.

Cami landed her job with *Impress* right after graduation. She knew what she wanted and she went for it. I, however, was still trying to make everyone around me happy, so I spent way too much time searching for a magazine I thought my parents would deem acceptable. I ended up in an internship for a smaller magazine and it wasn't bad, but it wasn't what I wanted. After about four years I decided it was time to make a change and right about that time the editor position opened up at *Impress*. Cami had a big hand in recommending me for the job and hyping me up, and it has been the best thing for our friendship.

"Fine, Cassandra," Charlie grumbles in that way of his. He pretends like he doesn't like her jokes, but he still plays along albeit begrudgingly. This is a weird bit they do. Charlie's name is not Charles and Cami's name is not Cassandra, but for whatever reason they do this every time they see each other.

"I am so glad you demanded bestie time," Cami says as she gets comfy on her side of the booth. "I was in major need of a margarita."

"Oh, is that all I'm good for?" Charlie scoffs.

"Of course not," she says dramatically. "But I would argue that it is a perk."

"Can't blame you there," I reply, grabbing a chip and dipping it in the salsa.

We each pick up the menu and look at it like we don't already know what we want. Almost every server here knows our orders. We end up here at least once a week to either catch up or talk through whatever problems we are currently facing. It's been a busy month though, so we've missed a few gossip sessions.

James, one of our favorite waiters, sidles up to our table and puts on his most charming smile. He always shamelessly flirts with us, knowing it won't go anywhere.

Actually, I take that back. I think he hooked up with Cami a while back, but she told me it was never going to happen again. Must not have been very memorable.

"*Hello* ladies," he says with a wink. "And gentleman. What can I get you?"

"The fact that you're even pretending to not know what we want is cute," Cami replies with an eye roll.

"Oh, so you think I'm cute?"

"James, come on," Charlie says. "You know neither of them is going home with you."

"Hey man, it doesn't hurt to give it a shot."

"I applaud your efforts. Three margaritas, on the rocks with salt, two orders of quesadillas, one order of chicken enchiladas," Cami replies curtly, ordering for the whole table.

"Thanks," I yell as he turns to walk away.

A few minutes later, James brings our margaritas and sets them down in front of us. I pick mine up and take a long sip, setting it back down with a sigh as the warmth of the tequila fills my body.

"Okay, fill us in."

I spend the next forty-five minutes telling Cami and Charlie about the meeting with Heather and Ian. I tell them about our trip to Paris, which earns me a jealous glare from Cami, and how freaked out I am about the complete change in plans for the next month of my life. I tell them vaguely about the panic attack, leaving out how bad it was. I tell them I *"freaked out,"* but that was the extent of it.

I cringe at the half truth as it leaves my lips, but something inside of me keeps me from leaning on them fully in this area. I know they'd be so mad if they knew I was dealing with this on my own, but I don't want to bring them into it. The less they know, the better. The less they know, the easier I am to love.

I tell them about Alex and how he was supportive through the freak out and all the bombs that were dropped today, and his new nickname for me. Charlie leans in with interest.

When I finally take a breath, I realize Cami is staring at me with her mouth hanging open and Charlie looks angry for some reason.

"That man is into you, Lan," Cami says as Charlie picks his margarita up and takes a very large sip, setting it back down quite harshly.

"Shut up, no he is not. He's just being a good friend. He's always been nice."

"*Nice,*" she says the words with air quotes, "doesn't give you your own special nickname and make excuses to touch you. He is *so* into you, don't be an idiot."

Alex might have given me more attention today than normal, but that can easily be explained away by our new assignment. Even if he does like me, it wouldn't last. Good men are extremely difficult to find these days, and the likelihood that Alex is hiding something is high. I don't even know what it would be, but I know there has to be something.

An extreme hatred for dogs.

A disbelief in womens' rights.

A toxic relationship with coffee.

A girlfriend.

A wife.

The possibilities are endless.

"Regardless, Cam, you know I'm not going to go there. I've sworn off men."

"Yeah, yeah. You've been saying that for an entire year. Don't you think it's time to get back out there and date a little?" she asks.

"No, I don't know if she's ready," Charlie quickly replies.

"You don't think I'm ready?" I ask, clear hurt in my tone. Not that *I* think I'm ready, but I crave my brother's approval.

"Lan, I think you can do anything, you know that, I just don't want to see you get hurt." He reaches over and squeezes my hand with affection. After a few seconds of tense silence he excuses himself to go to the restroom. He's always been like this, needing a moment to himself when emotions get high. Or maybe he hasn't *always* been like this, but he has since he joined our friend group.

It's been a while since I've been on a date and if I was honest with myself, I would admit that it has been a little bit lonely. Sure there are times when I wish I had someone to take care of me when I was sick or cuddle with me when a nightmare startled me awake in the middle of the night.

I miss those things about my relationship with Brad sometimes. I know there was so much bad, and I truly would never be okay with the way he spoke to me or treated me in the end, but I couldn't deny that it was nice having someone to lean on sometimes.

Even me, a strong independent woman, could admit that. Maybe not out loud, but I can admit that to myself.

Almost as if my thoughts have conjured the man himself, the front door chimes and I look up to see none other than my ex himself stride through it.

Alana

Brad walks in and passes the hostess stand, motioning to the bar to let her know he will be sitting there. He doesn't smile at her or tell her hello. He doesn't even speak words to her, just walks past like she doesn't even exist and he owns the place.

I know my brother is in the restroom, but we need to make a run for it. This restaurant is not big and it's only a matter of time before he notices us.

"Cam, do not turn around," I whisper under my breath. "Brad just walked in."

What does she do?

She turns around. And lets out the loudest gasp ever.

"Cam," I groan in frustration.

"Sorry, I was just so sure you were joking."

"Why would I joke about something like that?"

I get James's attention and he comes right over.

I reach up and pull at the collar on his uniform shirt, bringing his ear down to my mouth.

"Listen," I whisper. "You know that guy over there, the blond in the too tight suit?"

"I know the one."

"I need you to make this the worst experience he has ever had at a bar so he never comes back. If Angel has a problem with it, tell him to come talk to me."

Angel owns and operates the restaurant and he loves us. I know that if he knew the situation, he would fully support our alienation of this particular patron.

"And I also need you to box up our food and bring it to us to go."

"Woah," he says as he leans back away from my face. "What did that guy do to earn the poor customer service treatment and run you out of your booth?"

"He is a sorry excuse for a man. That should be all the motivation you need to help us out here," Cami whispers through her teeth.

He must see the stress on my face, because he nods stiffly and turns to get to work. I notice him speaking to the bartenders on shift tonight and subtly pointing my ex out.

None of them go over to speak to him, instead jumping around him to serve every other person at the bar.

"Good plan," Cami says while gulping down her margarita. "Get him to never come back and also hustle out of here so he doesn't see us. You have to chug your margarita now, though."

"There are worse things in the world."

I pick up my glass, remove the straw and suck it down.

I pull my phone out and shoot Charlie a text, telling him we have to leave but leaving out the reason why. He hates Brad and if he knew he was here he would come rushing out of the bathroom ready to throw down. I'm hoping he might make it out without even noticing Brad's presence and we can just tell him Cami has a stomachache or something.

James brings over the food and tells us it's on the house.

We stand and begin to make our way out of the restaurant. Unfortunately, the only path to the door is behind the bar. This means I have to walk directly behind Brad and pray he doesn't notice it's me.

I think I've made it. I pass where he's sitting on the barstool and I let out a breath that gets stuck in my throat as a warm and clammy hand wraps around my wrist.

"Alana?" There he goes using my full name again. "I thought I heard Cami's laugh. Always hated that laugh."

I'm pretty sure my best friend curses at him under her breath.

"I'm sorry," Cami pops her head into his line of sight, blocking his face from me. "Do we know you?"

I wish I could see his reaction to that line, but she's in the way.

He doesn't speak for a second, clearly taken aback, but he doesn't let go of my wrist either.

"Alana, why haven't you answered my messages?" he asks, like we didn't break up a full year ago.

"I didn't particularly want to. Please let go of my hand," I reply calmly.

He has never been physically aggressive with me. Verbally? That's another story.

Even so, the contact plus the environment and the fact that he smells like this wasn't his first drink of the night, is enough to have me on alert.

"Please, can we just talk? I have a lot I need to say to you."

"I don't want to talk, and I don't need to hear your excuses. We broke up a long time ago, let it go."

"Let it go? You were the love of my life. I could never let it go. I can't believe you would say that." He gets louder towards the end of the sentence, his hand tightening around my wrist and making me wince.

We have drawn the attention of the people around us and I can see James out of the corner of my eye starting to walk toward us. I raise my opposite hand up to stop him, not wanting to cause a scene.

"Brad, you're hurting me. Please let go," I say in an even tone.

He looks down and drops my hand like a hot iron, almost seeming like he didn't even realize he had tightened his grip.

"I'm sorry. Shit." He runs his hands through his hair.

Now that I am looking up close, he really looks like he is having a rough go of it. His eyes are sunken in, purple and blue underneath, and his hair is dirty and in need of a cut. Not that I cared.

"Brad, I am going to say this once and I don't want to have this conversation again. I have no idea how you can sit there and say that I was the love of your life. You treated me like absolute garbage and said the most disrespectful and hurtful things to me and about me. If that is how you treat someone you love, you need some serious help."

With that, I turn around and start walking out, only slightly registering the applause that has broken out in that section of the restaurant.

Out on the street I take in a deep breath.

"Babe," Cami says as she stumbles through the front door. "That was epic."

"I don't know if I'd call it epic but...it was something. I honestly just want to put on stretchy pants and watch a trashy reality show."

A second later, Charlie comes pushing through the front door and meets us on the sidewalk. I can tell from his relaxed posture and confused face that he didn't see Brad inside.

"Sorry we ran out on you. Brad showed up and I really didn't want to deal with it," I tell Charlie.

"Brad Buttehole?" he says with wide eyes, turning his body like he is about to walk back into the restaurant. The first time I told Charlie Brad's full name, he didn't stop laughing for a full five minutes. Even though it isn't pronounced like the word butt, I can see how the similarity is humorous. We joke about it often now.

"No need to go in and defend your sister's honor. She just gave him quite the verbal beating," Cami says as she grabs his arm and pulls him back towards us.

I can tell my brother isn't happy about not confronting my ex, but he nods his head.

"Want to come eat at my place?" I ask them as we start walking down the street towards our apartment building. I hold the bag of takeout containers in front of Charlie's face to show him we didn't leave without the food.

"Sure, Lan. I haven't been over to your place in a while," Charlie replies.

"Yeah, that's because we always hang out at your fancy apartment, Mr. Hockey Man," I say back with a smirk. He rolls his eyes and shoves me playfully.

"I'm down. I need to run to my place and change first, but I'll come over right after and we can eat."

Cami and I live in the same apartment building and it's only a few blocks away from where we work, which is only a few blocks away from the restaurant. It's pretty great.

"Okay, great. I think we are on the episode where Kristen finally admits to sleeping with Jax."

Charlie groans at the names I call out, realizing we intend to watch one of our favorite shows. He hates it.

"You're right, I forgot about that. I'll hurry, I'm excited."

"Can't we watch something we all like? Like, I don't know anything but *Vanderpump Rules*?"

"No," we reply in unison.

We reach the building, say a quick hello to the doorman, and ride the elevator up to the fifteenth floor. We split directions when we step off, Cami going left and Charlie and I going right.

I unlock the door, drop the to-go containers on the coffee table and walk to my bedroom to change. My apartment is in a really nice building, but the unit itself is pretty small, which is customary for New York City.

It's roughly 650 square feet and has enough room for a loveseat in the living room and a queen size bed in the bedroom. It's small, but it feels cozy and I like it.

As I pull my sweatshirt over my head, I hear the front door unlock and open.

"I brought beer!" Cami yells back to me.

"You're an angel. Will you pull up the episode?" I shout back.

I hear Charlie groan again through my closed door and I snicker to myself. He loves us enough to put up with our reality TV, which means he must love us a lot.

I finish getting dressed, push my feet into my slippers and step out into the living room.

Cami is already bundled up on the couch, Charlie sharing a blanket with her and their dinner in hand. She plated mine for me on a paper plate and has already popped the top of my beer.

Thank God for brothers and best friends.

CHAPTER 9
Alana

THIS IS ALREADY A DAY FROM HELL AND IT'S NOT EVEN eight in the morning.

My alarm didn't wake me up this morning, so I didn't have time to throw any makeup on besides some tinted moisturizer and a quick coat of mascara.

I washed my hair last night and slept on it wet, which usually leaves me with nice waves, but today it's giving Mia Thermopolis from *The Princess Diaries*, pre Paolo.

The shirt I had planned to wear today was dirty, so I threw on a random pink dress I found in my closet and ran out the door.

By the time I get halfway to the office, I realize I've forgotten to throw something in my bag for lunch. I'm already exhausted, so I decide that taking the extra time for coffee is necessary, even though I'm late.

I walk into the office thirty minutes past nine, coffee in hand, and remember that I have a mess waiting for me in my cubicle.

Great.

I walk past Alex's cube and give him a quick wave and a hello, which he returns.

I skip my section and hand Cami her coffee and tell her good morning.

I take a deep breath and brace myself for the mess as I head back to my cube. Except when I turn the corner, everything is tidy.

What in the world?

I left this office a complete mess last night. I know I didn't clean anything up here. I am so utterly confused. I look around, trying to figure out how this happened, when I spot a torn piece of paper with writing scribbled on it.

I sit down at my desk and pull the note up to my face so I can read the neat handwriting.

Told you we'd get everything sorted.
A

He must have come in here and cleaned up after me.

I stare at the note for a few more seconds, trying to decide if I should be touched by his kindness, or pissed that he messed with my stuff. I had lots of documents strewn about on the table, pens and notepads all over the place. I had samples out that needed filing and mock ups that needed to be put away. Even though it was a mess, I knew where everything was. The longer I think, the more frustrated I become. Now, who knows where all of my things are?

I start to frantically open and slam shut drawers and open up my filing cabinet. As I go about banging things around, a hand on my wrist halts my movements and startles me.

"The sticky notes are in the top left drawer, stacked by color. The spreads that were on the floor are organized by month and filed, and I color coordinated your pens," Alex says with a soft laugh behind me. "I also hope you weren't saving that banana. I tossed it."

I look up at him with wide eyes and then glance down at his

hand on my wrist. My anger and frustration dissipates almost immediately. He quickly pulls his hand away, awkwardly grabbing his other wrist, as if to keep his hand from touching me again.

I start to look around and realize he is right. Everything is where it's supposed to be.

Although I'm no longer angry, I feel unsettled that he was in my space and took on the task of tidying up my space. The gesture is extremely thoughtful, and I understand what he was trying to do, but it irks something in me that he took it on without asking. I don't want to rely on him to do things for me. Regardless, I decide to not make a fuss and be grateful. His intentions were good and even though it's a little weird, this does take a lot off of my plate.

"How did you know where everything goes?" I ask, my tone incredulous.

I have a very specific order to my desk space, and while I'm sure it isn't impossible for someone to know that order, I would say it's not likely. Keeping my desk space organized is something I've always done, ever since I was in my early elementary days, but it's not your typical organization. I have a method to my madness, and for as long as I've been doing it no one has bothered to learn it, that is until now.

"I pay attention." He shrugs a little as he says this and tilts his head to the side. It's endearing. "Meet me in conference room A in twenty minutes so we can get a game plan going?"

"Okay, sure." I nod my head yes and am certain I look like a bobblehead, just sitting there nodding long after he's left.

I can't figure him out. There is no way he has a thing for me. He's always acted this way towards me, but for some reason I haven't noticed it like I'm noticing it now.

Cami's argument that he wants me sits in the back of my mind and I think that might be the cause of my second guessing. Alex is just being a good friend. He saw I was overwhelmed, and stepped in to help. He needs my head clear just as much as I do.

I set my attention back on work. I am determined to get this promotion, and I can't do that if I'm preoccupied thinking about his jade colored eyes and strong hands.

CHAPTER 10

Alex

ALANA WALKS THROUGH THE DOORS OF THE SMALL conference room and sits across from me. I breathe in the addicting smell of her perfume. She smells like strawberries and vanilla and it reminds me of summers in Texas, picking strawberries out of a field and making fresh pound cake with my mom. I want to tuck her under my chin, hold her to me and breathe her in.

"All sorted?"

"Yeah, I think so. Thank you for tidying up my desk." She glances down and then back up at me. "I know I've been sort of a maniac since we got the news about Paris, but I swear I will calm down once we get everything figured out. I'm just a mess right now."

"Don't apologize. It's a lot for anyone to take in."

"I don't see the great Alex Ashford having a meltdown in the break room."

"You just haven't caught me." I wink at her and pull my laptop in front of me.

That earns me a small tug at the corner of her lips and I feel like I just won the lottery.

"Okay, let's get started." Alana displays her laptop screen on

🎀 53 🎀

the large monitor on the wall and pulls up our project management software. "So we have two options here for the December issue as far as spread designs."

We pitched four different designs to Ian and Heather at our meeting, and they chose their top two. We were left to make the final decision once we determined what all would be in the issue. The type of content on the page typically determines what spread we use.

"If this issue is going to be pretty photo heavy, we probably should go with the second one," she says.

"With the Anastasia Valentine feature I anticipate there will be mostly photos. Did we get confirmation from her publicist?"

Anastasia Valentine is an up and coming model in the industry and everyone is chomping at the bits to get her on one of their issues. Thankfully Ian knows her publicist personally, and has pulled a few strings.

"I just got an email about half an hour ago that we're good to go," she says.

"Look at you," I say with a smile.

"Don't inflate my ego. Ian did all the work."

I laugh and shake my head.

"Okay great, one decision made and a hundred more to go."

As we continue our discussion, I can sense Alana getting more and more anxious.

"We need to brief the rest of the editors on the shoot and the details, along with the spread content. Can you take care of that?" She starts fidgeting with the cap of her pen, snapping it on and off.

"Absolutely."

"I'll make sure all of our current projects are tied up and complete. I need to get with Caroline and check on where she's at with the November issue content." She starts to scribble frantically on her notepad.

She was relaxed when she walked in an hour ago, but she's tensed up now. Her shoulders and back are rigid and raised, she shakes her foot under the table and has taken a handful of very deep breaths in the last few minutes.

I have to physically restrain myself from reaching out and drawing circles on her arm or getting up and crossing the room to rub the tension from her shoulders. I want to ease her discomfort and I also constantly want to touch her. It's really not my place to do either.

I want to approach the topic of her anxiety so we can talk it through, but I want to do it with care. My mom suffered with anxiety growing up and I learned a lot about how to care for someone who struggles with it. Every person is different, but I want to take the time to learn Alana and how she best manages this.

"Why don't we take a break from work talk for a second?" I start with some simple questions to try and distract her. "What did you do after work last night?"

She is visibly a little confused by the change in conversation, but she goes with it.

"Um...Cami, my brother, and I went to the Mexican restaurant down the street, *Angel's*. We go there a lot."

"Oh no way, I love that place. What did you all order?"

"We get the same thing every time we go." I watch her shoulders drop a little as she talks. She's still wound up but I think this line of questioning is helping get her mind off of the stress. I think she can probably guess why I've turned this into a game of twenty questions, but she rolls with it.

"Wait, let me guess," I say, holding a hand up to stop her from continuing her answer. "I bet you both get a margarita." She gives me a soft smile. "And chicken fajitas to share."

She laughs and fiddles with the small gold chain on her wrist.

"You're close, but not quite. Margaritas and quesadillas."

"All three of you?" I ask.

"Well, no. Charlie gets a chicken enchilada. Pretty much the entire wait staff knows our order at this point."

"That's impressive. It's a great place and the staff is really nice. I can understand why you would make it a regular dinner spot."

She nods and smiles at me.

You might be thinking, *If you've worked with this woman for a year shouldn't you know the most basic things like where she frequents for dinner?* The answer is yes and no. Alana and I *have* worked together for a year, so I do know work-Alana well, but I don't know her at all outside of work. When she is in the office, she's a machine. She throws herself into her tasks and is one of the most determined people, often staying well past five. That was one of the reasons I asked where she went last night. I was surprised to see her leave so early.

We haven't had very many conversations that were about anything besides what goes on inside this office. I have always been fascinated by her, so these are all things I've wanted to ask, but until now I didn't feel that I could. I think the event in the break room changed the dynamic between us and now I feel like I know her on a deeper level and can let my curiosity out a bit.

"How was the evening besides the food?" Her posture has relaxed quite a bit in the last few minutes, but with this question she grows rigid again.

"It was fine."

Fine. Girl code for anything but.

"Want to talk about it?"

"Not really. It was stupid. My ex, Brad, showed up and we had to get our food to go and—"

"Wait," I say, cutting her off. "Is this the idiot that was bothering you the other day?"

She nods her head and looks down, picking at the skin around her pretty pink fingernails. Something in me snaps and I respond before really even thinking.

"I told you to let me know if you needed help."

I know as soon as I say it, it wasn't the right thing to say. I didn't even ask how that made her feel or if the prick tried to talk to her, I just jumped straight to what she should have done.

"Well, I didn't need help. I handled it on my own, thank you very much," she snaps at me. "No need to go all caveman."

I take a breath.

"I'm sorry, you're right. I shouldn't have said that. You are perfectly capable of handling that on your own, I just want you to know I'm here if you need or want help."

She looks up with wide eyes, clearly shocked by my response for some reason.

"Right, well anyways. He showed up and I really didn't want to get into a conversation with him, so we got our food to go and tried to sneak out."

"Didn't work?"

"Nope. Our covert mission wasn't quite so covert." She lets out a deep sigh and begins rubbing her wrist almost absentmind-edly. The motion causes her sleeves to ride up, and I notice small fingerprint bruises marring her porcelain skin.

"Lanie...I know I just told you I was sorry for going caveman on you, but if those bruises are from that jerk I swear I'm going to—"

"I'm fine," she hurriedly supplies, removing her hand from her wrist and tugging her sweater sleeves down to cover the marks.

"Did he put his hands on you?" I ask in a dangerously calm tone. My body feels anything but.

"I promise, Alex, I'm okay. Cami was there along with the entire restaurant. He just didn't realize how hard he was gripping my wrist."

It takes everything in me not to get up and go murder that man for putting his hands on her. Not only did he do whatever he did to get her to break up with him, but he clearly doesn't respect women if he feels okay leaving marks on their skin.

I close my eyes and take a deep breath, trying to ground myself. This isn't about me or my feelings.

"Okay. If you're okay then I'm okay. But please promise me if he messes with you again and you need help, you'll call me."

"I promise."

I nod, forcing my brain to be content with that and try to move back to my line of questioning to get us out of this emotionally charged space we're in.

"Right, so once you got back to the apartment what did you do?"

"We watched *Vanderpump Rules*. It's a reality TV show about a group of people who work at this restaurant."

"Oh yeah, I've heard about it. Did Cami and Charlie come over to your place?"

"Yeah they did. Cami actually lives in the same building as me, just down the hallway. We live in the building down on the corner there." She motions her hand in the direction of the only apartment building on this street, so I immediately know which one she's referring to.

"Not a far commute then."

"Not at all. That is for sure one of my favorite things about it."

We sit in companionable silence for a moment and it seems like things have lightened a little. I want to try and work through some of the major stress points of this whole Paris project we are assigned to, so I decide to push a bit.

"I know you're stressed about Paris. I assume you're trying to decide if you want to go?" I start. She gives me a small nod. "Do you want to talk about it? Maybe verbal processing might help."

"Have you been to therapy or something?" she asks in a teasing tone.

"All the best people have been to therapy, Lanie."

She stares at me for a moment, seemingly stares through me, and I can tell she's thinking. She takes a deep breath, then begins.

"Well, for starters I have some pretty bad flying anxiety. Once I get up in the air I'm okay but the getting up and the coming down are another story. I also love Christmas, it's my favorite holiday, and I have a list of traditions that my brother and I always do. Those will be pretty impossible to complete, considering I won't be home to do them." Her shoulders slump, giving away just how sad that makes her. "I also am not too excited to be visiting a city that inspires love stories, considering the one I *thought* I was living in turned out to be a nightmare. I mean, it's been over a year, so it's not like I'm hung up on it, but I haven't had anything else to replace those memories yet and I really don't want to walk around seeing couples in love left and right, when my own boyfriend didn't give me the time of day and constantly commented on what I was eating or how much weight I'd gained and ruined any hope that I'd ever trust a man again."

I see the moment she realizes she just word vomited and probably shared more than she meant to. Her eyes go a little wide and she takes in a sharp breath, staring straight at me.

I am trying to think through how to help her, but my brain is snagged on the part where she said her boyfriend thought she was too curvy for him. I honestly cannot imagine a body more perfect than Alana's, and I'm not just saying that.

She's short and petite in an endearing way, and she has the most delicious curves. Her waist isn't tiny by any means, but there's a dip in her hips that is perfect for someone's hand. *My hand.*

I shake my head and bring my thoughts back to the present conversation and away from her body.

Her lack of trust in men is surprising to me. It makes sense if she had an awful experience, and if the guy is leaving marks on her skin that tells me all I need to know about what kind of man he is. Still, it makes me sad that she doesn't feel like she can trust people. It causes me to look at our interactions through a different lens—one of caution and importance in every gesture. If this woman doesn't trust other men easily, then I need to work hard to make sure she *can* trust me.

I force myself back to the present.

"I can absolutely understand why you'd be stressed. That's a lot."

She laughs, but it isn't humorous. "Yeah."

She starts to close her laptop and I frantically search for something to say or do to get her to stop packing up. I'm suddenly desperate to keep her in this room and work through what's holding her back. I can't leave it like this. I reach out and softly touch the top of her hand, halting her movements. She flinches, not expecting my touch, and then relaxes. "Okay, let's start with flying."

She just stares at me, but after a second gives me a little nod.

"What part of flying specifically makes you anxious?"

"The tight space of the aircraft in general. It's so small and the seats are so close together that I feel like I'm suffocating."

As she talks, I begin making mental notes of things I can do to try and help. Surely Heather would approve first class seats if she knew about this. The company can afford it. I know Alana would never ask herself, but that doesn't mean I can't.

"I also really dislike the noises." She stops and thinks for a second. "The rattling makes it sound like the wheels are going to fall off the damn thing. Oh, and the turbulence."

"Do you have noise canceling headphones? Like the ones that go over your ear?" I ask.

"No...that might be a good idea to help with the rattling."

I nod my head and continue to think about the other things she mentioned. I give her hand a squeeze, then say, "I'll do some research on how we can tackle the other things."

"Oh, you don't have to do that Alex. That isn't your job."

"What if I want to?"

Her sapphire eyes meet mine and there is curiosity in them. She cocks her head to the side a little, as if she's trying to figure me out.

"Tell me about your Christmas traditions," I say, trying to move the conversation along.

"Oh that would take forever," she says with a laugh. "There are a ton."

"Then make me a list. I'd like to know about them."

She giggles, then nods. "Okay, Ashford, I'll make you a list. Maybe it will inspire you. Don't tell me you're a Scrooge."

"Oh, I could never be Scrooge," I say as I wave my hand in dismissal of her ludicrous suggestion that I don't like Christmas. "As for Paris being the city of love," I continue. "I think we can rectify that."

"What does that mean?"

I don't really know, honestly. Only that I want her to enjoy her time there and for the name of her ex to never cross her mind.

"Just let me worry about that part."

She laughs and sits back in her chair. *That laugh.* It's so beautiful and light and I realize at this moment that I would do anything to hear it. I would make any joke and move any mountain to see her smile and hear her laugh like that.

"How are you feeling now?"

"Better, thank you."

We gather our things, both of us seemingly happier with a plan of action, and head back out into the hustle and bustle of the office.

CHAPTER 11

Alex

THE REST OF THE DAY GOES BY QUICKLY AS WE START TO put our plan into action. I am scheduling meetings with the other editors on staff when my phone buzzes with a text message. I glance over and see Banks's name light up my screen.

Banks and I met on the first day of classes freshman year. We were both in English with Mrs. Thurr, and I was nervous and painfully awkward. He took pity on me when we were asked to pair up and share one fun fact about ourselves. I always hated icebreaker activities, but Banks was kind and didn't make me feel out of place.

A few weeks into the school year, I spotted his worn copy of *Catching Fire* sticking out of his backpack and that solidified the friendship. He followed me to Wisconsin for college and got his bachelors in education. Now, he teaches English at the same school we met at years ago.

After we graduated college, I really struggled with the decision of whether or not to go back home and be around for my mom or move to New York. I knew I could easily work for a small local paper in Texas and live with my mom and be fine, but Banks knew I wanted more for myself. He had planned to move back to be close to his family, they were all a tight knit bunch, so he told me to go and that he'd look after my mom in my absence.

About a year after he got started teaching, someone showed up at his doorstep with a kid.

Apparently a one night stand *can* change the course of your life. Now, little Hallie is one of my mom's favorite people and I know she loves it every time he brings her over.

It lifts a huge weight off of my shoulders to have him there. He has a great family, certainly a more traditional one than I had, but I think he needed a quiet place to land and somewhere to escape to when it got too loud at his house. My mom and I were able to provide that for him. He spent a lot of afternoons and evenings with us throughout high school, and I was grateful to have him around.

We would come home after a long day of learning to peanut butter and honey sandwiches on the counter and cookies in the oven. We'd sit and talk about books or play video games and after a while he just became a permanent fixture in both of our lives.

I know my mom appreciates having him around now. They always got along really well.

BANKS

Check this out

He follows the text with a link to a press release about the new *Hunger Games* prequel coming out in a few days. Even now, our love for the series lives on.

ME

That is going to be so sick. Do you think women all over the world will fall in love with President Snow even though he's the worst?

BANKS

Obviously. The guy they casted is way too dreamy.

ME

I'm going to save that text for future blackmail.

BANKS

I'm just speaking the truth.

ME

Lol. You got time for a quick phone call after I get off?

BANKS

Sure. I need to grade some papers before I pick up Hal. We can talk while I do that.

Banks doesn't date much, I'm sure it has something to do with having a kid and everything, but he gives solid advice. Of all of the people in my life, he's the most level headed.

I need to know how to move forward with Alana without ruining our friendship. I have to proceed with caution, because not only would living in an apartment with her be awkward if it didn't work, but I would lose her. Add to that, the fact that she has zero trust in men or people in general and I've got my work cut out for me.

I open the email app on my laptop and send an email to Lucy, Heather's personal assistant, asking for a quick half hour meeting. I want to discuss some of the concerns that Alana mentioned to me today. I think if Heather knew the severity of her anxiety, she would do what she can to help eliminate that barrier.

Lucy sends an email right back.

To: alex@impress.com
From: lucy@impress.com
Subject: Re: Meeting with Heather

Alex,

Thank you for your email. Heather has the next half hour open before her meeting with marketing. If you'd like to pop in and have a chat, she said that would be alright.

Have a great day,

Lucy Albright
Administrative Assistant
Impress Magazine

I stand and push in my chair, glancing over at Alana as she works with another editor on one of the spreads we pitched to Ian and Heather. She looks so beautiful and I long to walk over and wrap my arms around her. The side profile of her face showcases her wavy chestnut hair and the curve of her top lip. The urge to walk the few steps to her desk and pull her mouth to mine is almost too strong to resist.

I realize I have an audience when Cami clears her throat as she approaches. I rip my gaze from Alana and meet Cami's eyes as she moves past me and winks.

Great.

I knock twice on Heather's door before I make my way inside and sit down in one of the two leather chairs in front of her desk. She holds up a finger as she finishes a conversation on the phone, quickly telling them she will have to continue this conversation at a later time.

"I'm sorry, some designers really do just think everyone runs on their time." She takes a sip of her honey latte and faces me. "How can I help you?"

"It's in regards to the trip we're taking. I'm afraid I have a bit of flying anxiety and I was wondering if *Impress* might be able to do something to help alleviate that." I hold my breath. Heather isn't a dictator by any means, but she is intimidating. Initially, I thought I might tell Heather about what Alana was experiencing, but the more I thought about it the more it didn't sit right with me to share that personal information with someone and not run it by her first.

Knowing she struggles with trusting, I felt like that might be taking it a step too far. Instead, I figured I could fall on the sword this time and blame it on myself. I know Alana would never ask for this for herself.

"What do you think we could do to help?"

I breathe a sigh of relief.

"Well…" Now that I'm actually having this conversation I'm realizing I didn't think through how to discuss this without just demanding a seat change. "I tend to get pretty claustrophobic on planes."

The fact that I'm outright lying to her does bother me some, but if it helps Alana I'm willing to do it.

"Do you think a seat with more room would help?" Heather asks.

"I think that would be great. Maybe something in the exit row?"

"We'll upgrade your seats to first class," she says.

I hesitate, surprised by her words and unsure how to respond other than to immediately decline the offer. I know first class would definitely help, but it feels like too much to accept.

"First class is too much," I say.

"Nonsense. Is there anything else?"

"Um, no I guess not."

"Good, I have a meeting. Have a good day."

I stand in a daze and stand there awkwardly for a second before I remember I'm supposed to be leaving.

"You too. Thank you."

Well, that was easy.

I step out onto the icy sidewalk and slip my headphones out of their case and into my ears. Banks and I talked on my walk home every day when I first moved away, but we've since fallen out of the habit and it's been harder now that he has Hallie. It helps curb the feeling of loneliness that threatens to consume me sometimes, especially at first. Since we went to the same college, I never really felt alone until I moved to New York and he went back to Texas.

My apartment is only a few blocks and a subway ride away so I usually have about twenty minutes of uninterrupted time while I commute. I tap his name on my phone and wait for him to pick up.

"Hey, man," he says in greeting. He automatically switches our phone call to a FaceTime, something he does every time we talk. I accept and his face fills the screen. "Nice of you to actually call me. With the amount of time between conversations I could be dead in a ditch somewhere and you would have no clue."

"That's not true," I tease. "I would notice the decline in *TikTok* messages in my inbox."

"Get off my back, that's my decompressing time. Plus, you know you love them."

"Yeah, I sort of do," I say with a smirk. "How are things going there?"

"Not bad. Hallie is crushing first grade and taking names. She signed up for the holiday musical this year, so naturally I can't get "Rudolph the Red Nosed Reindeer" out of my head."

"Well, the legend did say he would go down in history."

"They weren't wrong. I've been thinking about bringing Hal up there sometime in early December to see the snow."

And that was all it took for me to remember the reason behind the phone call.

"Actually I don't think that will work. That's what I want to talk to you about," I tell him.

"Oh, so you didn't just call to hear my voice. You're here so I can fix your problems?"

"I am. You can bill me for the therapy session."

"You know I'm on call for you any time. What's going on?"

"It's about Alana."

"You mean the girl you've been obsessed with for the last year?" he asks with a roll of his eyes.

I've been gushing to Banks for months now about Alana and how great I think she is. I didn't realize I had been doing it as often as I had until he told me he had been keeping count of how many times I mentioned her name or brought her up.

Fifteen times in a month, apparently, but that's besides the point.

"We're going to Paris," I say, jumping straight to the point.

"Wait. Paris, France?"

"No. Paris, Texas," I deadpan.

He gives me an exasperated look through the iPhone lens and I continue.

"Heather and Ian scheduled a meeting with us this week and told us they want us to go there to help the European branch of the magazine. Apparently they think we're the top two editors, which I wouldn't argue with, and they wanted to give us the opportunity."

"That's insane. Ian is the guy above you right? Didn't you say he was leaving? Maybe they're putting you two to the test to see who to promote."

I was worried about that. It's not that I wouldn't be honored to receive a promotion, it would be a great move for me, but I really love my job as it is right now. I'm not sure I want the added responsibility.

"They haven't said anything like that, but I suspect that could be what they're doing."

"Okay, so the company is paying you to take a European vacation. What's the problem?"

"Well, it's just Alana and I going. We're going to be staying in an apartment together."

I'm met with silence and blank stares. He's so still, I think I might have lost connection, but after a few seconds I see him blink.

"You have to make a move."

"I don't think I can."

"Are you kidding me? You've been pining after this woman for a whole year and she has no idea. You're telling me you are going to keep her at arms length even when you're living in the same apartment? Come on man. Stop being scared."

This is why Banks is my best friend. He tells it exactly how it is and calls me out on my stuff.

"I don't want to mess up our friendship or make it awkward if she rejects me."

"It's not just that."

"What do you mean?"

His silence has me bracing for his next words and I know he's about to say something I don't want to hear. "Do you think..." He looks away from the screen.

"Just say it."

"Do you think it has something to do with your dad?"

"No."

He looks annoyed by my immediate shut down, but not surprised. We've been down this road before and it never goes well for him. I don't want to talk about my dad.

The only memories I have of my mom and dad together are ones involving screaming fights and slinging insults. Keeping the peace in my house was a constant battle and one I fought with everything I had. Anything I could do to keep my dad level headed and my mom happy, I would do.

My mom asked my dad to do the dishes after dinner, but she went to bed and he just sat on the couch? You'd find me at the sink.

My dad forgot to get my mom flowers and cards on Valentine's Day? I'd be using my allowance and signing his name.

Mom noticed there were a few hundred dollars missing? I'd be sure not to ask for a single thing that cost money.

Dad saw Mom talking to a man in the store? I'd distract him by pulling him towards the baseball cards and asking questions.

Neither of them were bad parents on their own, but together they were a tornado of chaotic emotions. All I could do was take shelter as best I could and pray I came out unscathed. I had, mostly, but I've allowed my dad's inability to be a present husband and father speak into my own beliefs about my ability in these areas.

"Okay, sure bud. If you're going to pretend like that isn't the reason you haven't let yourself work towards a relationship with Alana then I'll pretend with you. But eventually you're going to need to man up and face it."

"I really am worried I'm going to ruin our friendship," I say, trying to bring us back on track and further ignore his insightful words.

"Well, you can't just jump right in. You'll have to warm her up and slowly move yourself out of the friend zone. It's a delicate mission, but it can be accomplished. The guys in my first period have assured me."

I breathe a sigh of relief at his willingness to let it go and keep moving, even though I know there is some truth to his words.

"Do you mean the fifteen-year-old students in your class? Why are they talking to you about the friend zone?"

"You'd be surprised by the topics they choose for discussion."

I shudder thinking about spending my time around teenagers all day. Teachers are some of the bravest souls.

"So how do I move out of the friend zone?" I ask.

"You have to ease her into it. Innocent touches, excuses to be close to her, take note of the things she likes. You're already doing a lot of it, but you just have to kick it up a notch."

We spend the rest of my walk home talking about Alana and ideas for how to hint to her that I want more than our casual friendship. I mention my suspicions of her anxiety, but I don't tell him about the panic attack. That isn't my information to share.

"You're a good guy, Alex," he says as I step through the front door. "You went through a lot with your mom and her anxiety when you were younger and I know it wasn't easy on you. She tells me often how thankful she was to have you by her side. I don't have to talk to Alana to know she feels the same, she just might not realize it yet."

I set the phone down, propping it up against the backsplash so he can see me, and we continue catching up as I make dinner. I feel lighter now that I have a plan to slowly ease Alana into the idea of *us*, and after the conversation with Heather I think things are going to get off to an okay start.

CHAPTER 12
Alana

I hate Mondays. At some point I will write a petition to have Monday be included in the weekend and get every important person ever to sign it. Taylor Swift is at the top of my list. If I can get her behind me I'll have an army of Swifties fighting for my cause.

Cami and I always walk to work together, except for the few times one of us is running late, but on Mondays we leave early and stop by our favorite coffee shop before we head in. It's a bit out of the way to the office because we live so close, but we take the extra time because it's a necessity. It makes the slap in the face of an early start to the week sting less. Except this morning, three in the morning to be exact, she sent me a text telling me she wouldn't be able to walk with me to work because she wasn't home.

She told me yesterday she had a date, which wasn't surprising to me. Cami tends to date around, never staying in one place for long. Our weekly coffee trip is sacred, so it must have gone well enough that she'd stay over and skip.

I stop anyway and pick up coffee for the both of us, because I'm sure she's worn out if her date kept her busy last night. I make my way up to the office and set hers on her desk before sitting down and firing up my computer.

I spent the weekend alone in my apartment mulling over all of the reasons why I shouldn't go to Paris, then decided that I wasn't going to let my anxiety win. I was doing this. It's a once in a life-time opportunity and if I'm getting an all expenses paid trip to Paris, then I'm taking it.

I also spent the weekend thinking about Alex and the fact that I feel so incredibly comfortable around him, which is totally unnerving to me. I haven't felt that comfortable around a man that wasn't my brother since I dated Brad, and we all know how that turned out.

I sent an email to Heather and Ian on Sunday, letting them know of my decision to go to Paris. They had both replied enthusi-astically and a meeting with Heather appeared on my calendar for this morning. Alex is also invited, so I assume it's about our trip.

Cami waltzes in wearing the same top as the one she was wearing in the selfie she sent me last night before her date. I give her a look and point to the coffee on her desk.

"You are a literal angel sent from heaven." She takes the longest sip known to man and sighs so loud she turns heads. "Wow this is so good. Thank you, Lan, really."

"You're welcome. Wild night?"

"You could say that," she says with a wink. I wait for her to give me details, but none come. Normally when Cami hooks up with someone I can't get her to shut up. She usually tells me way more than I want to know and I have to remind her that some things aren't meant to leave the bedroom, but today she is very tight lipped. *Weird.*

I look through my schedule for the day, noting meetings and tasks that need to be done. After that, I start working on a spread that one of the other editors and I started on Friday. I am startled out of my work-induced stupor by a *knock knock* on the wall of my cubicle.

I smell the cedar and sandalwood before I even see him. Looking up, I immediately get lost in his flirty gaze. My eyes begin their slow descent, taking in the strong set of his shoulders and the deep red collared shirt that makes his eyes pop. He's lounged casually against the side of my cubicle wall, one foot crossed over the other and a hand in his pocket. How men can make something so simple, like leaning against a wall, sexy I will never understand. Finally, my eyes make their way back up to his and I see it. Just a slight tug of the corner of his mouth. He's smirking at me and he is absolutely the most gorgeous man I've ever laid my eyes on. I want to take a photo of him right now and hang it on my fridge like a piece of artwork. I realize I've missed something when Alex clears his throat.

"I'm sorry," I say, willing my voice to not betray my thoughts. "I missed that."

"I just said good morning. Struggling to break through the weekend fog?"

"Oh yeah, something like that." He knowingly smirks and my cheeks burn.

"Our meeting with Heather is in ten minutes. I'm going to grab some water from the break room and then head in there. Diet Coke?"

"I thought I'd taught you not to ask stupid questions," I deadpan. "I'll meet you in there, thanks." He smiles at me and tosses today's chocolate onto my desk. White chocolate caramel, yum.

As his broad shoulders disappear around the corner I take a cleansing breath and a sip of ice cold water from my bottle. What is happening to me? Alex has always been gorgeous, but something is pulling me to him now that I haven't felt before. I don't know what's changed, but something has.

This is the worst possible time for this to happen, because not only am I apprehensive about being in a relationship, I am about to be forced to live with this man for at least a month. Not to mention, he doesn't even like me like that.

I groan in frustration and finish up what I'm working on, then head into Heather's office. Alex is already there, a Diet Coke placed in front of my chair. He and Heather are chatting about what they've done over the weekend and they look over at me simultaneously as I walk in.

"Sorry to keep you two waiting," I say with a small smile.

"No sorry necessary, Alex here was early. Have a seat, Alana."

I sit down and fold back the cover on my notebook. I sift through my bag and find the pink pen I've been using lately. I uncap it, write "Meeting with Heather - Paris" as the header, add the date and a few doodles before looking up.

Heather is busy opening her laptop and getting it set up, but I look over at Alex and find him staring at me, eyes glowing with enjoyment.

"I like your drawings. Flowers and hearts?" he asks, his voice a low whisper that causes me to shiver. I try to mask the effect his voice has on my body, but the smile in his eyes tells me I wasn't successful.

"Thanks. It makes the page happier," I whisper back. His quiet laugh and the sparkle in his eyes at my response catches me off guard.

"Alright, let's get started," Heather says, bringing us back to the present. "I just wanted to chat with you two about your trip and the logistics of everything. You fly out in two weeks on Thursday." I can feel my palms getting sweaty just thinking about flying. "Because of this one's flying anxiety," Heather nudges Alex and the color drains from his face. "*Impress* has decided to put you two in first class. The seats in coach are quite small for the seven hour flight. You will be much more comfortable there anyways."

I school my features before my jaw hits the floor. First class flights are not cheap. I know because a few years ago Cami and I wanted to take a girls trip to Cancun and I looked at the tickets, thinking it would be the only way I could get over my fear.

We couldn't afford them at the time so we ended up driving to Florida.

Not to mention, *this one's flying anxiety*? Alex doesn't have flying anxiety, I do. Did he lie to her and blame it on himself so they'd get us better seats that would help me be more comfortable?

While I understand he was trying to help, it feels invasive and sneaky and I don't like it. I give him a look that I hope communicates 'we will be talking about this later' and he glances away. He looks embarrassed, an emotion I don't think I've ever seen him wear.

I turn my attention back to Heather, nodding along as she shares more details.

"We are thankful that the two of you are uprooting your lives for a month or so to help us."

That *or so* makes the anxiety return and I wipe my sweaty palms on the material of my skirt and restlessly stroke the arm of the chair. There is a proposed end date to this trip, but each time there is always mention of a possible extension. The control freak inside of me rears her ugly head and I desperately try to tame her, while listening to what Heather has to say.

I haven't noticed that my left knee is bouncing until I feel a warm but firm hand press it down to still it. From where we are sitting, Heather can't see either of our laps or legs. His hand resting on my knee isn't visible to her, but it's currently burning a fire through me.

I know he can tell I'm frustrated with him, but he still can't help but try to calm my anxious fidgeting. The ratcheting up of my anxiety this week has been extremely frustrating, because I thought I had it under control, but his ability to ease it is almost more startling. Against my better judgment, I realize I miss the warmth of his hand when he pulls it away

"Thank you, Heather, for switching our seats," he says. "I am immensely grateful."

"Enough thank you's," she replies, waving her hand in a dismissive gesture. "Back to the plans."

Oh good. I love plans.

"Each of you will likely be assigned something different when you arrive at the office. Amélie is wonderful and will guide you well."

"What is it that they are needing the most help with right now?" Alex asks.

"Mostly hiring and catching up on the work the editors left behind when they jumped ship."

I begin taking notes in my notebook, and it's like the scratch of my pen on paper is a natural form of anxiety medication. With every swipe of ink, my heart rate lowers.

"Your flight will be overnight. You'll depart from JFK on Friday evening and arrive in Paris early the next morning. Your driver will pick you up at the airport and take you to your flat. His name is Marco and he will be with you through the duration of your time in Paris."

The more Heather speaks, the more excited I become. My pen moves feverishly over the paper, jotting down each important detail she mentions and adding questions that come up as she speaks.

She stops to take a phone call and Alex glances over at me.

"I'm mad at you," I whisper.

"I know. We'll talk about it."

"You better believe we'll talk about it."

"Careful, you're going to burn a hole through that paper," he says playfully.

I stick my tongue out at him and continue writing as Heather hangs up the phone.

"My apologies, where was I?"

"The driver will take us to our flat," Alex supplies.

"Oh yes, so you will be staying in an apartment that has two rooms and an office. The office has two desks in case you both have a need to work in there. Obviously you can each take a room and then you will share the living spaces and kitchen."

My pulse quickens as she talks about how close we will be while we are there and I can't determine if it's from excitement or nerves.

"You will have the weekend to adjust to the time difference, settle in and do a little sightseeing if you'd like to. Then you will both start at the office on Monday morning." She takes a sip of her coffee and leans forward, as if to emphasize that what she says next is important.

"Now, the situation at *Impress Europe* is a bit touchy. One of their top editors was in contact with the editor-in-chief of a French magazine called *Fameux*. They offered her a nice amount of money and a higher paying job if she left *Impress Europe* and brought all of the other editors with her. There are two that chose to stay, but other than those two they have no one else."

"Yikes. That had to hurt," I say, stunned. Editors have a huge role and I couldn't imagine our magazine functioning without that vital branch of our company. I knew the majority of their editors had left, but I wasn't aware of the circumstances surrounding it.

"Exactly, which is where you two come in. Your job will be to help interview and hire a new team of editors, then train them to work as fabulously as the two of you."

That sounds like an overwhelming task, but I know Alex and I can tackle it.

"What about the other two editors who stayed? Did the magazine consider having them help with the hiring and training?" Alex asks.

"Great question, Alex." Heather taps her fingernails on the top of her wooden desk and seems to be thinking about how to answer. "Let's just say, there was a reason these two weren't welcomed in the mass exodus of employees. They aren't the most popular in the crowd and can tend to be a bit snide. You will have to have some tough skin, I'm afraid. I've interacted with them on only one occasion and could feel the ice through the computer screen."

Alex and I share a look of apprehension.

"Lanie will just share a bit of her sunshine. That should warm them right up." The comment would usually make me cringe, but for some reason it doesn't.

I don't know about sunshine, though. I think about my work family here and how I always feel so supported and championed. I guess that isn't what I should expect at *Impress Europe*. I want that promotion, though, so I push past the worried thoughts of workplace mean girls and straighten my shoulders.

"It's nothing we can't handle," I say as a sense of strength flows through me.

"Right, that's why we asked you two. We knew you were perfect for the job." Heather begins clicking around on her computer, our half hour with her almost up. "Let me know if either of you have any questions, I know you will both get everything in order here before you go."

I tell her I will follow up with my questions in an email and we say our goodbyes.

Before heading back to our cubicles, I pull Alex by the elbow into a vacant office and shut the door behind him.

"What the hell was that?" I ask. "Why did you tell her you have anxiety?"

He reaches up and rubs the back of his neck in a move of apprehension.

"I just wanted to make it better for you. I didn't want to break your trust and tell her about your anxiety, but I knew you wouldn't ask for it yourself."

"You're damn right I wouldn't have. I'm a big girl Alex. I can take care of myself."

"You're absolutely right. I know you can and I'm sorry I took it upon myself to fix a problem that you didn't ask for help with."

I take a deep breath in and do my best to breathe out the frustration.

"Thank you. I know you were just trying to help and I appreciate the fact that you care enough to want me to be okay. I just want to be in on the conversations about how we're going to accomplish that."

"Completely fair."

After a heavy pause, I decide to move on. I've made my desires and issues known and if he crosses that boundary again, I'll say something.

"Well, Ashford, looks like we're going to be living together for a month."

He stares at me with a half smile on his face.

"Looks like we are, sunshine. I can't wait to find out if you snore loud enough to hear it from the next room."

I smile at him and shove his shoulder playfully. He laughs and we head back to our desks. Instead of separating and going to his, he grabs his chair and pulls it into my space. He points to my notebook.

"Why don't you pull that bad boy out and we can debrief that meeting."

I appreciate that he doesn't make fun of my obsessive note taking. Doing as he says, I take out my notes and we talk for the next hour about our excitements and worries. For the first time in a while, I feel this bubbling of anticipation of the future. After my ex, I really didn't know what to do with myself. I wasn't able to see the good in anything and I couldn't get myself to feel excitement over even the small things. That all seems to be changing and it's a really good feeling.

Over the next two weeks we will be running at one hundred miles per hour getting everything here settled so we can go to Paris, and as we plan how to accomplish everything, I find myself becoming more and more enthralled by him.

No matter how intriguing I find him or how good he makes me feel, I keep reminding myself that I cannot go there. He might be a great guy, but in my experience, relationships and men only lead to pain and heartbreak.

I repeat the mantra to myself.

I will not fall for Alex Ashford.

CHAPTER 13
Alex & Alana

Wednesday, November 15

ALEX

What's your favorite TV show?

ALANA

Why are you asking?

ALEX

Because I want to get to know you.

ALANA

New Girl.

ALANA

I've probably seen it at least five times through. It's the perfect background show and it's insanely funny.

ALEX

YOUTHS.

ALANA

You get me. What's yours?

ALEX

The Office 100%.

ALANA

I haven't seen that one. Maybe I need to give it a try.

ALEX

I'm sorry, we can't be friends any more.
Gotta go.

ALANA

Oh, whatever.

ALANA

…

ALANA

Okay, seriously. I promise I'll watch it, you big baby.

Saturday, November 18

ALANA

Omg, have you seen these huge croissants? << sends link to TikTok >>

ALEX

Giant croissants? Do you seriously think I would have kept this incredible knowledge to myself if I had known?

ALEX

Do you think they'll let us leave early? Because I think I need that right now.

ALANA

That thing is bigger than my head! And I bet it's buttery and flakey…

ALEX

Buttery, flakey crust.

ALANA

Huh?

ALEX

Have you not seen that video?

ALANA

...

ALEX

I'll see myself out.

Sunday, November 19

ALANA

I hope we see Timothee.

ALEX

Who is Timothee?

ALANA

...you're joking?

ALEX

Is that like a long lost friend? Your grandpa's butcher? An old neighbor? Oh, I know! Tiny Tim from A Christmas Carol?

ALANA

Yes, Tiny Tim from A Christmas Carol.

ALEX

Gotta love Charles Dickens.

ALANA

Seriously, do you not know who Timothee Chalamet is?

ALEX

Should I?

ALANA

Have you not seen Wonka?

ALEX

You know I don't keep up with actors' names.

ALEX

And no, why would I purposefully put myself
through Wonka?

ALANA

You have no idea what you've just gotten
yourself into. Wonka is a great movie and I will
be proving it to you.

ALEX

I'm looking forward to it.

ALEX

But wait, isn't Timothee American? Why would
we even see him?

ALANA

You're outing yourself right now…

ALANA

I don't know why we would see him, I think he
literally grew up in New York, but his name is
French, so.

Tuesday, November 21

ALANA

I downloaded Duolingo.

ALEX

That was a great idea. What have you learned
so far?

ALANA

Brace yourself, I think you're going to be
wowed by my level of knowledge.

ALEX

Hit me.

ALANA

Une femme et un homme.

ALEX

A woman and a man.

ALANA

Tu manges une pizza.

ALEX

You are eating a pizza.

ALANA

And my favorite one, Chien.

ALEX

How did I know dog would be your favorite word? Incredible work, I can't wait to see you put it into practice when we get there.

ALANA

Watch out because I will be looking like a pro. I already have a two day streak.

ALEX

You learned all of that in two days? Look at you go! As long as we end up in a situation with a man and woman eating a pizza with their dog, you'll be all set.

ALANA

I guarantee you we will be in that very situation at least once.

CHAPTER 14
Alana

"Coming," Charlie yells as he walks to my front door to let Cami in.

I leave tomorrow morning for Paris, and I haven't packed a single thing. Even though I'm excited for the trip, I'm also terrified, which has led to ultimate levels of procrastination.

When I told Cami I still needed to pack, she did what she always does and vowed to make it fun. She declared tonight was a packing party and called Charlie to invite him. She told me he was excited to hang, but I overheard the conversation and it sounded a lot more like force.

Not that it takes much to convince him to hang out with us, he just always pretends like he doesn't want to. We know the truth, though.

The more I think about leaving Cami and Charlie, the more nervous I get. They are my safe place, and while I've grown increasingly more comfortable around Alex in the last few weeks, nothing amounts to the level of comfort I have with my two best friends.

The three of us haven't really discussed the fact that I'm leaving and I'm perfectly okay with that, but the closer we get to tomorrow morning, the more real it's becoming.

Last night I was feeling particularly panicky, so in an effort to help me sink further into denial, I wrote out the list of traditions that Alex requested. I didn't allow myself to think about the reasoning behind the list. I pretended I was doing it for the sake of nostalgia and put pen to paper as I stared out the window at the falling snow and sipping hot chocolate.

Growing up, we always had a good time around the holidays. It seemed like the only time my mom and dad put aside their clear favoritism for one child over the other and actually brought us all together to celebrate. I'm not sure why that is, maybe it was just to keep up appearances, but as a little girl starved for attention I didn't question it. My mom created lots of small moments of magic throughout the November and December months through these traditions, but now the only way to keep them alive is with Charlie.

We started taking over the traditions list when we were in college. Our parents became empty nesters and they took full advantage of that. Whereas before we would spend holidays and the weeks surrounding them together, now it was just Charlie and I alone in our childhood home. Our parents always wanted to travel the world and with us gone, they made those dreams a reality.

My parents were distant from me in every way, except for during the holidays, so it felt like the last strand that held us together snapped when they stopped spending the holidays with us. We used to speak on the phone every few months and they'd acknowledge my existence at least, but once we went to college it was out of sight out of mind.

Even with Charlie, they stopped calling as much. They never visited and the more I let myself care about it the more it hurt. Eventually, we decided we were going to make our own Christmas magic and thus the list of traditions was born. Some of them were ones we carried through from when we were kids, and some were brand new.

I left it on Alex's desk at the end of the day today. I'm not sure what his intentions are with it. He played it off like he just wanted to know about my traditions, but I would be lying if I said I wasn't suspicious.

"Hello, Charles," I hear Cami say from around the corner.

"Cassandra," he replies curtly.

Cami comes barreling into my room with a huge smile on her face, Charlie following closely behind.

"Alright, what do we have here?" Cami asks as she starts wading through the pile of clothes I've thrown onto my bed.

"I honestly have no clue what to bring. It's going to be cold, so I threw in some coats and sweaters."

"Ugh, I love this one," Cami says as she hugs an oversized red, black and green Gucci cardigan to her chest. It was gifted to me from one of last year's shoots and I'm always too terrified to wear it, but this might be a good occasion.

I take the cardigan from her and start going through the rest of my items, but get distracted when my phone lights up with a text message.

ALEX

Winter or summer?

He started doing this about a week ago. He said if we were going to be living together, we needed to know more about each other, so he started asking me random questions. I know a lot about Alex because we're friends and we've worked together for a year, but I've been surprised by the amount of things I didn't know.

Despite my fears of growing closer to Alex, it feels nice having someone take the time to get to know me. To know my ins and outs, but also the simple things like what season I might like.

I never know the time of day that the message will come, but he hasn't missed a day since he started. I find myself looking forward to them and sometimes hovering around my phone waiting for the specific chime that I've set up for his contact.

I type back a reply, hit send and toss my phone to the bed.

ME

Winter. Always.

I can feel the heat rise to my cheeks and the smile spread across my face without my permission.

"What are you smiling at?" Charlie asks, glancing from the phone and back to me, a frown on his face.

"Nothing, I'm not smiling," I say, and walk out of the room to avoid his questions.

"Yeah, right," I hear Charlie whisper under his breath. A minute later I hear a thud and peek my head back in to find him on the floor. He curses under his breath and I giggle to myself because I know Cami likely put him in his place for trying to snoop.

I grab my cosmetic bag and begin filling it with countless serums, toners, face washes and moisturizers. Next, I add my makeup and make my way back to my bedroom. I decide to keep my face clean for the flight, considering I will be sleeping for most of it and don't want a full face of makeup on.

I continue packing my two huge suitcases, throwing in as much fashionable workwear as I can find. As I'm folding things up and placing it in my suitcase, Cami hands me a red Valentino mini dress that I haven't worn since it appeared on my desk one day after a particularly long work month. Sometimes Heather gifts us items from the fashion department and I always take full advantage.

It's a simple dress, but at the shoulders there are two small red bows that connect a kind of cape that covers my arms and hangs down the back. It's so beautiful, but it isn't office appropriate at all. It's way too dressy. I tell Cami as much, but she scoffs at me.

"You never know...maybe Ashford will take you out and you'll need a sexy red number," she says with a wink.

"Yeah, right. Never going to happen."

"Still, you need to bring this with you. If not for a date, then for drinks or a work event. You never know."

She makes a good point, so I add it to the things I'm bringing. I pack a garment bag with all of the hanging items that would be wrong to fold, including the Valentino, and decide to carry it onto the plane.

The beginning notes of *"Best Day"* by Taylor Swift hit my ears and I reach for my phone. I press next just as she begins to sing about a time when she was young and her mom helped her put her coat on. My mommy issues mixed with the high emotions of today will not survive that song.

As I'm setting my phone back down, I notice a text.

ALEX

Reasoning?

ME

I can layer on as many articles of clothing as I want to get warm. I can only take off so much. Also, the snow is pretty.

After I press send, I automatically regret my choice of words.

'I can only take off so much'? Seriously Alana? Might as well have said, *'Are you free tonight ;)?'*

I'm about to double text to assuage my anxiety and embarrassment, but he responds before I get to.

ALEX

Makes complete sense. Are you currently trying to pack your entire wardrobe into two suitcases, or is that just me? I am a chronic overpacker.

I giggle and take a deep breath, thankful he didn't read too far into my response.

ME

Not so fast, you didn't answer the question. Favorite season?

ME

And yes, I am doing exactly that.

ALEX

Thrilled you'd want to know my answer as well. I would say autumn. I love the weather and the leaves and the smell of the air. Well air that isn't in the city.

I react to his message with a heart and tune back into the conversation Charlie and Cami are having. They're talking about seeing *The Nutcracker* ballet and a twinge of sadness hits as I realize I won't be going with them this year. I must be visibly closing in on myself because they both notice that I've gone quiet.

Someone who didn't know Charlie fully might say these traditions were completely out of character for him, and they wouldn't necessarily be wrong, but they were about something other than just the event to him. Back before he turned into stormy Charlie, the way I refer to him when discussing his high school transformation with Cami, he was all about the holiday stuff. This is one of the only ways he shows that old version of himself to me.

"Hey, Sis, don't be sad. The ballet is boring anyways. Plus we can FaceTime you so you can watch it with us. I don't care about the no phone rules," he says as he gets up and envelopes me in the biggest bear hug.

"Don't let Mrs. Lewis hear you say that," Cami replies, referencing our theater loving neighbor down the hall. "Let's finish up here and then I'm commissioning an emergency feel good movie. Which one are you thinking we should watch tonight?"

My three favorite comfort films are, in no particular order: *13*

Going on 30, The Devil Wears Prada, and *Father of the Bride.* Tonight I am thinking I need a little Mark Ruffalo in my life.

"Let's watch *13 Going on 30.*"

"You got it."

Before I can zip up my suitcase, I notice Cami slip in a handful of black fabric.

"What is that?" I ask, picking it up and holding out...a black bikini? "Cami, why in the world would I need this? What is this even covering? There's barely any fabric here."

"Exactly. You need a saucy little number if you and Alex get cozy and you want to close the deal. It's sexy."

I can't deny the bathing suit is sexy, but just thinking about putting it on makes me want to throw up. I haven't shown that much skin in...I don't think ever. Despite my knowledge that my ex is scum of the earth, his words still sit in the back of my mind. This bikini is a painful reminder of the thoughts that swirl when I consider showing off more of my body than normal.

"I don't need this. Paris is freezing and he doesn't need to see this much skin. We aren't like that."

"Okay first of all, there are indoor hot tubs," she says, ticking off on her fingers, "and second, you know you want him deep down. You'll be glad you have it with you if you decide you want to make a move. Come on, just take it."

I roll my eyes and let her put it back in my bag, knowing I won't be utilizing it. It's easier not to fight it.

We zip up my suitcases, weigh them to be sure they aren't over the limit and pile together on the couch, me in the middle and Charlie and Cami on either side of me. We cuddle and watch the movie, laughing at all of our favorite parts and singing along to the soundtrack.

When the movie is over we throw blankets onto the floor in front of the TV and fall asleep to *The Father of the Bride.* I feel content and safe and, for one night, the scary changes that are about to take place in my life don't exist. Within these walls and with these people I am so happy.

The sun rises, morning comes, and they each hug me before they leave to go to work. I make it through the entire goodbye without crying, but I feel the first tear slip down my cheek just as I shut the door and stand in my empty apartment.

I turn my back to the door, lean against it, and slide down. The hot tears begin to fall in streams down my face and I use the back of my hand to wipe at them. As I work to calm myself down, Cami's name lights up my phone screen. I look at it and let out a small laugh.

BESTIE FRIEND

You are allowed to be sad for 10 minutes. I'll text you when they're up.

I thumbs up her message and allow myself to feel my emotions, knowing they will pass. I feel my way through the fear, the uncertainty, the sadness. Then, exactly ten minutes later, my phone dings.

BESTIE FRIEND

Alright, no more crying. Time to fly to freaking Paris! I am so excited for you.

ME

Thanks. I love you.

BESTIE FRIEND

I love you too, bestie friend.

I take a deep breath, get up off the floor and head to the bathroom to shower. This is going to be a good day.

Alana's Christmas Tradition List

 Pick out ornaments for each other

 Decorate the tree together

 Watch Elf with cookies and cocoa

 Look at window displays

 Advent calendar Christmas countdown

 See The Nutcracker ballet

 Go ice skating

 Have a gingerbread house making competition

 Gift each other a set of Christmas PJs to wear on Christmas Eve

 Bake homemade cinnamon rolls with Charlie on Christmas morning

CHAPTER 15
Alex

My least favorite thing about traveling? The security line.

You might be thinking, not all of the people? The check in line? The crying babies?

The answer would be no. I hate all of those things considerably less than I hate the security line. There is something about it that ratchets up my stress and it's like I can't relax until I have crossed that item off of the traveling to-do.

I'm standing just outside of the line, having already checked my bags, eyes peeled for a flash of chocolate brown hair. I've been here for about thirty minutes and it seems like the longer I watch the chaos of the line in front of me, the more antsy I become.

In an effort to distract myself, I pull out my phone and scroll on the local news site. I click on an article about turbulence, thinking it might come in handy later, and skim the information. I am so engrossed in the article that I don't notice the two feet standing right in front of me until Alana clears her throat.

I glance up from my phone and into the bright blue eyes staring up at me and smile, and just the sight of her removes all of the stress I was feeling just moments ago.

"Hey, Lanie."

She's wearing white tennis shoes, black leggings that hug the curves of her legs perfectly and an oversized gray sweatshirt with the college letters "UCMH" on the front in blue and gold embroidery. Her hair is down and in loose waves that I want to sink my fingers into. She looks at me quizzically, probably wondering why I'm staring at her.

She's so beautiful, it's impossible not to.

"UCMH?" I ask, referencing her sweatshirt.

"It's from a book," she answers with a soft smile.

"How are you feeling?" I ask, taking note of the tension in her shoulders.

"I'm nervous," she says with a self-deprecating chuckle. "I feel better than I thought I would, but I'm still a little anxious. Just hoping I'm masking it somewhat."

"No need to mask it. Admittedly, I'm nervous about the whole trip too. I guess I'm in good company."

"I don't know about that." Her cheeks go pink and she looks down at her feet.

"There's no one else I'd rather do this with."

Her eyes widen a little in shock before going back to normal and I realize I might have just been a tad too honest. Oh well, I'm not going to backtrack. I'm trying to get myself out of the friend zone and per the article I read last night, *subtle flirty comments can communicate to your love interest that you want to be more than just friends.*

We chat about logistics as we move through the security line and wait for our turn.

The closer we get, I notice Lana starts to take things out of her bag and pile them into the crook of her left arm. Her iPad, laptop, and Kindle all rest in between her arm and her chest.

"What are you doing?" I ask

"It stresses me out to have to get all of my stuff out of my backpack when I get to the X-Ray machine, so I try to do it back here. Then I can just place it in a bin and I'm not rushed."

Huh. That does sound less stressful. I start pulling my laptop and iPad out of my backpack and balance it in my arm like she does.

She smiles at me and moves forward to a TSA officer to show her boarding pass and passport. I move to the one next to her to do the same.

We each go through security and make it to the other side without any issues. I walk up to her as she is reassembling her backpack and putting her shoes back on.

We make our way to the gate and just before we get there, we walk past a small store with every snack you could imagine. We veer off in that direction and split up, she goes towards the fridge of drinks and I head towards the snacks.

A few minutes later I'm still trying to decide on what to get when I notice her walking up to me holding a Diet Coke and a sparkling water.

The amount of satisfaction I feel from her knowing what I want should worry me, but at this point it's par for the course when it comes to this woman.

"Well, well, well. How the turn tables."

"Did you seriously just quote Michael Scott?"

"The one and only."

"You must be watching the show."

She shrugs and hands me my water before turning towards the wall of snacks and I decide this is the perfect time for a question, but before I can ask she reaches up and grabs a blue bag of Doritos for herself and a bag of Combos.

"Are those for me?" I ask, surprise clear in my voice I'm sure.

"They are," she answers matter-of-factly and hands them over.

"How did you know I liked Combos?"

"You've gotten them a few times from the vending machine at work."

"Maybe twice." I try to meet her eyes, to tell her without words how touched I am by this simple gesture, but she just shrugs and turns to walk down the aisle to the candy.

I hesitate, but eventually follow her and shake off my reaction. It's just Combos. Not that serious.

"Who even likes Combos? What a weird snack."

"Weird? They're hollowed out pretzels with cheese in the middle. That doesn't sound like the perfect salty snack to you?"

She turns and looks at me over her shoulder, raising her eyebrows and narrowing her eyes as if to say *what do you think?*

I shake my head disapprovingly and go back to the question I had planned to ask earlier.

"Sweet or salty?"

Her eyes jump to mine and she smiles bigger than I've ever seen her smile. I love it.

I haven't asked her any of these daily questions in person until now. Usually I text them in the evening after we've gone home or early in the morning before work. It's clear by her visible reaction that she enjoys this game. Obviously it's fun to get to know one another better, but she's more delighted by it than I anticipated.

"Well, I'm not sure if that's a fair question. Can my answer be both?"

"Only if you can explain why."

She smirks at me and opens her drink, taking a sip.

"When I'm anxious, sometimes I like sour candy," she answers. "Apparently there is something about the shock of the sour taste that can distract your brain. My therapist suggested it to help with panic attacks. Right after Brad, I was having them a lot and..." she trails off, and I can visibly see on her face the moment she starts to overthink whether she should continue going down this path.

"And did the sour candy help?" I ask softly, encouraging her to continue.

"It did," she says with a shy smile. After a deep sigh, she pushes on. "Anyways, I tried it and it did help. Obviously it isn't one hundred percent effective and doesn't really remove all of the panic, but it does ease it a bit."

"So, sweet then?"

"Sweet and sour during a panic attack," she says with a wink. "But if I'm choosing a snack, I would choose something salty." She holds up the blue bag of chips. "What about you?"

"My answer would be sweet."

"Because..." she says, leading me to explain.

"When I lived at home, my mom would always bake these incredible cookies. They were pumpkin cream cheese and she would bake them all year, not just in the fall. She would roll the dough in cinnamon sugar before they went in the oven and it gave them this really nice crunch. Literal heaven in a cookie."

I get lost in the memory of sunny afternoons in the kitchen with my mom, laughing as we listened to '80s music and she let me stir the batter. Alana's voice brings me back to the present.

"I am formally requesting that you teach me how to make those cookies at some point. For now though, I have an idea."

"I'm listening."

She takes my hand again and drags me over to the area where the books are. There are all kinds of books in front of us. Horror, fantasy, romance, comedy, autobiographies, thriller— you name it, this tiny airport store has it. I'm honestly impressed.

"Okay Lanie...what are we doing in front of the books?"

"We each get to pick one book for the other person to read on the trip," she replies, eyes already scanning back and forth through the rows.

"I haven't read a book in a long time. I used to love reading when I was a teenager."

"Oh yeah? What was your drug of choice?"

"I was particularly interested in "The Hunger Games." Still really like it."

"That series is phenomenal."

"You're not wrong about that." I start looking at the selection and have a thought. "I'm adding a rule."

"Tell me your rule and I will decide if we are adding it."

"Okay, bossy." She rolls her eyes. "We each surprise the other and don't reveal our book choices until we are on the plane."

"Okay, I like it."

"That was easy."

I wander back over to the snacks to finally make a decision and give her time to choose her selection for me. After she lets me know that she has purchased it and it is safely tucked away in a bag, I move over to the books.

I have a secret weapon in this game. I look over my shoulder one more time to make sure she isn't watching, then I pull out my phone and open the reading tracking and reviewing app I know Lana uses.

She has mentioned it to me before and I've seen her leaving reviews or marking her progress at the end of lunch when she's had time to read. I found her account and started following it a few months ago. While poking around, I discovered that there is a spot where you can mark books you want to read, so I navigate to that section of her profile and start looking to see if any of the books on the app are on the shelves here.

I see a book about a single dad who plays baseball and grab it off the shelf. I quickly pay and find her looking at the neck pillows towards the front of the store. We make our way to the gate and take a seat. As I busy myself with getting settled and pulling my laptop out, I notice Alana making a call.

She is FaceTiming Cami and I'm staring at my emails, but not really reading them. It's impossible to focus with her as close as she is. I can't take my eyes off of her, and thankfully her attention being on Cami allows my stare to go unnoticed. The outfit she chose today is so casual that it has me picturing Saturday after-noons at home with a certain brunette woman curled up on my couch. I'm imagining her wavy tresses piled atop her head in the most beautiful messy bun that she throws her hair into when she's annoyed with it after a long day. I would get dinner started and she'd light a few candles and turn on the perfect soundtrack for the occasion, because that's something she's weirdly good at.

I'm snapped out of my daydream when Alana waves bye to Cami through the phone and pulls out her Kindle. I go back to staring at the email I've had open for the last twenty minutes.

Before I know it, the gate agent speaks into the intercom to let us know we're about to begin boarding. I start to gather my things and she packs her bag and stands, pushing her arms through the loops. I notice her reach into her bag and grab the sour watermelon candy she bought as we get closer to the gate. She pops a few in her mouth and chews, then lets out a deep breath.

A sense of pride blooms in my chest at the way she cares for herself. She was nervous about this trip, but she's got this. I'm glad I'm here if she needs me, but she needs to prove to herself that she can do it.

They call group one and we step up, scanning our tickets and moving forward to walk down the tunnel that leads to the plane. As we get closer to the entrance, I notice her breathing deeply a few times. I reach over and squeeze her hand once before letting it go. She smiles at me and continues forward, looking her fear right in the face.

I remember this feeling of helplessness with my mom. When you care so much about someone and see them struggling through panic and anxiety, the need to quiet it for them is overwhelming. But I can't quiet it *for* her, she can do that all on her own. I need to just be here to support her.

"You can do this," I whisper in her ear. She nods up at me and the look of determination in her eyes makes me proud.

When we make it to the entrance of the plane, we turn toward the left to the first class cabin, instead of towards the right for business and economy seating. There are two kind looking flight attendants directing people to their seats.

Each of our seats are like little pods with a seat that lays back flat, a small screen and an area to keep all of our items. We're seated next to each other, but there's a divider in between us that lowers to just below waist height, so we can make it one big pod if we want.

Alana sits in her spot and I go around to the other aisle to find mine. We each get started putting our bags away and settling in for the long flight ahead. I press the button to lower the divider so I can see her, and she startles a little at the movement.

"That's nifty," she says, watching it's slow descent.

"Now we can play cards or something."

"Play cards? What are you, eighty?"

"People play cards," I say and narrow my eyes at her.

"Whatever, Ashford."

She's still munching on those gummy candies, but I can tell she's calmed a bit now that we're settled and in our seats.

"Hey, before we take off do you want to exchange books?" I ask.

"Oh, yes. I completely forgot. Me first." She pulls a thin book out of the bag and hands it to me. It looks to be a thriller about a therapist that went missing and after reading the back, I am actually very excited to dig in.

"This looks great."

"I think you'll like it. The twists and turns are so good. I can't wait to see your face when you get to that part."

I grab my book and hand it over to her, then pass her today's chocolate square. She smiles at the chocolate, but as she looks at the book I chose her eyes widen in surprise and she looks up at me.

"How did you know I wanted this book?" she asks in wonder.

"I looked at your reading tracking app and picked the one with the highest rating in your want to read section."

"You did not. That is one of the sweetest things anyone has ever done."

For not the first time, I find myself irritated at her ex. The fact that she dated him for years and he still treated her like she had no real place in his life is infuriating. She deserves so much more and I'm determined to give it to her.

"I'm happy to do it, it's quite the app. You've got some pretty interesting books on there Lanie."

Her entire face turns pink and she glances away. I laugh. A little while later, the pilot tells the flight attendants to prepare for takeoff and I notice Alana shift in her seat a little.

The noises in the plane start to get louder, the vibration growing stronger as it picks up speed down the runway. She takes another breath and closes her eyes, then holds her hand out towards me.

"Don't read into it Ashford," she says, eyes still closed. "For whatever reason the anxiety isn't so loud when I'm touching you."

I say nothing, because what the hell am I supposed to say to that, and silently grab her hand. She squeezes, as if to say thank you, and pulls her headphones on with her opposite hand. I do the same and sit back. We take off and she breathes through it, then pulls her hand away. By the time we get up in the air, she's relaxed.

She picks her book up, opens to the first page and starts reading.

CHAPTER 16

Alana

I'm DOING IT. I'M IN AN AIRPLANE IN THE AIR AND I'M flying. Well, sort of.

I am trying so hard to concentrate on my book, but I keep getting distracted by Alex next to me. He's been flipping the pages on the thriller I chose for him pretty quickly, which isn't surprising to me. That book is addicting.

My single dad baseball romance is also incredibly captivating, but I can't stop thinking about how Alex knew which book to get for me.

You might be thinking: *Alana, why are you freaking out over the fact that this man did one nice thing?* To that I'd say, I'm not sure. It just felt like a big deal to have someone recall a conversation we had months ago and go to the trouble to download an app just to get the answer to what book I might like to read. It felt intentional. It felt like he cared enough to put effort into it, rather than just appeasing me and moving forward. It made me feel like I meant something to him.

His actions have me questioning my *all men suck* stance, making me think maybe there are good men out there. Ones that are nothing like my ex and my father. Ones that support you. I so desperately want to let Alex in and open up to him, but the fear stops me from fully letting go. Despite the fact that he's been nothing but phenomenal, there's a wall in my heart that refuses to fall. It does feel like it might be crumbling a little at the edges, though.

I wiggle a bit in my seat and vow to read for the next twenty minutes before I take another break to stare off into space. I set a timer on my phone, start my playlist and draw my eyes down to my book.

The next time I look up, I realize way more than twenty minutes have passed and I've made it at least halfway through the book. When I get immersed in a really good story, time doesn't exist, but I need to stretch and rest my eyes for a minute. I slide my *Gilmore Girls* bookmark in place and set my book down.

Before long, the first class attendant is coming around to bring us our dinner. I've never flown first class, mostly because I never fly, so I haven't ever eaten a meal on a plane like this before.

She sets down a warm plate with some sort of pasta dish covered in tomato sauce. There's a small slice of warmed bread on the side, along with a chocolate chip cookie. My stomach betrays me by growling and Alex lets out a chuckle.

"You must be hungry," he says to me.

"I didn't have much for lunch today, just ate a quick protein bar before I left for the airport, so I am pretty hungry."

The attendant brings me a glass of white wine and I take a sip before digging into my food, humming after the first bite. Airplane food has no right being this good.

"Is yours as good as mine, or am I just so hungry that anything would taste good at this point?" I ask.

"No, mine is pretty good for airplane food. I'm sure we will find much better once we get to Paris, but it definitely isn't bad."

I nod and keep eating, but as I get to the end of my plate I start to think that maybe I should leave a little pasta behind so it doesn't look like I ate too much. I leave a few bites worth on my plate and move to the cookie. I split it in half and slip the other half back into the sleeve it came in and set it aside.

I finish half of the cookie and then look down at my plate, recognizing I'm still hungry and really want to finish it, but feeling like I can't. It's irritating when I do this.

I've talked to my counselor about these moments. It will happen randomly. Brad's voice flashes through my head, all the comments he made throughout the years coming back, and I experience an overwhelming feeling of *not enough*.

Today, and most times, it's finishing my meal. Sometimes it's trying on new clothes or trying something a bit more form fitting. Other times it's messaging a guy on a dating app.

There's no way that's going to fit you.

Your hips are really feeling fuller.

Do you really think you'd be able to find anyone but me? I remember him saying after a pretty nasty fight where I threatened to leave.

I've done so much work to move past the way he affected me, but it still paralyzes me sometimes, especially when my anxiety is high—which it absolutely has been today. It's frustrating to be a year past the breakup and still struggling with this, but I'm further along than I used to be so I have to give myself *some* credit.

I pull out my journal that Dr. Rodriguez gave me and write down my actions and the thoughts that came up. I notice Alex looking at me out of the corner of my eye, but I ignore him and continue to jot down the phrases that came to mind as I was working on finishing my food. I think he might ask me about it, but he doesn't.

After I've finished writing everything down I put my small notebook back into my backpack, take a deep breath and begin eating again.

I eat slowly, assessing how I feel after each bite, and stop once I am actually full, which is after I've finished the pasta dish and eaten the slice of bread, leaving half of the cookie behind. I slip it into my backpack for later and then grab the small blanket and pillow the airline provided and tap Alex on the shoulder.

"I'm going to try to get some rest."

"Okay, sure. How are you feeling?"

"Better than I expected. A little jittery but nothing too terrible."

His grin would have knocked me over had I not been sitting down. I was nervous about this trip, but each step I've taken today has felt like a huge accomplishment and it feels good to prove to myself that I *can* do this. Just because something seems scary doesn't mean I can't do it.

"That's great Lanie. I'm so proud of you."

My unstable emotions can't handle his kindness.

"Thanks," I say with a smile before turning to face the opposite way and settling into my seat. I close my eyes and drift off to sleep thinking about Alex's hand in mine and his words of encouragement whispered into my ear.

CHAPTER 17

Alex

THIS IS ONE OF THE BEST BOOKS I'VE EVER READ. THE only other books I've read recently have been required reading for high school and college.

This one has me on the edge of my seat and I can't put it down. It's been a few hours since we boarded and I've had my nose stuck in it this entire time. Every so often I get distracted by the sleeping beauty next to me. Her lips slightly parted, soft breaths in and out. She has the most peaceful look on her face.

I've been satisfied with our friendship being the extent of our closeness, but this trip feels like a nudge in a direction I had convinced myself we would never go.

After another hour or so, I decide I should try to get some sleep. Most passengers are resting or watching a movie and the cabin is dark. I reach up and turn off the light above my seat, place a gum wrapper where I was in my book and lay my seat into the flat position.

Eventually I drift off, only to be awoken by the jostling of the plane. The cabin is shaking and vibrating, cluing me in to the fact that we must be in some turbulence. I hear the chime that alerts the passengers that the pilot has turned the fasten seatbelt sign on and see the seat belt icon above my chair light up.

Lana.

I turn to check on her and feel automatic relief when I realize that she is still asleep. It's short lived, though.

The plane shakes and jerks, sending passengers just a tiny bit airborne. I see heads bounce up out of their seats and hear a few shouts of surprise. Alana must have heard them as well, because I notice her startle awake. She jerks upright and the peaceful expression that was on her face is replaced with one of terror.

"Alex?" Her eyes dart around until they find me. I lean over and place a hand on her arm gently, in an effort not to spook her further. She's been so strong today, but this amount of shaking would unsettle anyone.

"Hey, Lanie shh. It's okay, just a bit of turbulence." I see the war in her eyes and it seems like she wants to ask for something, but she hesitates. The bumps continue and another bad one sends us jumping. Her breathing escalates even higher and I curse under my breath.

"Can you hold me?" she asks quietly, so quietly that I wouldn't have heard if my entire attention wasn't focused on her right now.

I freeze and stare at her. We hit another bump and I have to reach out to steady myself so I don't fall over.

"Shit," she breathes. Her hands start to shake and she looks at me with so much fear and frustration. Not with me, but with herself. "Please, if you just hold me and sort of squeeze a little, it will help."

She hasn't asked for one single bit of my help today, so the fact that she's asking now must mean she really needs it. I don't hesitate for another second. I stand and awkwardly climb over the barrier between us, then nudge her shoulder.

"Scoot over, Lan." She turns away from me and scoots to the edge of the chair. I lay down behind her and put my arms around her trembling body. I'm almost certain that what we are doing right now is not allowed or at the very least frowned upon, but I'm not concerned about that right now. No one could pry me away from her at this point.

I reach around her and grab the seat belt. Safety first.

"You've got this," I whisper in her ear as I snap the seat belt around our hips.

"Oh shut up Ashford," she breathes through trembling lips. She has full body shivers now, but the more pressure I apply to her arms the more she seems to calm down. "Everyone rides on airplanes and no one I know needs their hot coworker to spoon them and provide deep pressure therapy."

I ignore the hot coworker comment and rub my hands up and down her left arm, trying to stifle my laughter. All of the flight attendants are sitting back in their seats because of the commotion, which allows me to stay here with Lana a bit longer.

I start talking in a low voice to her about what I did this morning. I go through my whole morning routine, talking in a soothing voice. Then I have her walk me through her morning. As she talks, her breathing slows and the trembling halts. The turbulence has died down and the plane is steady.

"Can I scratch your back? My mom always used to scratch my back when I couldn't fall asleep."

She hesitates for a moment and then nods her head. I begin scratching her back lightly and the longer I do it the more relaxed her body becomes.

I notice her breathing start to deepen, alerting me to the fact that she is asleep again. I know I should get up and move back to my seat, but I take full advantage of having her in my arms and stay put for a few more minutes.

Finally I determine it's time to get up before a flight attendant comes over and wakes her up again. I slowly slip my arm out from beneath her, unbuckle the seatbelt, scoot out from behind her and snap it back in place. I grab the blanket that has fallen and cover her up. Hopefully she will sleep for the majority of the rest of the flight.

I lay back down on my chair and my fingertips tingle. I fall asleep thinking about how good it felt to have my hands on her.

CHAPTER 18

Alana

My nose is practically glued to the window of the town car as we drive through the city.

The rest of the flight was uneventful, thank the heavens. I woke up when the pilot announced our descent and immediately remembered begging Alex to hold me.

I didn't say anything to him about my mid-flight panic attack and he seemed content to leave it as well. I was thankful.

After we collected our luggage and walked outside, we found a short man with graying hair holding a sign with our names on it. He introduced himself as Marco and led us to a beautiful black town car.

I think Alex has tried to start a conversation with me a few times, but I am completely distracted by the hustle and bustle happening outside of our car as we drive. My eyes are peeled just in case I see a famous monument or something.

Once I got off the plane I automatically felt so much lighter. I am away from my ex, away from the city that was starting to feel suffocating and I have a clear path forward to level up my career.

I am also accompanied by one of the few people on this earth who doesn't bother the hell out of me. My eyes aren't on him, but it's impossible to ignore his tall frame next to me. Impossible to ignore the heat of his body and the way mine wants to reach out for him without my permission.

I take a deep breath and remind myself why I'm here. I am not going to think about him. I am not going to think about how good it felt to be held by him or the way he makes me feel seen or the cute little smile he has when he looks at me like we share a secret. Thinking about those things will only lead to feelings that I do not want to allow myself to have.

I repeat the mantra to myself.

I will not fall for Alex Ashford.

Not only is this the most complicated time to start something with Alex because we are about to be roommates, I am dealing with way too much from my ex's reappearance. It's shaken me and brought up feelings that I thought were resolved.

I'm snapped out of the trance as Alex nudges his shoulder into mine.

"Lanie, look."

He motions out his side of the window and there it is. The Eiffel Tower. *Oh my gosh.*

I told him this was one of my most anticipated things to visit and see while we were here. He had asked during one of our daily games of question and answer what I was most looking forward to in Paris.

I practically lay down in his lap trying to see through his window. I can only see the bottom part of it from the car and I almost ask Marco to pull over so we can get out and take a longer look.

Alex must see the torment on my face, because he grabs my hand as I sit back.

"Don't worry, I'll take you to see it tonight."

"Really?" I ask.

"Really." He smiles at me.

It's currently around seven thirty in the morning, so we have the entire day ahead of us. I slept for most of the flight, but I feel groggy and dirty from the airport.

"You may want to be sure you pack a coat," Marco says. His thick french accent sounds so sophisticated. I had almost forgotten he was in the car with us considering how quiet he'd been. "You've arrived in the middle of a winter storm."

The white flakes fall gracefully as I watch from the safety of the car. It's not usually this cold in Paris at this time of year, typically it's just pretty rainy. While the snow can be a bit of a pain, it's painting the city in the most beautiful blanket of white.

We pull up to a tall tan building that must be where our apartment, or flat I guess, is located. There are multiple balconies all along the front and there's ivy climbing up all around them.

"Right, here we are," Marco tells us. He opens my door and I follow him to the trunk where he removes our bags. We head inside behind him and are greeted by a doorman who introduces himself as Albert. He's older, probably in his late sixties, and is wearing a suit and white gloves. His eyes are kind and the smile he gives me seems genuine.

I forget all about the friendly doorman though as I step into the lobby. My mouth drops open as I take in the space.

The room around me is adorned in gold colors. The ceilings are incredibly high, at least fifteen feet but probably more, and there is gold trim lining the walls. They're covered in a deep forest green color with swirls of gold throughout them. The most beautiful artwork is hung all around the space and I feel like I could get lost for hours down here.

Marco walks us over to a woman standing behind a desk labeled registration.

"Maura, these are the two with *Impress*. They have unit 4B," he tells her.

"Here are your keys," she says with absolutely no emotion. "Elevator is on the left, fourth floor. If you need anything, I will not be here most of the time so try to catch me when I am."

Alex and I exchange a look and thank her. She doesn't respond.

Alex shakes hands with Marco as he walks back through the door held open by Albert and we head to the elevators. He turns to me as the doors close.

"Two things. One, this building is insane. Two, what is with Maura?"

"No kidding," I say. "The building *is* insane. I can't even imagine what the inside of the apartment looks like. This feels like a dream. Someone pinch me. "

Alex reaches out and pinches me on my arm, causing me to jump.

"Ouch," I say, rubbing the spot.

"You asked for it."

Before I can come up with a response, the elevator dings and we step off and into a hallway with beautiful carpet. It's a deep maroon with all different sorts of flower designs dancing down it, and the walls are lined in that same gold trim that I saw in the lobby.

We walk down the hallway and see a forest green door with '4A' written on it in gold. Across the hall is door '4C'. We move further down, dragging our luggage behind us, and finally come to our door.

Alex inserts his key into the lock and we step inside.

I then do a complete repeat of the whole song and dance I performed in the lobby. Jaw dropped and eyes wide, I survey the space in front of us. Neither of us speaks or moves for a solid minute.

Heather told us her friend owns this flat and is allowing us to stay here in exchange for our plant watering abilities, but that suddenly doesn't feel like nearly enough payment after seeing this gorgeous space.

"Holy..." Alex breathes.

"Yeah."

"The rent here has to be like..."

"A lot," I say.

The floors are a deep wood, placed in a design that makes them look like alternating arrows. There are two teal velvet couches in the center of the room with a glass table between them. Beyond the couches are two floor to ceiling doors that lead out to the balcony.

Looking up, I find a huge chandelier that twinkles as the sun hits it from outside. The walls are a sort of salmon pink that highlights the gold in the room so well. The corners of the room are decorated with the same golden trim, but in here it swirls around and makes circular and winding designs in all of the corners. There are paintings on the walls and a huge golden mirror on one with a fireplace below it. I can't help but think about Alex and I sitting on one of these couches, cuddled up by the fire.

I will not fall for Alex Ashford.

Moving into the dining room, there is a long glass table with ten placements and gorgeous velvet chairs in front of each one. There's a large vase of flowers sitting in the center and green plants all around the room.

The kitchen has shiny marble floors and all of the decor and appliances are black and white. The refrigerator is stocked with all of the essentials, as is the pantry. There are double ovens and a large island with eight stools lining one side. I think about baking while Alex sits at the island and works or talks to me about our day.

I will not fall for Alex Ashford.

"Lanie, come look at this view," he calls from the balcony. Every time he uses that nickname it does something to my stomach.

I head out onto the balcony and gasp as I look out on the city below us. We aren't too high up, but we're just high enough that we have a pretty great view of the street and shops below us. This is a prime people watching location.

"I wish we were on the other side of the building. I bet they have views of the Eiffel Tower."

"Are you seriously complaining?"

"No, absolutely not. Just making an observation."

He laughs as we head back inside and down the hallway to find a room. There are two bedrooms in the flat and one office. The primary is the first one on the left. It has a huge bed, bigger than a king, that has an opulent blue velvet quilt draped over it. There are nine of the fluffiest looking pillows on earth piled against the headboard and I almost moan as I think about slipping down into them.

Right across from it is another bedroom, slightly smaller than the first but still much bigger than my bedroom at home. This one is topped with a white duvet that reminds me of a marshmallow.

A little further down the hallway there is an office with two desks, just as Heather promised. There are two large cherry wood desks that probably weigh two hundred pounds each, facing one another. There are built in bookshelves lining the walls that are full of all kinds of books from vintage looking copies of Shakespeare, Jane Austen, and Agatha Christie to more modern historical fiction and romance.

I know I'll be spending lots of time roaming these shelves and I feel giddy as I run my finger along the spines, taking in all of the titles.

"Why don't you take the primary Lana?" Alex says as he continues down ahead of me.

"Oh no you can have it, I don't care which room I get."

"You look like you want to live in those pillows," he says to me as we stand in between the two rooms. "Go on, I can take this one."

"Are you sure?" I ask, hesitating to take the best room from him.

"Positive. But as payment, I'm throwing you into those pillows." He lunges toward me and I squeal, darting away from him on instinct. I begin to run around the room, laughing as I go, only to be snatched from behind by Alex's strong arms.

He carries me bridal style and I cling to him with my arms wrapped around his neck.

"One...two..." he swings me back and forth as he counts, his hands tightening around my body before he shouts "three!" And tosses me onto the bed.

I land in the pile of pillows and they go flying all around me at the impact. I'm giggling, tears flowing from the corners of my eyes from laughter, and Alex leans against the doorframe with a smirk on his handsome face.

"Okay fine. I'm just going to take a quick shower and I might rest my eyes for half an hour or so, then we can go sightseeing."

"Sounds good to me."

He turns and closes the door behind him as he leaves. I lay on the bed for a few seconds more and squeeze my eyes shut, trying to stop thinking about the fact that he's going to be sleeping just a few steps away, right across the hallway from me.

Talk about temptation.

I repeat my mantra to myself.

I open my suitcases up on one side of the room, pulling out my toiletries and head into the bathroom. I make quick work of the shower and find a robe that feels like a cloud hanging in the closet. I wrap my hair in a towel, pull on the robe, and practically run face first into the bed.

I'll just close my eyes for a little bit and then I'll drink an espresso and be on my way.

"Lanie? Hey, Lanie girl. Open your eyes."

My eyes blink open and I feel a warm hand resting on my shoulder. After a few seconds, I remember where I am. I look up through my lashes at Alex standing above me. I have the sudden urge to sit up just a few inches and touch his lips with mine, but thankfully I snap out of it when my eyes move to the window and I realize it's no longer as bright and sunny out.

"How long have I been out?" I ask, rubbing my eyes. I realize, then, that I am still wearing my hair towel and robe. Awesome.

"It's been about seven hours," Alex whispers softly to me.

"Seven hours? Why didn't you wake me sooner?"

"You looked so peaceful and I know the flight this morning was pretty draining. There's no way you got good enough rest. You needed it and I fell asleep too." He is sitting on the edge of the bed next to me now. His hair looks perfectly messy and I have to physically restrain myself from reaching out and running my fingers through it.

"What time is it?"

"Around three thirty in the afternoon. I didn't want you to miss the Eiffel Tower and I figured you might be hungry." As if on cue, my stomach growls and he laughs. He remembered that I wanted to see the Eiffel Tower tonight. That does stupid things to my heart.

"Good idea. Let me get changed and see what state my hair is in. After being up in this towel for so many hours, who knows what it will look like."

Alex gets up and heads for the door, pausing to look back at me once he reaches the threshold.

"I'll wait for you in the living room." He turns to leave, but pauses. I think he's about to say something else, but then he keeps walking and shuts the door behind him. I almost don't notice the chocolate square waiting for me on the bedside table.

CHAPTER 19
Alex

I HAD A MINOR LAPSE IN JUDGMENT AND ALMOST TOLD her she looks pretty when she sleeps. Thankfully, I remembered myself and kept walking.

When I first discovered she had fallen asleep, I sat there watching her breathe for probably longer than was acceptable. She just looked so peaceful, like she did on the plane hours earlier. She looked like she felt safe and at ease. I would do anything to see her looking like that all the time.

It's already been difficult to be near her and not treat her like she's more than a friend, but I am desperately trying to. I don't want to cross a line she isn't willing to cross with me.

I walk through the insanely large house and head to the living room where the two teal couches sit facing one another. I was absolutely shocked when we walked into this place. I assumed *Impress* would set us up nicely, but I wasn't expecting anything close to this.

I grab the copy of *Impress Europe* off of the coffee table and start flipping through it. I like their style. It's pretty similar to the US version, because it has to be, but it has its own flair. *The maga-*

zines are sisters, not twins, Heather told us in one of our debrief meetings before coming here.

We know very little about what we are walking into on Monday besides the fact that there is little staff and high tension. I'm feeling nervous about the whole thing, but Lana seems okay for the most part.

I glance down, checking to be sure that we leave with enough time to catch the first lighting of the night. Our flat is a short walk to the Eiffel Tower and, if my research is correct, the first sparkle should be in about an hour. The high today is around 30°F and since we've arrived the storm has picked up and snow has covered the ground in a thin layer, turning everything white.

I chose some dark jeans and a knit sweater with boots and a heavy coat. It's not exactly the best weather to picnic on the Champ de Mars in front of the tower, but I know Lana wants to sit out there for a little while, so I grabbed some warming packets for her hands and to slip into our boots.

While I wait, I decide to call and update my mom. She and I talk on a pretty regular schedule and she was so excited to hear about this trip. I wish I could've brought her with me, but maybe one day I'll bring her back.

"Hi, sweetie." Her cheerful voice makes me smile and sends a pang of longing through my chest.

"Hi, Momma. How's your day going?"

"Pretty good so far. Are you settled in your new place? How is it?"

"It's absolutely gorgeous. You would love it."

"FaceTime me so I can see."

I hear the chime of the FaceTime ring and pull my phone away from my ear to accept. Her kind face and warm eyes meet mine and I wish I could reach through the phone and hug her.

"Well, it looks gorgeous and I can only see the ceiling. Turn me around and give me a tour."

I do as she asks, starting from the front door and making my way through the entire flat. I don't show her Alana's room, but I do show her the door.

"And how are things going with your coworker?" She says the word like it's a joke, and I quickly turn the volume down.

"Things are good, Mom. Our flight was a bit bumpy," I say in an effort to change the subject.

"Really? I hate it when there's turbulence. Really shakes you up."

"It didn't last very long, but it was pretty rough for a little while."

"I'm sorry to hear that. What plans do you have for the rest of the day?"

I hear Alana's door open and her feet begin to shuffle down the hallway.

"I can't say right now, it's a secret and Alana is on her way out here. I'll send you pictures, though."

"You better, or else I'll get real mad. I love you."

"I love you too."

I hang up just as she waltzes into the room and I have to remind myself not to stare. She's got on black leggings that must be fleece lined—otherwise she's going to freeze—and she's bundled up in a light pink sweater and a beige coat.

The top half of her hair is pulled back into a hair tie with her bangs messy and hanging near her eyebrows. She's wearing a knit hat on her head that matches the color of her coat and she looks absolutely adorable. She pulls her mittens out of her coat pocket and throws them at my head.

"No staring. Let's go."

"Sorry," I mutter, grabbing her mittens off of the floor and chasing after her. "I grabbed a few of these for you. You can put them in your pockets and boots to keep your hands and feet warm. Here," I kneel down and grab one of her feet and prop it on my knee. She startles, not expecting me to make contact or kneel in front of her, I guess, but I keep moving like I didn't notice.

I shake the warming packets and then slip them in between her calf and her boots, then I do the same with the other leg. I stand back up and meet her wide eyes.

"Th-thanks," she stutters, and I pretend not to notice her flushed cheeks.

"Sure. Let's get going or we'll miss it." We head out of the flat and into the elevator. The tension in the air between us is thick and I fight the instinct to pull her close to me as we ride down. We get to the lobby and I wave to Albert as we pass. Sucking in a deep breath, we step out into the chilly air. I glance over, my eyes immediately finding hers, and see the biggest smile I've ever seen on her face. It brings out my own.

"What?" she asks me.

"Nothing. I just like it when you smile."

"Oh," she says, looking down at the ground to hide her blush.

I nudge her shoulder with mine and continue walking, leading her around the building to the other side. As we round the corner, the Eiffel Tower comes into view and it's absolutely breathtaking.

"Wow," Lana breathes as she stops, frozen in place.

"I know, it's beautiful. I thought we could watch the first sparkle happen, which should be soon, and then grab a bite to eat somewhere close where we can watch."

"That sounds perfect."

Alana

WE'RE STANDING IN FRONT OF THE EIFFEL TOWER AND I'm trying to be in the moment, but my brain keeps snagging on the things Alex has been saying and doing within the last twenty-four hours. Maybe it's the love in the air that's causing me to read into his actions, but it suddenly feels like we are a lot closer than we were when we got on the plane this morning. Our friendship has always been easy and casual, but the innocent touches and small comments are confusing me.

It could be because I forced him to spoon me...*ugh* I don't think I will ever get over the embarrassment I feel regarding that, and I've been so thankful Alex hasn't brought it up, but he keeps doing things that has my heart forgetting that my brain has decided we are swearing off all men.

Waking me from my nap so I don't miss this.

Thinking about my hands and feet being cold and bringing warmers.

Kneeling in front of me and slipping said warmers into my boots...won't be forgetting that one for a while.

Planning out our evening so I don't have to do any planning.

Typically I'm the one making plans for our group and figuring out the logistics. I like knowing where we will be when and making sure everything is planned out well. I didn't anticipate, however, how good it would feel to let someone else make the plans for once.

Maybe it's because I'm starting to trust Alex, or maybe it's the jet lag and the weird seven hour nap I just woke up from, but I am along for the ride and happy to let him pull me around to wherever he sees fit for tonight.

There aren't many people on the grassy area in front of the Eiffel Tower, the Champ de Mars, tonight. It makes sense because it's absolutely freezing and literally snowing, but I wanted to watch it sparkle from here, so here we are. I sit down on a bench and Alex walks up to a street vendor to get us hot chocolate. I pull out my phone and see more than five missed texts in my group chat with Charlie and Cami. Things have been so busy I haven't stopped to check my phone.

I snap a picture of my view and send it. It's a picture of the Champ de Mars, with the Eiffel Tower in the distance.

ME

You two will be so jealous.

BEST BROTHER IN THE WORLD

First of all, the fact that this is the first update and it's been multiple hours is ridiculous.

BEST BROTHER IN THE WORLD

Second of all, you're right. I am so jealous.

BESTIE FRIEND

Lana I thought I gave you the mom speech before you left. You cannot go hours without updating us. We haven't heard from you since you told us you were taking off. How did the flying go?

Cami's next message comes in, and it's a photo of her sitting at my desk. It's taken with the back camera on .5 width and she's sticking her tongue out. She's wearing my sweater, which I have no idea how she got because I could have sworn I left it at Charlie's, and she's got her arms spread like she owns the place. A bit of longing tugs in my chest.

BESTIE FRIEND

Also, I'm not jealous, you are.

ME

Aww, I miss you two.

ME

The plane ride was better than expected. I did have a panic attack during some pretty bad turbulence and I might have asked Alex to hold me. But now we're here in Paris and everything is great.

BEST BROTHER IN THE WORLD

I knew I was going to have to get on a plane to come punch that guy.

BESTIE FRIEND

EXCUSE ME?

I groan. I knew I shouldn't have told them about this. They are going to blow it way out of proportion and the only thing a relationship with Alex is going to lead to is further disappointment and hurt feelings. I really can't afford for anyone to encourage the side of me that is deciding to look at him as anything but a coworker and friend. I'm having a hard enough time reminding myself that this isn't going anywhere and I really don't want to have to remind anyone else.

ME

It was nothing. Please don't make a big deal out of it.

BESTIE FRIEND

Nothing?

ME

Drop it or I'm disappearing again.

BESTIE FRIEND

Ugh. Fine, whatever. Okay so you're at your dream spot, isn't it a little cold to be sitting outside?

BEST BROTHER IN THE WORLD

Wait, I don't want to drop it.

ME

It's pretty cold, but I'm all bundled up. Alex just brought me a hot chocolate so that's helping.

BESTIE FRIEND

Alex brought you a hot chocolate...

ME

You are so annoying.

BEST BROTHER IN THE WORLD

Everyone always ignores me.

I lock my phone and slip it into my coat pocket. The hot chocolate is warm on my tongue and Alex's body heat next to me makes it feel at least ten degrees warmer than it is. My nose is freezing, though and has to be red. I lift one of my hands up to my face and press it against my nose.

"I know I look like Rudolph," I tell him, and he chuckles.

"A cute Rudolph."

If it's possible, the red on my cheeks and nose definitely deepen at that comment. We both go quiet and I search for something to change the subject.

"How did you like your book?" I ask.

"The twist was crazy. She killed the therapist and I had no idea. Never saw it coming."

"Right? I was so shocked," I reply, excited to talk about this book with him.

"It was pretty shocking. A great recommendation." He hesitates, as though he isn't quite sure what he wants to say next. I wait and give him space to decide, and eventually he speaks again. "I won our bet," he says.

"You sure did," I reply, unsure where he's going with this.

"What do I get?"

"What do you mean?"

"I won. What do I get if I win?" he asks.

Oh. Why does that sound suggestive? "You win...a high five?" I say it like it's a question.

"A high five?"

"That will have to do for now."

"Alright, Lanie, that will do," he says, and he winks at me. *He winks.*

The sun is almost fully set and I know the lights have to come on any second now. We both go silent and turn forward. Sure enough, a few minutes later the Eiffel Tower starts to sparkle in the most magnificent way. The lights are a golden yellow and it feels almost like a dream sitting here.

We both sit and stare in awestruck silence. I can't see my face right now, but if I could I know it would reflect the absolute happiness I'm feeling. After watching it for a while, Alex turns to me.

"Come on, let's get you warmed up. I looked up some places to grab food and found one that looks good."

He grabs my hand and threads it through the crook of his elbow. I follow willingly, happy to take some of his body heat.

We walk away from the Eiffel Tower and he leads me down a few streets and a handful of blocks away to a small restaurant that looks cozy. Snow weighs down the red awning that sits over the door and the candles inside on the tables create a warm glow.

Alex opens the door for me and I step inside, immediately hit by the warmth of the restaurant.

"Bonsoir, my name is Alex Ashford. I called ahead."

"Ah, oui. Right this way, Mr. Ashford, to the table you requested."

Called ahead? The table he requested? He's speaking French?

I am so done for.

We follow the man just a few steps to our table that sits nestled in the corner and up against the window. I sit down first and notice how I can see all of the people walking by. This street is beautifully decorated for the holidays. Pine garland is draped along the tops of the buildings and there are large velvet red ribbons tied to the lamp posts. It looks like a scene from a Hallmark movie.

I realize that while I've been looking out the window, Alex is still standing next to our table.

"Are you going to sit down?" I ask.

"Actually, why don't you sit on this side?"

"Oh I really don't mind which side I sit on. I'm good either way."

He continues to stand, shifting awkwardly from foot to foot.

"What? Are you one of those people who needs to be facing the entrance at all times? Because if you are, that's totally fine. Charlie is that way and it's like a protective instinct or whatever."

"No. I mean, yes I prefer to see the door, but that's not why I asked."

"Oh...okay then."

"Just switch with me, Lanie."

"Alright, fine."

I stand up and slip out of the chair, moving to the other side. He slides the chair out for me and tucks it back under with me in it. I situate my napkin back in my lap and look up.

Wow.

I realize the reason why he offered me this seat. Outside the window, far off in the distance, I can see a beautiful view of the

Eiffel Tower sparkling in the night sky. He chose this restaurant, asked for this table, and had me sit in this seat, so I could see the Eiffel Tower while we ate.

"Alex...this is..." I trail off, not having words.

"I just thought you'd enjoy the view. I know how much you were looking forward to seeing it and it's so cold out so you can't really sit out for long and look."

"It's perfect," I say, reaching over and placing my hand over his, giving it a squeeze. "Really, thank you."

Alex

SHE LOOKS SO INCREDIBLE TONIGHT. AS SHE GETS COZY in her chair and gazes out the frosted window, she pulls the knit hat off of her head and smooths down her hair. Her cheeks have this beautiful red tint from the cold and I find myself wishing for many more nights like this.

I don't know what the rest of our time here is going to look like once we start working at the office, but I selfishly hope that we get our evenings so I can continue to spend one-on-one time with Alana.

"Look." She uses the back of her hand to swat me on the shoulder. "It's sparkling again." She bounces in her chair happily. She's adorable when she's excited like this. I've only seen it a few times in the office, usually when she gets new office supplies or with Cami, and every time I want to bottle up her happy and save it for a rainy day.

Despite her demand to look and the violence that followed, I don't take my eyes off of her. I can't. Eventually, I turn my head to look over my shoulder and out the window to see the glittering tower. It really is beautiful.

"It's gorgeous." *Just like you* I almost say, but stop myself.

Our waiter brings bread and olive oil, and we order. We each get a different pasta dish, because duh, and dig into the bread.

"So how did you get into editing?" I ask.

"Mmm good question," Lana replies through bites of bread. "*The Devil Wears Prada.*"

I choke a bit on my surprised laughter and her eyes widen at my sudden outburst.

"Sorry, I wasn't expecting that," I say.

"What were you expecting?"

"Oh, I don't know. You had an aunt who got you into the fashion world. You loved magazines as a young girl. You were an editor for your high school paper."

"Oh yeah, none of that. Just Anne Hathaway and Meryl Streep."

"Respect. They're incredible."

"They absolutely are. But in all seriousness, my mom showed me the movie when I was young, probably too young to be honest, and it hooked me. I loved the fast-paced environment and how glamorous everyone looked."

"But that isn't reality."

"No, it definitely isn't. Eventually I came to terms with that, but the movie is what got me interested in the industry. I started researching and then eventually ended up at NYU with a major in journalism and a minor in media, culture, and communications which is like a whole program with all three of those wrapped in. It was really great."

"Where did you work after you graduated? Did you jump right into the industry?" I knew she hadn't worked at *Impress* right out of college.

"I got an internship for a small lifestyle magazine and then they hired me. I worked there for four years before I wanted something different in all areas of my life. That's when I made the switch to *Impress.*"

"And how lucky they are for it."

Lana blushes a little and breaks eye contact as the waiter places our meals in front of us. The food smells incredible and has my mouth watering instantly. We both dig in, a minor pause to our conversation, and the most tempting moan leaves her mouth as she takes her first bite. I clear my throat.

"Taste good?"

"Oh my gosh, it's incredible. Here you have to try." She rolls up some of the pasta on her fork and holds it out for me. I lean in and take the bite she offers, chewing and nodding in agreement.

"That is maybe the best pasta I've ever had."

"Right?"

I do the same for her and gather a bite on my fork, holding it out for her to taste. She leans forward and wraps her lips around the fork, pulling back and humming in delight.

"I think we need to come here at least twice a week," she says after chewing.

I chuckle and smile at her. "We can make that happen."

We spend hours at the restaurant just talking about work and what we might be walking into on Monday morning. Our conversation moves to the shows we've both been watching and stays there for a long while.

We eventually order decaf coffee and our waiter brings out dessert pastries. Both of us indulge, although I'm not sure how I find the space for it, and he ensures us that we can take our time. They close late on Fridays, which is why I chose this restaurant. By the time our conversation starts to dwindle, it's around 11:30 p.m. and Alana yawns.

"Starting to feel sleepy?"

"Yeah, I am, which would be good because then I'd be on a somewhat normal schedule. Doesn't really make sense considering I just napped for hours, but I'm not complaining."

"Maybe your body is registering the fact that it's dark."

After each ordering a second decaf coffee to take with us and using the company credit card to pay, I lead her out of the restaurant and onto the snowy street.

The streets are mostly empty at this time of night and with the temperatures being so low, it feels like we are in our own little world.

I resist the urge to reach out and grab her hand, instead placing mine on the small of her back as we move past another couple on the sidewalk. There isn't really a reason to keep it there after we pass, but I do.

"I hope you remember where we're going," she says. "I'm currently in a food coma and can't be trusted to hold any responsibility."

"Don't worry Lanie. I've got you."

CHAPTER 22

Alana

"Don't worry, Lanie. I've got you."

Six simple words that stun me into silence. I don't recall a time anyone has ever uttered those words or even words of that sentiment to me. I can't remember the last time someone took care of me. Sure, Charlie and Cami try but I don't make it easy and they don't push.

Alex's hand presses into my back to move me forward and I go blindly, following his lead. We continue walking and as we turn a corner, he moves me so I am on the inside and he is closest to the street. It's a move you hear about in books and see on television, but not one I have ever experienced in real life. Not that I've dated at all in the last year, but Brad didn't even care enough to do that.

I get lost in thought as we walk. Most of the differences between Brad and Alex are obvious, but the subtle things that Alex does to make sure I'm cared for aren't as loud. I'm starting to learn that he shows his care in small gestures and kindnesses, and it makes me feel all warm and fuzzy inside.

The Eiffel Tower is on my left and I gaze at it as we walk. Even though I stared at it through the window for hours at dinner, it's beauty is still breathtaking. Every hour on the hour, the tower sparkles in yellow lights for about five minutes and I know we're coming up on another top of the hour mark.

"Let's stay and watch the last one. It's about to go off," Alex says as he tugs my hand towards it. He must have done his research to plan out this evening and the timing of it all.

We stand there, side by side waiting, and minutes later the show begins, except it's different from the times before. It isn't shining the yellow lights like it has the rest of the night. This time, all of the lights on the tower are turned off and the only ones shining are white. They sparkle and shimmer in the evening sky and light up the shadows of the Eiffel Tower and it is absolutely incredible.

"Oh my," I gasp. "Did you know it did this?"

Alex's cheeks go a deeper shade of pink and he shrugs his shoulders. He timed this perfectly.

This show lasts about ten minutes instead of five and I stand there shivering for every second, the warming packs he gave me long worn off, unable to peel my eyes away.

When they stop and the tower goes dark, I turn to him and smile.

"Thank you for planning this. I feel like I'm living in a movie. It was perfect."

"It was nothing," he says with a self deprecating shrug. I notice his hands ball into fists at his sides and it makes me wonder if he's just cold or if he feels the draw towards me that I'm feeling towards him, and is making an effort to resist that.

"Ready to head back?" he asks, breaking the tension of the moment.

"Yeah absolutely. I'm freezing."

We walk back in silence and I turn the night's events over and over in my head. I think we are becoming closer and deeper friends, and I also think I might be feeling things towards him. Things I haven't felt in a long time. Things that, the last time I felt them, lead me to intense heartbreak. Things I swore I wouldn't feel for someone again.

And that terrifies me.

But after everything he's done and shown me in these short twenty-four hours—really ever since that first day in the office when I got turned around and he offered me chocolate—I'm wondering if he might feel something more than friendship too. And I'm wondering if it might be about time for me to work on overcoming these fears and start to trust him.

CHAPTER 23

Alana

5 *MISSED CALLS FROM* UNKNOWN

I groan and throw my phone onto the bedside table. It's Brad again. I block one number and somehow he gets another one and continues bothering me. Why he is calling me, I have no idea. I don't want to know. I wish he would stop.

Last night was absolute perfection and I fell asleep thinking about Alex's hands on me, woke up thinking about it too. Then I saw the five missed calls and the happiness bubble popped.

I throw back the covers and sit up, rubbing the sleep from my eyes. I actually slept through the night and feel like I am somewhat adjusted to the time change, which I'm thankful for.

I slide my cold feet into my fluffy pink slippers, grab my robe and mindlessly tie it on while heading to the kitchen for coffee. I can't think about my ex or work or anything until I have coffee.

I pad into the beautiful black and white kitchen and freeze when I see the back of Alex, facing the coffee pot. The very naked back of Alex.

He's only wearing a pair of boxers and his back is rippled with muscle. I haven't ever seen him shirtless, because *hello* coworker, but wow have I been missing out. I have to physically stop myself from reaching out to touch his sun-kissed skin.

I realize I have been staring for too long when he clears his throat and I notice he's turned around. Except I can't look away because *oh my word* the front of him is more gorgeous than the back.

His abs are defined and his boxers are slung low on his hips, revealing the deep V there. Suddenly I need a glass of ice cold water.

"Earth to Lana?" Alex says, waving his hand in front of my face.

"Um, hey," I clear my throat. "I mean, good morning. Making coffee?"

He hesitates a second, shooting me a puzzled but amused look. I can only imagine what I look like right now. My hair is always a mess of tangles when I wake up and I haven't even brushed my teeth yet so there's probably drool on the side of my mouth. Awesome. This look practically screams the opposite of *Hey, Alex. I'm super mysterious and sexy and you should totally have more than friends feelings for me.*

Which is absolutely wonderful because I definitely *do not* want him to think I'm mysterious and sexy and I *only* want friendship feelings between the two of us. Yep, that is exactly what I want.

He continues on like nothing is amiss.

"Yeah, I just made myself one with the espresso machine. I can make one for you too?"

"You don't have to do that. I'm sure I can figure out how to use this thing."

"It's a little difficult with lots of steps. I really don't mind."

"Good because I would have no clue what to do and my need for coffee is higher than my need for independence right now."

His shoulders shake with his chuckle and I take a seat at the large white marble island, watching his back as he works. He grinds the beans, uses a fancy thing that looks like a stamp to press the grinds down and then he hooks it into place, hits a button and it roars to life.

"Hazelnut latte?"

"Huh?" I ask, shaking my head to try and clear the fog. What is happening to me? I haven't had a man distract me like this in a long time.

"Do you want a hazelnut latte?"

"Oh, yes, thank you. But can you do it with—"

"Oat milk?"

I short circuit. About a week ago I switched to oat milk in my coffee instead of almond because the texture is so much better. Brad got me hooked on almond milk when we were dating because of the lower calorie count. That was something he did a lot while we were together and he did it slowly and subtly enough that I didn't notice until after.

Lower carb breads, light sour cream, reduced fat cheese, sugar free chocolate...the list goes on. A few weeks after I broke up with him I was at the grocery store doing my normal weekly shopping and looked down at my basket only to realize that I had almost exclusively "diet" type foods in my cart. I got so mad.

I started at the front of the store and went all the way back through, placing the items back on the shelf and replacing them with foods that I actually wanted to eat. It was a freeing moment, but it's pretty crazy to think about how even now the small ways I changed myself for him still linger.

Like almond milk in my coffee. And let me be clear, if you like almond milk in your coffee I am so happy for you. I liked almond milk in my coffee until I tried it with oat milk and now I will never go back to the watered down devils milk ever again.

"How do you know that?" I ask as he pulls out the syrup and oat milk, adding it to a metal tin and steaming it with the steamer on the machine.

"I pay attention," he answers, and it transports me back to a few weeks ago when he picked up my office for me and everything was in the exact right spot.

He hands over my latte. I take a sip and sigh happily, and it is the most delicious coffee I have ever had. All of my problems automatically disappear.

Brad? Gone.

Work? Easy.

Parents? Who needs 'em.

Ridiculous sexual tension with your hot coworker who is just a friend and needs to stay just a friend?

Unfortunately the world's strongest coffee cannot fix *that* problem.

"Alex. This is incredible. I think I may need you to come make me one of these every morning when we get home. I'm going to get used to them."

"That can be arranged," he says with a wink.

He really shouldn't be winking. It doesn't help the whole just friends thing.

"So, how should we spend our Saturday?" *Hello* subject change.

"I don't have any major plans, but I figured we might do some sightseeing. Grab a bite to eat and maybe stop for some groceries. I think there's a little market not far from here."

"That sounds good. Let me get ready and we can head out in about an hour?"

"Perfect. I'll be ready."

I walk back down the hallway towards my room and swipe my phone off of the side table. It buzzes with an incoming text and I close my eyes and take a deep breath to try and steady myself.

UNKNOWN

Alana answer the phone. I want to talk to you.

In the past, a text like that would have me obeying immediately, but those days are over. It's the middle of the night in New

York. But I'm not surprised because staying out at the bar until the early morning hours became a habit of his. He's likely drunk.

ME

Leave me alone, Brad.

I really shouldn't even give him a response, I know that. He wants to get a rise out of me, he thrives off of it, and with that one text I have given him just enough momentum to continue.

UNKNOWN

Wow. How kind and hospitable of you. I want to speak with you. Be an adult and pick up the phone.

I stare down at the hypocritical words and my phone starts buzzing with an incoming call.

"Ugh. Leave me alone!" I shout at it before tossing it across the room. It flies through the air and almost hits Alex right in the face if not for his incredibly quick reflexes.

"Oh my gosh, I'm so sorry, I had no idea you were standing there." I fall back onto the bed and shut my eyes, willing the problem away. "Just leave me here, I'll pick the phone up eventually. You can be on your way, nothing to see here."

I feel the bed dip on my left and I open one eye to peer up at Alex.

"Who is the unknown number?"

I groan again in frustration and realize I'm not getting out of this conversation. He cares way too much and is way too good of a friend to let this go. I haven't told anyone about the text messages from Brad except Cami and Charlie. I know eventually he will stop, but this is the third number I've had to block and I'm just tired of it.

"It's Brad, my ex."

"That guy seems pretty awful."

"You could say that. His last name is Butte. B-U-T-T-E. I don't know why I ever gave him the time of day to be honest."

"No, it isn't," Alex says with wide eyes.

"It is."

We both sit there staring at each other for a second, and then burst out in laughter at the exact same time. He falls back onto the bed next to me, holding his stomach as he laughs. Tears prick my eyes, but what starts out as laughter slowly morphs into real tears and now I'm crying. *Great.*

"Lanie." Alex's tone is pleading. I can tell he doesn't like seeing me this way. He is a fixer and has been trying to fix ever since we started this Paris journey together. It goes against everything I've been preaching to myself since my breakup to let him in, to let him care for me.

Charlie and Cami love me, but they have their own lives going on too. They do what they can and love me through the hard times but I purposely push them away sometimes so they don't feel like I have to lean on them 24/7. They don't deserve that.

It's made our friendships and relationships healthy because they aren't in danger of ever crossing into the codependent territory, but it makes me feel like I don't have *my* person who is there for me no matter what. I thought that was Brad at one point, but boy was I wrong.

Alex is starting to feel like that person and that scares me.

He brings his hands up to cup my cheeks and swipes his thumbs under my eyes to wipe away the tears.

"I'm sorry, I don't even know why I'm crying. It's just some dumb texts and he won't stop calling. I haven't had to deal with him since I broke up with him and I guess seeing him again and hearing from him constantly is catching up with me."

"He won't leave you alone?" Alex asks. His demeanor suddenly changes and he goes stiff.

I nod my head and sniff, trying to stop the flow of tears. "I keep blocking the numbers, but he gets new ones."

He is about to say something else, but he is cut off by my phone buzzing again in between us.

"You've got to be kidding me. The balls on this guy," he says with a shake of his head. "I'm going to answer this."

"No, Alex, please don't. I told you before, I'm a big girl. I can handle my own problems. I've got this."

"You clearly don't if he isn't leaving you alone."

The hurt and shock in my features must cause him to rethink the words he just said, because he backpedals.

"That isn't what I meant." He runs his hands through his hair in frustration. The phone stops buzzing.

"Then what did you mean? Because it sounded to me like you don't think I can handle my problems on my own."

"That's not what I think at all, Lanie. You can handle any problem that comes your way. What I mean is, Brad is clearly not the type of guy to take no for an answer and that isn't your fault. You've been blocking the numbers and that's all you can do, all you're in control of." He takes a breath before continuing. "I know you can handle this on your own, but that doesn't mean you have to."

"You can't do everything for me. We talked about this."

"I know I can't and I wouldn't want to. You're your own person, but let me help where I can." The phone starts buzzing again and I take a deep breath. "Please, let me help you with this? I'm just going to tell him to leave you alone."

I sigh and stare at the ringing phone. What's the worst that could happen? I never let anyone help me with anything. Maybe it's time I start trying.

"Okay," I whisper.

Alex swipes his thumb across the screen to answer the phone and holds it up to his ear without speaking. The volume is loud enough, and so is Brad, that I can hear him even though it isn't on speakerphone.

"You don't have to be such a bitch, Alana. I call and you pick up the phone. That's how this works," he shouts. Alex's jaw clenches at the name Brad calls me and I feel bad for dumping this on him. The fact that Brad is acting like we never split and he has a right to demand my attention is appalling and frustrating.

"Bradley. Nice to hear from you." Alex's voice is eerily calm.

"Who is this?" I hear Brad ask.

"That doesn't matter. I'm going to need you to stop calling my girl."

"My girl?" I mouth at Alex, eyes wide. What is he doing?

"Let me speak to Alana," I hear Brad demand.

"Can't let you do that Bradley. You call or text her again, and we're going to have an issue. Got that?"

Is it hot in here? Did someone turn on the heater?

"Listen here you—"

"Glad to hear we understand one another. Have the day you deserve," Alex replies, cutting him off and ending the call.

He hands me my phone and stands like nothing out of the ordinary is happening. Meanwhile, I am reeling.

"What was that?" I ask.

"What do you mean? Hopefully he'll stop bothering you now."

"Well he would be an idiot not to. What with the 'we're going to have an issue'," I say, lowering my voice and mimicking his.

"I do not sound like that," Alex says with a roll of his eyes.

"So not the point. He definitely thinks you're my boyfriend."

"Sorry, sunshine. Didn't think, just said it. I figured he would be less likely to keep bothering you if he thought you were with someone."

Sunshine? *What is happening?*

I reach for my coffee and take a huge sip, hoping it will bring me back to reality because there's no way I'm currently in it.

"If he gets in contact with you again, I need you to let me know. Okay?"

I nod and Alex walks out of the room, leaving me to get ready.

I hear his door slam behind him and I wince. I can tell he's off, likely frustrated by the conversation we just had, and part of me wants to go to him and check on him, but something holds me back.

I stand and pace the room, trying to decide the best course of action. He's been there for me so much these last few weeks, I ought to return the favor at some point.

CHAPTER 24
Alex

I SHUT THE DOOR MORE GENTLY THAN I FEEL CAPABLE OF and storm down the hallway. I'm itching to punch something, but I think if I made a hole in the wall Maura from the front desk would have my head. Instead I sit down on my bed and take five deep breaths, thinking through five things I can see, four things I can touch, three things I can hear, two things I can smell, and one thing I can taste.

It helps, but not by much. I don't remember the last time I was this angry.

I thought Alana's ex was a sucky guy, but I didn't realize how bad he really was. The fact that he keeps getting new numbers to bother her with is not normal and I didn't want to scare her, but it doesn't sit well with me. That plus the bruises he left on her dainty wrist weeks ago has red flags flying high.

I'm just thankful she's thousands of miles away from the city so he can't physically get to her right now.

I was impressed with the level of calm I maintained throughout that phone call, because all I wanted to do was go find the guy and run him through a wall. I'm not sure if I helped by implying that we were dating, but Brad can think whatever he wants if it keeps him away from her.

My hands shake with anger and I take a few more deep breaths, trying to calm them. A soft knock at my door startles me and I hesitate. I'm not sure why, there's only one person it could be.

"Alex," she says softly through the closed door. "I just wanted to check on you."

I smile to myself as I stand, most of the frustration and anger disappearing when I see her face as I pull open the door. I gesture her into the room and she follows me to the bed, sitting next to me.

"Are you okay?" Her voice is timid and apprehensive, but full of concern. "You seemed pretty upset when you left a second ago."

"I'm okay, that guy just pisses me off."

She laughs a sad laugh.

"You and me both." She plays with strands of her hair, fidgeting nervously. "What helps you when you're angry?"

"I usually try to get my mind off of it." She nods in understanding and starts to glance around the room. Her eyes snag on the baseball cards I have lined up against the wall on my bedside table. I take those cards with me everywhere—the only real piece I have of my dad—so naturally they made it in the luggage.

"Do you collect those?" she asks, gesturing to the cards. "I've seen them in your office at work and always wondered."

"I don't really collect them anymore. Back when my dad was still around, baseball was kind of our thing. He used to take me to games and we'd talk about all the players and their stats. He had a big collection of vintage cards and let me keep a couple. I can't seem to get rid of them."

"That makes sense, they mean a lot to you."

"They do. It's strange, though, I have so much anger towards my dad for leaving but I can't seem to let go of this piece of him. I'm so mad at him, but it feels like if I don't carry these around those memories don't exist. Almost like he was never even there."

She hums in contemplation and we sit with the words for a few moments before she speaks again.

"It's okay to remember the good parts of your dad. He gave you some good memories and just because there were bad ones it doesn't mean you aren't allowed to acknowledge the good ones."

I meet her eyes then, wanting to look into them and see the emotion behind her words. Since I was a kid, I've been taking care of all of the people around me. It has always been my job to hold the weight of everyone's emotions on my shoulders and do what I can to neutralize them, but right now Alana is doing that for me. She's taking my emotions and putting them on her shoulders for a second. She's helping me carry the load.

"Are you a therapist or something?" I tease, trying to lighten the mood.

"No, but I've been to a lot of therapy." She bumps her shoulder into mine and places her hand on my knee. "I'm serious though, don't feel guilty about enjoying the good moments you had with your dad. The world is dark enough, there's room for some light."

I smile at her and place my hand on hers before giving it a squeeze of gratitude. We seem to come to a mutual understanding to move on and I realize that the overwhelming anger I was feeling has mostly dissipated.

"Thank you for that by the way, all the stuff with Brad."

"What exactly happened with you two? You don't have to share if you don't want to."

"No, it's probably good you know. I want you to know."

She picks at an invisible piece of lint on her shirt, not making eye contact with me. After taking a deep breath, she starts talking.

"We dated for three years and it was pretty serious. I thought we were going to get married after a year or so, but he started changing." She takes a breath and I wait until she's ready to continue. "It's hard to notice changes in someone who you spend so much time with, especially when those changes are gradual.

We were really happy in the beginning. I was happy in the beginning.

"Somewhere along the way, he started making comments about my body. I shouldn't wear form-fitting clothes because they aren't flattering on my figure, I need to swap my foods out for lower calorie ones, I should go see a personal trainer, stuff like that. I should have recognized it for what it was, but I was too close to see it. He told me it was because he loved me and he wanted the best for me, but what he really wanted was for me to be his puppet and trophy that sat on the shelf while he made all the big moves and got all the recognition."

Suddenly, her frustration with my attempting to help her makes more sense. I can understand how, when she felt like she had no control of her life, it would be uncomfortable to allow anyone in once she gained her independence back.

"He began climbing up the ladder at work and that just fed his ego. He started being a jerk to not only me, but everyone else, and Cami and Charlie hated him. It put a huge strain on our relationship."

Tears well up in her eyes and give in to the urge to reach across and hold her hand. She doesn't react, so I leave it.

"Anyways, at our three year anniversary dinner he bought me a dress that was purposefully too small and told me that if I fit into it, he'd propose to me. I was so fed up and embarrassed so I broke it off there at that table. I haven't told anyone about the dress situation, it was way too mortifying, but I haven't regretted walking out for one second. It was the best thing I could've done for myself."

"I don't know if I've said it already, but I hate that guy."

She huffs a laugh.

"You and me both."

"I really am so sorry you had to deal with that, Lanie. I'm so proud of you for walking away when you did and building yourself up into this incredible woman."

"Thanks." She sniffs and reaches up to swipe the tears from

her cheeks. "It feels good to get that out. To tell someone else all of it. Thanks for listening."

"Right back at you. I feel better than I did fifteen minutes ago."

"Happy to help." She squeezes my hand. "Now I really do need to go get ready."

She stands and crosses the room to the door, opening it and stepping out into the hallway. She starts to close it, but looks back at me before she does and smiles.

We have lunch at a small bistro nearby and after we eat we head to the market where we do some light grocery shopping for the week ahead. Neither of us quite knows what to buy, considering we just arrived and aren't sure what our day-to-day will look like, but we get a few essentials and I grab some ingredients for dinner.

On our way back through the lobby Maura stops us.

"Mr. Ashford, Ms. Cade. I was asked to inform you that Amélie has made reservations for tomorrow at 7:00 p.m. and a car will pick you up promptly at six thirty."

"Okay, great. Thanks for letting us know," Alana replies with a sweet smile.

Maura doesn't acknowledge her, she just continues doing whatever it was she was doing before we arrived.

"I don't think she likes me," Lana says once we're inside the lift.

"I don't think she likes anyone. I wouldn't take it personally."

We enter the flat and I grab her hand before she takes off towards her room to call Cami back after missing her call earlier in the evening.

"I was thinking I'd make dinner tonight. Pasta sound okay to you?"

"Is Taylor Swift the greatest songwriter of our time?"

"Yes?" I answer hesitantly.

She raises her eyebrows as if to say *exactly* and turns to walk to her room, leaving a trail of sunlight in her wake.

CHAPTER 25
Alana

"Oh my gosh, it's about time. I've been staring at my phone waiting for you." Cami's face fills my screen and I settle down on my bed, holding my phone up so she can see me.

"Sorry, Cam. We got stopped in the lobby and then Alex offered to make dinner tonight so it took me a little longer to get back to my room."

"Oh he's making dinner for you," she says with a smirk.

"Yes and he talked to Brad."

"Wait. He *what*?"

"Mmmhmm. He implied we were dating and called me his girl."

"He what?" she yells.

I stare blankly.

"Explain."

"I was sitting in my room and saw that I had some missed calls and texts from another unknown phone number and got frustrated. I threw my phone without looking, not expecting him to be standing in my doorway, and I almost hit him with it. He saw the texts when he picked it up and I explained a little about what was going on."

"You told him about the breakup?"

"Well in the moment, no. I was giving him the SparkNotes and I tried to go further, but I started crying so..." I trail off.

"Aw, babe."

"Yeah I know. Anyways in the middle of him consoling me, Brad calls again, and Alex says 'I'm going to answer this' to which I tried to tell him no."

"Naturally, because you'd rather die than let someone help you."

"Exactly so then that sparked an argument because, like you said, I don't let anyone help me and he's been doing it *so much* lately, but he reassured me and said please and of course I caved."

"Understandable. Hot guy tells me he wants to help me with something and I am folding so fast. So he picks up the phone for you and what does he say?"

"He was all *'I'm going to need you to stop calling my girl'* and *'You call or text her again we're going to have an issue. Got that?'*" I use my Alex voice, which I have to say is pretty close to the real thing, and continue. "So now I'm sure Brad thinks we're dating, which is fine, maybe that will keep him away."

"He absolutely thinks you two are dating. Ugh I wish I could've been there to witness this. Did you block the number?"

"Yeah I watched Alex do it after he hung up."

"He is so into you."

"No he is not. He just saw a problem and tried to fix it. He's a fixer." Even as I deny it, I know I'm wrong. Alex and I are moving into uncharted territory and it's unnerving.

"Yeah, a fixer who is into you."

"Whatever."

We continue talking and she catches me up on the happenings back at the office. It seems like things there are running smoothly, which is good. I hear the door open and close in the background and someone shouts at her.

"Who's that?"

"Oh, no one."

Weird.

"Well, it's obviously someone. Wait, are you seeing someone?"

"Trust me if I was seeing someone you'd know. It's just the neighbor bringing some dog food and treats. They asked me to watch their dog for them this week."

Cami watching a dog? Voluntarily? Nothing about that seems right.

"Okay...I guess I'll let you go and talk to that neighbor."

"Love you Lan," she says brightly.

"Love you too."

She hangs up the phone before I can even get the sentence out, which is so strange because she never rushes me off the phone. I usually have to force her to hang up so I can get things done. I brush it off, she's probably just busy.

I set my phone down to charge and change into a comfy lounge set. We don't plan on leaving the flat again today and we have a few hours before dinner, so I grab the book Alex got for me and sit on the bench at the window in my room.

The view of the snow covering the ground outside my bedroom is absolutely gorgeous. I could sit here for hours reading and people watching. As I look down at the street, I can't help but think about how snow blankets the ground, concealing the seeds and roots that will sprout and grow in the spring. Brad was like my snow and now that the snow has melted, Alex might be my spring. The thought is equal parts scary and exciting.

A few hours later I hear clunking happening in the kitchen and decide to venture in and see what's going on. My eyes are blurry from staring at my book for so long, so I rub them and slide on my slippers.

Walking down the hallway, I hear the telltale signs of cooking and pause at the entryway. Alex is so gorgeous it's unfair. He grabs for a pot and turns around, spotting me staring.

"You should take a picture. It'll last longer."

"Ha ha, very funny," I reply, tossing a hand towel at him playfully. "How can I help?"

"You can help by sitting down at that island and keeping me company. I told you I was cooking for you tonight."

"I feel weird just sitting here and watching you do all the work," I confess, sliding onto one of the barstools.

"Don't. I am going to force you to do the dishes, so we'll be even."

"Ah, okay. I see how it is."

He continues busying himself. It looks like we're eating something with a cream sauce and it smells peppery and cheesy and good.

"Ready for a question of the day?" he asks.

"Hit me."

"Tell me about one of your favorite childhood memories."

"Oh goodness. Give me a second to think about that one."

"I'll share mine first and give you a few minutes to think." He turns back to the sink and towards me. He washes his hands and grabs a towel, drying his hands and then draping it over his left shoulder.

"One year, around the holidays, my mom picked me up early from school and we went to this Christmas tree farm about an hour away. We stopped on the way and got hot chocolate and snacks at the gas station and she made it feel really special. After that year, we always took a mini road trip to go get our tree from that farm." He pauses and slides a glass of wine he's poured towards me. I lift it and take a sip, never breaking contact with his green eyes. "It was the year that my dad left, and I know she was trying to distract me and make it feel special. Clearly it worked to some degree because those years going to that tree farm are some of my favorite memories growing up."

"Did you hear from him again after he left?" I ask in an almost whisper. This might not be the right time for these questions, but after our conversation this afternoon I'm curious.

"He tried to reach out a few years ago, but I never returned his call."

I nod my head in understanding. I don't think I would want to call him back either.

"Alright, your turn, sunshine."

I ignore the way the term of endearment sets off fireworks in my chest and continue with my answer.

"I'll follow your lead and share a holiday memory I love. When I was in high school, I took this food and nutrition class. They used to teach us all of these healthy recipes packed with nutrients and things that were good for your body, but they made an exception for the holidays.

"Around November we made these incredible homemade cinnamon rolls. They were melt in your mouth delicious and I loved them so much that I went home and shared the recipe with my mom. We had already started making cinnamon rolls each Christmas morning, but we always just did the ones in the can. That year though, we made the homemade ones that I learned in class and every year since we've made them. Of course we've refined the recipe over time, but I loved baking them with my mom each year. She usually isn't around on Christmas anymore, but Charlie and I still make them."

"Well, I am officially requesting them for Christmas morning."

I'm grateful he doesn't press me on my mom not being around for the holidays. I don't want to get into that particular topic right now.

"Already planned on it," I say with a wink.

He continues cooking and we chat about random things—a new movie in the Hunger Games series he saw recently, our coworker Caroline's new husband, and our screen time. That last one came about after we both got notifications alerting us that our weekly average had gone up. Not like either of us really wanted to know.

Eventually he gets close to having everything ready and I stand having decided I'll cut up a salad.

"Hey, where do you think you're going?" he asks when he sees me get up from the island.

"Calm down, big guy. I'm just cutting up a salad." He narrows his eyes at me, but relents.

"Fine, I'll allow it."

I open the fridge and pull out the ingredients I need, then grab a cutting board and a knife from the knife block. I get lost in the methodical work of cutting up the veggies and Alex moves around me as he finishes up.

"Just going to grab this," he says as he reaches past me for a spoon he left on the counter. As he pulls back, his arm brushes my waist and I jump at the contact, causing my hand to slip just as I'm pressing the knife down on the carrot I'm chopping.

"Ouch." Blood starts pooling from the cut and I quickly pull my hand back so it doesn't drip down onto the counter or any of the food.

"I'm so sorry, Lanie, I didn't mean to bump you. Here let me see." Alex reaches out for my hand and I pull away. It wasn't his fault, but I'm flustered and my emotions feel all over the place. I need some space.

"It's fine. I'm fine." I rush down the hall and into my room to get a little bit of distance. I push my thumb under the cool water in the sink and watch the water run light pink. Once it's clear, I dry my hand and squeeze some ointment over the cut, topping it with a Band-Aid.

I sit down on the edge of the giant tub and let out a breath, running my hands through my hair. I decide that I'll take my dinner and eat in my room. I just need to put some space between us right now. Things are moving a bit too fast for my liking and if

I'm going to be open to this at all, it's going to need to move slowly.

Feeling slightly more centered, I stand and head back to the dining room.

When I walk in, he has already taken everything but the bowl of salad to the table. He's set the table and placed us on either side of it, facing one another. I wince, knowing me pulling away right now isn't the kindest move after he set this up for us, but I don't see another option right now.

"You okay?" he asks, concern clear on his face.

"Yep, all good," I say, holding up my hand with the Band-Aid on it. "But I need to look over a few things before we meet with Amélie tomorrow. Do you mind if I grab a plate and eat in my room?" I'm being a jerk. I know I'm being a jerk.

"Oh. Um, yeah that's fine. Of course." I can tell he's disappointed, even I'm disappointed and I'm the one pushing him away.

I grab a plate and load it up with pasta and salad. Alex grabs a slice of sourdough bread that we got at the market and tops it with garlic butter, then places it on my plate for me. Always taking care of me, even when I'm being the worst.

"Thanks for cooking," I tell him as I turn to go and hate the way my voice wobbles.

"Hey, Lanie." I turn back to look at him. "You sure you're okay?"

"Yep, totally fine."

He nods, looking back down at his plate and I take that as my cue to go.

I walk down the hallway and shut the door behind me quietly. I don't actually have anything I need to look at for our meeting, but I sit down at the desk and flip open my notebook anyway. Before I start doodling, I twist a few pieces of pasta on the fork and take a bite.

Heaven. That is the only adequate way to describe this pasta.

As I chew, I can't help but think about Alex and the effort he put in. I was so dismissive, I barely even thanked him. My appetite suddenly plummets and I set the plate aside.

I draw and journal until late in the evening, and as I'm getting settled in for bed, the expression on Alex's face when I left him alone at the table is at the forefront of my mind. It's made worse when a milk chocolate and caramel square, wrapped in gold foil, slides under the crack in my door.

Alex

I haven't seen Alana since she ran away from me last night. I'm not going to lie, it hurt. I was excited to spend the evening with her and I knew she'd love the food I made, but after the incident it was like she totally shut me out.

I sat at the table alone and tried to figure out where I went wrong and ultimately decided she probably was just feeling the pressure and the cut on her finger heightened that. She needed some space and I could understand that.

Our conversations that afternoon had been pretty deep and with her phobia of relationships and trust, it makes sense that she freaked out a little, I think I probably would have too. So, even though it hurt, I try to put it out of my mind.

I stretch my arms above my head and throw on a long sleeve tee with my boxers, then head into the kitchen to make myself a latte. I wrestle with whether or not I should make her one, not wanting to upset her further.

Things over the last few days have gotten a little more serious, I can see the light at the end of the friend-zone tunnel, but I know that's what's scaring her. I know this thing with her ex has her shaken up, but I'm willing to be patient and prove myself to her. I'm here for the long run.

I walk into the kitchen and find a sticky note covered in her handwriting.

Went for a run, be back in a bit.
Alana

A run? It's insanely cold outside. I remember her telling a story once, back when we were working in New York, about a race she was planning on running. We got to talking and apparently she picked up running as a way to de-stress. She told me to give it a try, but I am certainly not a runner. I like to unwind in other ways, like playing Candy Crush or doing a puzzle.

Running at home, where she knows the area and what to expect from the weather is one thing, but running in an unfamiliar city when the temperatures are below freezing doesn't sound like the safest situation.

I try to shove down my concern. She is a big girl, as she keeps reminding me, and she knows how to take care of herself. Even if my first instinct is to have Marco canvas the streets to find her and bring her home, I can't do that.

About a half hour later, she comes bursting through the door, nose and cheeks pink and snowflakes still frozen and stuck to her hat. She's wearing a long sleeve hot pink athletic top and long black leggings that stretch all the way down to her ankles. Her pale pink socks are pulled up over the leggings, leaving no skin showing, and she's wearing mittens.

She walks into the living room where I am sitting and starts pulling articles of clothing off one by one. She rips the mittens off and throws down the two heating pouches she was holding in either hand, then she pulls off her top leaving her in a sports bra.

"Why are you stripping in the living room?"

"Have you ever run in the cold? All the clothes keep you warm while you're out there, but the second you come inside it's like you're burning up."

"Can't say I've experienced it, but I'll take your word for it."

She makes her way into the kitchen and I hear the ice machine working. A few minutes later, she comes back into the living room and plops down on the couch holding a tall glass of ice water in her hand.

"How was your run?" I ask, unsure if I should bring up last night or just leave it. Ultimately, I decide to follow her lead. I don't want to push.

"It was great. It's super cold out there, but it was nice to clear my mind for a little while. Running always helps with that."

I nod and we fall into an awkward silence. I don't like it. Things between us have never been awkward.

"Listen," she starts. "I'm sorry about last night. It wasn't fair of me to walk out on you like that after you went to all that work to make dinner. I was a jerk and I'm sorry."

"Did I do something that made you uncomfortable?"

"No, not at all. It's not you." She fidgets with the band of her leggings, not meeting my eyes. I can tell she's trying to decide whether or not she wants to keep going. Eventually she does. "I struggle sometimes, with letting people in. And as much as I appreciated our conversations yesterday, I think they just spooked me a little. I opened up a lot and I wanted to, but I needed a little bit of space. I hope you understand, though, that it wasn't your fault and you've been great. I just needed to hit the brakes for a second."

My heart breaks for this woman who is so closed off to anyone outside of her inner circle, that a few deep conversations spooked her so much that she stepped back. It's not her fault, though. Most of the important people in her life have let her down, so it's going to take some work for her to trust me. When I eventually tell her how I feel, I want to be sure she's going to believe me.

"That makes sense. It did get a little heavy, but I learned a lot about you and you learned a lot about me. That's a good thing." I nudge her shoulder with mine and she finally meets my eyes, smiling.

"It is." She takes a deep breath, then stands. "I'm going to go grab a shower. We need to leave for dinner by six?"

"Yep, sounds good to me."

I walk with her down the hallway and we turn opposite directions once we get to our doors. Once I shut the door behind me, I take out my phone and look over the surprise plans I have for tonight. When Alana first gave me the list of her traditions, I had an idea to do something special with it, but I didn't want to overstep. I have to remind myself that, while I have been slowly falling for her for the past year, she has been healing from an awful break up and relationship. I need to let her catch up to me.

I pull up the website of the tree farm we are going to tonight. It happens to be close to where we are meeting Amélie, which worked out perfectly. They're open late, so it should work for us to drop by there before they close. I don't know that our car can hold a big tree, so I shoot off a text to Marco asking him to bring supplies to tie whatever tree we choose down to the car. He responds and lets me know he has it handled.

As the plan forms in my mind, my excitement grows. I want to make this year magical for Alana and I want her to feel special and cared for. I'm not going to let her cold shoulder from last night scare me away. This girl deserves the world and I am going to work to earn her trust, so she'll let me give it to her.

I don't hear from her for the rest of the day. She came out to make a peanut butter sandwich, but took it back to her room and hasn't come out since. I know I'm going to spend the entire evening with her, so I let her be. About ten minutes to six, I head out of my room and into the living room to wait for her to be ready.

I sit down on the couch and scroll through my phone, checking in with mom and Banks. Everything at home seems to be going okay and Banks says mom is doing well. I'm reminded of how thankful I am that he is there and checking in on her. I know if something was actually wrong there is no chance she'd tell me while I'm here and unable to do anything about it.

I hear a door shut and the tap of boots on the marble floor and I look up just as Alana is entering the living room. She looks stunning. Her long legs are covered in tights and she's wearing a black skirt and a blazer.

"Wow, you look great, Lanie."

She blushes. "Not so bad yourself, Ashford."

"Ready to head out?"

"Yep. Let me grab my coat and purse real quick." She walks over to the small mud room that houses all of our coats and grabs hers. I already have mine on, so I cross the room and take hers out of her hands.

"Here, let me help. You've got stuff in your hands."

She smiles up at me and passes her purse, phone and lip gloss to one hand, freeing the other arm to slip into the coat. I hold it out for her and she slides one arm in and then the other. I spin her around to face me and tug the coat forward, then without even thinking I start buttoning it up for her.

"Oh, I can do that," she says hesitantly.

"Let me."

She doesn't protest, but I am aware of her rigid posture. Whatever is happening inside of that beautiful head of hers is causing her to pull away and it's frustrating.

We walk out of the flat and down to the car. When we get outside, we're in a different car than usual. This one is a black suburban that is a lot bigger than the small sedan we've been driving in. I know why, but Lanie doesn't.

"I wonder why they switched cars," she whispers to me, not wanting to make a big deal out of it I assume.

"Maybe the other car needed servicing," I supply, keeping the secret a bit longer.

She shrugs and I reach to open her door, waving off Marco and helping her in.

The drive to the restaurant is short and quiet. I assume we're both in our heads a bit about this dinner, neither of us really know what to expect. Just as I am about to say something, Alana speaks.

"I'm a little nervous," she says, brushing an invisible piece of lint off of her skirt. "About the dinner."

"Yeah, I am too."

"I'm excited to know more about what exactly she wants us to do while we're here, but it feels like a lot of pressure. Hiring people and training them just feels like a lot."

"I agree, it does feel like a lot of pressure. You're better at explaining things, so I'm sure they'll want you to head up the training."

"Oh, whatever Alex. You're good at just about everything, including cooking."

We arrive at the restaurant and I turn to her.

"Stay there. If you even think about trying to get out of this car before I open the door for you I will pelt you with snowballs when we get done with this dinner."

Her laugh is beautiful and shakes her head in earnest.

"Yes, sir," she says with a mock salute.

I jump out, walk around to her side of the car and open the door for her. I hold out my hand and she takes it, stepping out onto the sidewalk.

I reluctantly drop her hand and we walk into the restaurant.

Alana

WE STEP INTO THE CROWDED RESTAURANT AND ALEX speaks to the maître d'. After an exchange, he leads us to a table in the back corner. It's much quieter here and it's dark, the candle-light flickering on the tables is some of the only light. It creates little bubbles of golden glow around the faces at each table and reminds me of a scene from a movie.

As we approach our table, an older woman with white hair stands to greet us.

"Amélie, so good to finally meet you," Alex says, taking her hand and bringing it to his lips for a kiss. I smile next to him and put my hand out for her to shake. She takes it, and tugs me forward, capturing me in a hug.

I let out a small *oomph* as my body meets her's, but her embrace is comforting. As I pull away, she moves her hands to my arms and squeezes them before letting go.

"Alex, Alana. It is so lovely to meet you." Her accent is beau-tiful and adds to her grace. She's wearing a black Chanel dress and short heels. Her hair is tied back with a gold clip and she has pearl earrings hanging from her ears. She is the very picture of elegance.

"Likewise. Thank you for having us for dinner," I reply with a smile. We all sit down and the waiter brings us water and tells us about some of the menu items, he takes our order and Amélie gets right to it.

"I am sure you are both anxious for any information about our office and your tasks for the next few weeks."

"We are excited to get going," Alex answers her. I give a nod in agreement.

"Excellent. Well, as you know we are in a bit of a predicament." Amélie pauses and takes a sip of her water. She takes a deep breath and continues, "Almost our entire team of editors was poached by a competing magazine and it's left us with only two."

"How many editors do you typically have on your team?" Alex asks. It's a good question, because the European version of the magazine operates on a much smaller scale than the US does. Our office has upwards of fifty different editors because we branch off. We have beauty editors—which is Cami's title—features editors, short story editors, and a few more. There are usually a team of two editors for each category and underneath each of those is a team of ten or so more that work with the lead editors and support them.

Alex and I are both features editors, but we sort of flip flop around and help where needed. Our team under us is currently running ship back in New York while we're here.

"We typically have a small number of about seven total. Someone takes on each of the branches, beauty, fashion and so on, then we have a few others to support and assist. However, right now only two are taking on the whole magazine alone. It's been...challenging."

"I can imagine that would be tough. I'm sorry you've been having to juggle all of this."

"Thank you, Alana. It has been. But I feel confident that, with your help, we can overcome these challenges and put our magazine back together."

The waiter arrives with our food and we talk as we eat. Amélie asks about our backgrounds and she shares a little bit about her family. She is much warmer than I anticipated her being and I think it will be really easy to work with her.

"Can you tell me a bit more about the other two editors that are still with you?" Alex asks. I've been wanting to ask this as well, but haven't had the courage. Heather mentioned to us that they weren't the kindest, so I am anxious to know Amélie's thoughts on them.

"Those two are interesting. They are not the most warm people you'll encounter in the office and I anticipate them making your time a bit difficult. They don't welcome outsiders and even when our team was intact, they often split off on their own and didn't engage with others."

"We aren't scared of a little challenge," Alex says, looking over and winking at me. *He really has to stop doing that.* His eyes are so warm I want to get lost in them, but I can't because I'm at a work dinner.

"I'm sure we can handle it," I say with a nod. "So will you have us interviewing new hires or helping train them? We can help with the workload as well as assisting with the hiring of a new team, if that is how we can best be helpful."

"Ah, yes. I would like to have at least one of you in each of the interviews, but they will likely be done in French so I'm not sure how beneficial your presence will be if you don't understand what they are saying."

"I know a small amount of French. I'm not fluent by any means, but I could probably pick up on the general flow of the conversation."

"That would be fantastic, Alex. I will plan to have you sit in then."

I suddenly feel a small panic at the need to prove myself worthy and helpful in this situation. Right now it seems like Alex is the only one with any initiative. If I want this promotion I need to step it up.

"I am happy to train whoever you choose to hire. I've already started mapping out what they might need to know and creating onboarding materials."

Why did I say that? I have no onboarding materials.

Alex looks over at me with a surprised sort of approval and I shrink a little in my chair.

"Oh Alana, that would be wonderful. It seems like you two really are the dream team. Heather wasn't lying when she spoke of your abilities."

Heather is always our biggest champion. I find myself missing her, which says so much about her leadership style considering people don't typically miss their bosses.

We finish up our conversation over a shared dessert and then gather our things and head out.

"Thank you both so much for meeting with me. I look forward to seeing you in the office on Monday."

Alex reaches out to shake her hand, but she pulls the same move from before and tugs him in for a hug. I go straight for the hug this time, knowing that's what she'd prefer, and she waves goodbye as she walks down the street. Our car is already pulled up out front, so we climb in and buckle up.

As we drive, I notice we aren't headed back in the direction of the flat. Not that I know where we are, but I know our flat is near the Eiffel Tower, and we are currently driving away from it.

"Where are we going?" I ask Alex, hoping he has more knowledge than I do.

"It's a surprise," he says with a shy smile.

"A surprise? For me?"

"Yep. Just sit back and relax, we should be there shortly."

I want to ask more questions, but he seems so excited and I don't want to force him to tell me what we're doing, so I do as he says. Normally, my need for control would prevent me from enjoying whatever Alex has planned for us tonight, but for some reason the worry eases with him.

Resting my head back on the headrest, I look out the window and watch as we pass buildings and people all bundled up. All of the light posts are topped with green wreaths adorned in gold and red ornaments. The snow is falling lightly, dusting the wreaths and streets in a slightly transparent white blanket.

I notice the car slowing down and turning onto a street that is pretty deserted looking. We continue driving down the road and there's only a few street lights placed a couple hundred yards apart.

"Are you driving out here to kill me and dump the body? Seriously, where are we going?"

"Relax, Lanie," he says and reaches out, placing his hand right above my knee and squeezing three times. He does that a lot, squeezes three times. "We're nearly there."

After about five more minutes of driving in dark nothingness the car turns onto a street, and as it does, lights come into view. The long drive we're headed down is lined with short evergreen trees leading to a small red barn at the end. Behind the barn there are rows and rows of tall, short, fat, and skinny Christmas trees. I feel like we've left France and crossed over into a Hallmark movie. The roof is covered in a blanket of snow, the temperatures having dropped so the snow is now sticking to the surfaces, and there are yellow lights framing the barn.

The whole thing reminds me of one of my favorite romance novels and I pinch myself because it doesn't feel real. There's a sign on the barn that says 'ferme de sapins de Noël'.

"Wait, where are we? What does that mean?" I ask, peering through the window looking for clues. Alex clears his throat before speaking, a bashful expression on his face.

"Um, it's a Christmas tree farm." The blush on his cheeks is endearing and makes me smile.

"A Christmas tree farm?" I ask in wonder. I didn't notice we'd pulled up to the front, lost in thought, until Alex hops out of the car. He doesn't even have to threaten me to keep me in my seat this time, the shock has frozen me as I stare out the front window. The door startles me when he opens it and I take his hand in a daze, stepping out of the car.

He doesn't let go of my hand, instead he uses it to pull me forward and towards the small building.

I think this man is going to get me a Christmas tree.

Alana

"How did you find a place like this in France?" I ask incredulously.

"It's not hard to use Google, Lanie." He continues pulling me forward. I take note of the fact that we are still holding hands, and although it would probably do us both some good if I let go, I don't. It's getting harder and harder to resist the pull between us.

We walk in and I take in the tiny store inside of the barn. There is a fireplace in the corner that makes the room feel warm and cozy and there are all kinds of different ornaments lining the shelves. I walk around and browse—touching the sparkly glass balls and admiring them—as Alex exchanges a few words with the man behind the counter.

"We just head out this way," Alex says, as he gestures to the back door, "and point out the one we want to one of the staff members. They'll cut it down and wrap it up for us. I don't think we can get anything too big, because it won't fit on the car, but we can get a pretty good sized one. Come on, let's go." He takes my hand again and I let him.

We walk outside into the cold and stroll down the rows and rows of trees.

"I haven't ever had a real tree before, we always got artificial ones. They all smell so incredible." I lean in and take a deep breath, inhaling the pine and snow.

"That's funny, we're the opposite. After that trip to the tree farm my mom took me to, we never went anywhere else. Once I moved away, though, I bought her one so she didn't have to go out and deal with the hassle of getting a real tree in the house. It was too much for her to do without me and I didn't want her to have to wait for me to put her decorations up. She's a November first decorator," he says with a laugh.

"You and your mom have a really good relationship," I say as a statement, not a question, because it's obvious they do.

"Yeah, we do. She's great and we got a lot closer once it was just the two of us." We continue forward, making comments about certain trees and keeping track of the top contenders. "What about you?" he asks. "You don't talk about your family much."

"Yeah," I shrug. "They're good parents, they just don't really acknowledge my existence most days." I laugh a sad sort of huff. "Then once my brother and I moved out they sort of stopped coming around at all and that was the last straw for Charlie. He tried to keep up a relationship with them and hoped for the best as far as their relationship with me, but it never got better and he got bitter."

He doesn't say anything else, just lets the silence hang between us, and it makes me want to keep talking.

"I think they really embraced the empty nester lifestyle. Charlie started playing hockey when he was five and my dad was his biggest supporter. My parents were obsessed with his hockey career, and I wasn't into sports so I fell to the wayside. They weren't bad parents, they just clearly favored one child over the other."

"One might classify that as less than ideal parenting," Alex says under his breath. I continue like I didn't hear him.

"Charlie liked the attention, but once he realized they

weren't giving it to me as well he came to resent it. Then, once we left for college, they completely gutted and renovated our rooms. Mine turned into mom's athletic studio with a full wall mirror, more yoga mats than you could ever want, and a cycling machine. Charlie's is now Dad's man cave, which I guess he gets to take advantage of if we ever go home. I don't know, it's weird. In college my friends would talk about going home for breaks and getting to stay in their childhood bedrooms, but I just slept on a springy pull out couch. They still keep up with his career and my dad calls to debrief every game, although Charlie never picks up."

At this point, we aren't really looking at the trees. We came across one a few rows back that I think is the winner, so now we're just strolling. I feel so safe with him and it feels like I can tell him anything. I notice, not for the first time, how different this feels from my previous relationship.

Brad never actually listened to me when I shared anything about how I felt about my parent's dismissal of Charlie and I. He would tell me my feelings were dumb and I should be grateful I even had parents and then move on to whatever he wanted to talk about.

It made it difficult to decipher exactly how I felt about the situation, because any time I started to get frustrated with them or sad they weren't around more, I'd feel guilty. Guilt that I wasn't just grateful for the fact that they took care of Charlie and I, and put us through college.

I've been learning though, through lots of therapy, that I can hold space for my thankfulness for a good childhood and also acknowledge the pain that I feel at being thrown to the side as I got older.

"Did that bother you?" Alex asks. "That they changed your rooms?"

"I acted like it didn't bother me, but if I was honest with myself it probably did more than I let on."

He squeezes my hand in solidarity and we continue walking. He stays quiet, so I continue.

"Soon after we left for college, they took this year-long road trip and drove all over the US. It looked like they were having a ton of fun, but it was weird for the holidays and breaks. Charlie and I came home to an empty house every time, and that was fun at first, we would get the whole place to ourselves and we had a few parties with Cami and some other friends. Eventually though, when everyone else was spending Christmas with their parents and loved ones while we sat home alone eating delivery pizza it lost its excitement pretty quick. I felt like that scene from *Home Alone,* when Kevin is walking on the sidewalk at night and he looks into the window of one of the houses and it's a glowy and happy picture. The whole family is crowded around a dinner table enjoying a meal together and laughing. I could imagine what he felt like at that moment.

"I thought after that one weird year it would be back to normal, but they loved traveling so much that they were gone for most holidays, off to the next exciting adventure. They raised us well and loved us and I don't doubt that they still do. It just feels like they don't care as much about our lives now as they used to. I think that's why Christmas is such a big deal to me. When we started having holidays alone, just Charlie and I, we had to come up with things that made the holiday feel special again, things that were just ours. So not doing those things feels weird."

Alex nods his head and hums in understanding, but continues walking without saying much. I don't say anything else, but the silence is nice. It allows me to think and reflect.

After a while of walking, still hand in hand, Alex finally speaks.

"I'm sorry your parents didn't stick around, Lanie," he says, brushing his thumb over the back of my hand.

"It's alright. We got by okay."

"It isn't alright though. Parents are supposed to love and

cherish you. They brought you into this world and they have a responsibility to nurture and love you, even in adulthood."

He pauses again, collecting his thoughts.

"I'm sure their dismissal made you feel like you didn't matter to them, and that might make your other relationships, like with Charlie, all the more important. If he makes you feel loved and like you matter, I bet you'd want to hold that relationship close."

I nod, because he took the words right out of my mouth, and turn to him.

"I think you're right. Charlie has always made me feel like I was the most important person in the world to him. He is an incredible brother." I pause, lost in thought. "Thanks for listening. It means a lot." I know I'm blushing, I can feel my face heat, but I don't really care. This man is so sweet and genuine that I can't help it.

"Always." He pulls me in for a hug and I melt against him. He smells incredible, and before he pulls away he places a gentle kiss to the top of my head. It feels like the most natural thing in the world, for him to place a chaste kiss there. Like we were made to fit together in this way. It's a sobering thought and takes me by surprise, but I don't hate it. It feels good. The embrace ends and he continues forward, pulling me along with his grip on my hand.

"Come on, let's go tell them which one we want."

We walk to one of the staff members at the farm and Alex points our tree out. They get to work bundling it up for us and we head back inside the small building at the front to pay.

"Before I pay for the tree, we need to get some ornaments. I figured we could each pick one out for the other person."

I don't say anything for a beat, trying to figure out what he's doing here.

"That's the first item on my traditions list," I say, narrowing my eyes at him. "Picking out ornaments for each other."

"It is," he says, nonchalantly.

I stare at him for another few seconds and he finally breaks out in a smile.

"We're completing your list, sunshine."

Completing my list?

"Why?"

"What do you mean why? It's important to you, is it not?"

I nod my head.

"That's all I need to hear. Now pick out an ornament, they close soon. And no peeking. I have an idea for the perfect one for you."

He turns around and starts browsing the aisles, leaving me behind. There's nothing to do but go along with it, but as I walk up and down rows and rows of ornaments, I'm resigned to the fact that I don't think I am going to make it out of this month without falling for this man.

CHAPTER 29

Alana

THE TREE IS BUNDLED UP ON TOP OF THE CAR AND AS WE pull up to the door of our building, Alex turns to me, a serious look on his face.

"Okay, so one thing I didn't do before we went out on this little adventure..."

I raise my eyebrows and wait for him to continue.

"IdidntexactlyclearitwithMaura," he says it so fast and so jumbled together, it's impossible to understand.

"Say that again?"

"I didn't exactly clear it with Maura," he says sheepishly. "So we are going to have to sneak this tree into the elevator without her seeing, because I doubt she is going to want a live tree with pine needles in one of the building's flats."

"And how do you suppose we get this tree upstairs without her seeing it? It's huge!"

"Well, Albert is going to help me carry it upstairs. He doesn't know that he's helping me, but I know he likes me and he doesn't much care for Maura so I should be able to convince him. While we're getting it through the lobby, you're going to distract Maura."

"Excuse me?"

"You'll be great at it. She loves you." Yeah, right.

We climb out of the car and Alex walks over to Albert, talking to him in hushed tones. Before I go inside, he looks over at me and uses his index and middle fingers to form a peace sign and then points them from his eyes to mine, in an 'I'm watching you' sort of gesture.

"What are you doing?" I ask.

"I don't know. I'm nervous. Get in there tiger," he says to me and pushes me through the door. I stumble into one of the decorative trees at the entrance, making it wobble and gaining Maura's attention.

I make my way in slowly, trying to figure out what I could say in order to get her to look the opposite direction for a few minutes. I glance behind me and see that Albert and Alex have gotten the tree off of the car and are just waiting for me to distract her.

I walk over to the elevator and push the button so it's at least on its way down, then I make a big show of remembering something and walk over to the desk where she is ignoring me.

"Hi Maura," I say cheerfully. She doesn't respond, just looks up at me with a bored expression.

I spot a stack of papers on the counter, so I lean over them as I speak to her.

"I was wondering if you had an extra key to our flat? I seem to have misplaced mine."

She starts talking in French, no doubt putting some kind of curse on me for losing my key, and bends down to look in the drawers. Alex and Albert start making their way in just as the elevator doors slide open, but it looks like Maura found the key because she starts straightening back up.

Before she can stand up fully and see the illegal decorations, I sit up off of the counter and "accidentally" push the papers in front of me down on top of her head and onto the ground.

"Fils de pute est bon," she says in an angry tone. I don't know what it means, but I'm sure it isn't kind.

I turn around and see Alex standing in the back of the elevator snickering, the tree pushed just out of view. Glancing back at Maura, I see she is crouched down, gathering the strewn about papers back into a pile. Her distraction makes this the most opportune time to get away, so I run and jump into the elevator, standing in front of Alex. Just as the doors close, Maura straightens and looks more angry than I've seen her so far.

"Found it," I exclaim, holding up my key. Once the doors close, I lean back against Alex and let out a large breath. After a second of silence, we both break out in laughter.

"She might hate us even more now than before, but at least we have a tree."

Our laughter has subsided as we reach our floor and I help Alex carry the tree inside. We talk for a while about where best to put it, but decide on the living room because we've been spending most of our time in there anyways.

After we get the tree set up in the corner, Alex moves to work on something on the TV, and I start unboxing the lights that he had Marco pick up for us while we were out at dinner. I get to work untangling them and plugging them into the nearest outlet, but get distracted when I hear the beginning music from the movie *Elf*.

I smile as I realize he really is planning on completing some of the items on my list, and I wander over to the couch and take a seat to watch the opening credits. Alex says nothing, but sets the remote down on the table and walks off to the kitchen.

It's about twenty minutes later when I see him walking back into the room and look up. He is carrying two mugs that look like gingerbread men. They each are piled high with whipped cream and red and green sprinkles. He sets his down and hands me mine without a word, then heads back into the kitchen.

"Alex, did you seriously make hot cocoa?" I yell at his retreating back.

"I don't know, take a sip," he shouts back.

I cautiously bring the mug to my lips and tilt it back, careful not to burn myself, and I close my eyes when the chocolatey goodness hits my tongue. This tastes like absolute heaven, probably the best hot cocoa I've ever had.

"What did you put in this?" I call out.

"My mom's special recipe," he answers, loud enough for me to hear him.

"I am going to need that recipe when we get back."

"I'm sorry, family secret." He's smirking as he returns to the room.

"I bet I can get it out of you."

"You probably could," he says with a laugh.

The way he balances the plate of cookies in his hand is impressive and he holds it out to me. There are chocolate chip, sugar with different holiday sprinkles, snickerdoodle, chocolate with white chocolate chips, and gingerbread men.

"The list didn't say what kind of cookies you usually eat, so I made a few different kinds just to be safe."

I stare up at him, speechless.

"What's wrong? I missed one didn't I?" He lets out a sigh of disappointment. "I knew I should have made peanut butter. I just didn't—"

I stand and place a finger over his mouth to get him to stop speaking. It works, but now I'm distracted by the softness of his lips beneath my finger. Mission accomplished, I pull my hand back into the safety of my space and continue.

"This is incredible, Alex. You didn't have to do all of this."

"I wanted to."

He holds the plate out to me again and I grab a snickerdoodle, taking a small bite.

"Are you just good at everything?" I ask. "First you cook an incredible meal, then you make some of the best hot chocolate I've ever had and now I find out you make incredible cookies too. What *can't* the man do?"

"Own a hermit crab."

"Huh?"

"I'm terrified. My mom got me one when I was little and after a few months it changed shells because it was growing. The sight of the naked hermit crab unsettled me so much I made her take it away immediately."

I'm laughing now, imagining a small Alex screaming at the shell-less hermit crab.

"There, there, big boy. No hermit crabs in sight," I tell him and pat him on the shoulder in a comforting gesture before sitting back down on the couch.

He shrugs me off and sets the plate of cookies down on the coffee table before grabbing one for himself and sitting down next to me.

"When did you even have time to make these?"

"While you were getting ready for dinner. You holed up in your room a lot the last twenty four hours."

He's right, I did. I wasn't trying to be a hermit (pun intended), but I needed a break from the whirlwind that is Alex Ashford. I've been trying my hardest not to fall for the man, but I'm starting to admit to myself that I might not be able to stop it.

The constant back and forth I feel is so frustrating. One minute I'm ready to say 'to hell with it' and lean in for a kiss, and the next I want to run and hide.

Regardless, I make a decision to put this out of my mind for the rest of the night and just be in the moment. Alex has gone to great lengths to make this a fun night full of holiday traditions and warmth, so I am going to let it be that.

We sit and laugh at the movie and eat cookies for a while longer before getting up to continue working on the tree. Alex and I drape the lights from the top to the bottom and then get to work placing the red and green ornaments that he purchased a set of at the shop.

I'm about to get the star we picked out, but Alex stops me with a gentle hand on my wrist.

"We need to exchange the ornaments we picked out," he says, placing a box in my hands.

I completely forgot we even got each other ornaments.

I start to unwrap the paper protecting it from breaking and open it to unveil a mini sized Diet Coke covered in glitter.

"Oh my gosh, this is perfect," I say as I look down at the ornament. It seems we were on the same wavelength with our ornaments because the one I chose for him is similar. Always in each other's heads lately.

"I saw it and it reminded me of you."

I smile up at him.

I move towards the tree and start to reach up to place it on a branch, but I'm just a tiny bit too short to reach the one I'm aiming for. I go to move to a lower branch, but just before I do a hand snakes around my waist to hold me steady and I feel Alex's body heat pressed behind mine.

"Here, let me help."

He reaches up to where my hand is holding the ornament halfway onto the branch, and moves his hand over mine, helping to push the ornament fully onto the branch. Once he's got it securely in place, I lower off of my tip toes and turn around, trying to get a little more space between us, but Alex doesn't back up. He also doesn't remove his hand from my waist, instead keeping it on my body as I spin around and letting it glide over my stomach as I turn.

Now I'm pressed in between him and the tree, and I can't step back without risking an ornament falling and breaking. I remain trapped, breathing heavy from first stretching to place the ornament and now the close proximity to Alex.

"Thanks for the help."

He reaches up and brushes a strand of hair back behind my ear that had fallen forward. "Any time, Lanie."

A smirk lands on his face before he turns around and pretends like it never happened. His self-assurance is charming and I fall a little harder down the path I'm desperately trying to avoid.

"Alright, my turn," he says, breaking the spell. He turns and grabs the bag that houses the ornament I chose for him, and begins to unwrap it. I suddenly find myself feeling nervous.

"If you don't like it, you don't have to—"

He stops unwrapping and looks up. "Lanie, stop. I'll love it because you picked it out, no matter what it is."

I don't respond, but he must be happy with whatever he sees in my silent reaction, because he continues unwrapping.

He pulls out the small glass bottle of Topo Chico, the sparkling water he always drinks, and immediately bursts into laughter. He looks up at me with the happiest expression I've seen on him in a while and I wish we could stay in this moment forever.

"This is perfect for me. Thank you." He winks at me and turns to hang the bottle on a branch on the opposite side of mine and a bit further down.

For the rest of the night we laugh and talk, taking bites of cookies and sips of cocoa as we finish decorating the tree. Eventually we make our way back to the couch to finish the movie and I don't even realize I'm drifting before I've fallen asleep.

CHAPTER 30
Alana

I'M BEING LIFTED AND THE ONLY REASON I CAN TELL IS because I feel the air brush against the small strip of exposed skin on my back where my pajamas have ridden up. Strong warm hands cradle me close and I breathe in the familiar smell of cedar and sandalwood.

I subconsciously realize it's Alex and cuddle closer to his chest, leaving my eyes shut tight. I am halfway between asleep and awake, not sure if this is a dream or reality. I must make a noise to alert Alex of my consciousness because he speaks.

"Just taking you to your room."

"You smell like my favorite aisle in the bookstore."

"That's a weird thing to say," he says with a chuckle.

I peer open my eyes and look up at him through my eyelashes.

"No it isn't. It's comforting."

He smiles down at me, his features softening. "Close your eyes and go back to sleep, sunshine. I'll tuck you in."

I obey and he places me onto my bed. He pulls the covers up to my chin and starts to pull away, but before he can, I grab his hand.

I think I ask him to stay, but I can't be sure. My sleep drunk brain makes its own decisions and I'm a bystander. I'll find the energy to be embarrassed about this in the morning.

I hear him mutter something that sounds a lot like 'You have no idea how much I want to' but then he's placing a gentle kiss on my forehead and walking away. I hear the snick of the door closing as I cuddle into my blankets and pillows and drift off into a dreamless sleep.

I wake up thankful for a good night's rest, considering today is our first day at the office. I'm nervous, but also really excited and honestly just anxious to get started. The lead up from the last few weeks has been brutal. I'm ready to stop talking about it and just do it.

I reach over to turn off my alarm and freeze. I don't remember setting an alarm. I don't even remember falling asleep here last night.

What happened last night?

I flop back down onto the pillow and rack my brain trying to recall the events of the last twelve hours.

Alex took me to get a Christmas tree.

He brought me home and made me cookies.

He gave me hot chocolate and we watched *Elf* while we decorated.

I remember sitting on the couch with him while we watched the movie and I must have fallen asleep. The memories that come back are foggy, but I know what happened.

Alex picking me up, carrying me into my room, whispering to me. Me asking him to stay and sleep with me.

Oh goodness.

I asked Alex to climb into bed and cuddle with me. I press my fingertips to my eyes and groan. He clearly said no, which is somehow more mortifying. If he had said yes and stayed with me at least it wouldn't have felt like an embarrassment *and* a rejection.

It's seven in the morning in Paris, which means it's just after one in the morning in New York, but I still grab my phone and call Cami. Hopefully she either hasn't gone to sleep yet or is sleeping light enough that she hears her phone.

"Please pick up. Please, please pick up," I whisper into the phone.

"There better be a good reason why you're calling me. I just fell asleep."

"Oh thank you baby Jesus."

"What's going on?"

"I think I want to jump into bed with Alex and I need you to remind me why I decided not to."

"I'm not going to do that. And why are you whispering?"

"Because I don't want him to hear me. Just be a good friend and go get the letter I put in your junk drawer in the kitchen."

"You've got to be kidding me." Cami groans, but I hear her throw the covers back and stand. The sound of the drawer opening and the rustling of paper makes me breathe easier. "When did you even put this in here?"

"That's not important. Just read it." Her sigh is heavy with annoyance.

"Alana, it's Alana Cade from *Impress Magazine* speaking to you through Cami, friend and beautiful editor," she reads. "Wait, is this from *Parks and Rec*?"

"Just keep reading. Leslie Knope won the presidential election for a reason."

"Do not do anything with Alex. Be responsible, no matter how cute his mouth is. Your job is on the line."

"Great delivery. You're exactly right, thank you," I reply.

"You're forgetting Leslie and Ben end up together and become arguably one of television's biggest power couples."

"I need you to help me stay strong. I just put myself back together, Cami."

The conversation quickly turns heavy as the emotion is thick within my voice, and she must be able to hear it.

"Lan, babe, this isn't that."

"How do you know? I want to believe he is different, but every time I think about giving into this pull I feel towards him I freak out. It hasn't even been that long. We've only been in Paris for three days."

"Okay slow down," she says, in a gentle tone. "Tell me what's been going on. You asked him to cuddle you on the airplane, he took you to the Eiffel Tower and literally created a scene from every romcom movie ever, he stood up to Brad... anything else?"

"Last night," I say with a groan.

"Oh my gosh what happened last night?"

"Well I gave him my Christmas traditions list before we left New York and thought nothing else of it, until he started checking items off of the list yesterday."

"Wait, what do you mean?"

I tell Cami all about how Alex created the most special and magical night. I tell her about the tree, the hand holding, the ornament, and falling asleep on the couch.

"Last night I woke up as he was bringing me back to my bedroom and I asked him to stay. He turned me down. That's weird isn't it? Why wouldn't he stay?"

"You asked him to stay with you?"

"Yeah, I think I wasn't really aware of what I was saying. I was half asleep, but clearly it doesn't really matter because he rejected me anyway."

"Sometimes you are such an idiot."

"Oh. Thanks."

"Lan, he absolutely wants you. He's just being gentlemanly and not crossing boundaries. You two haven't gone there yet and he's not going to just sleep in your bed with you when you weren't even fully conscious enough to make that decision."

What she's saying makes sense, but the rejection still stings, even if it wasn't a total rejection.

"Don't you think it's fast?" I ask. This is another insecurity of mine. Even though it feels like I've known Alex my whole life, we only arrived in Paris a few days ago.

"It isn't fast. I know you just started spending more time together recently, but you've worked right next to him and on the same team for a year now. It isn't like you were strangers before this, you two are good friends. He is observant, he probably knows you better than you realize."

"That's a good point."

"I know. I'm extremely smart. I'm also extremely tired and I need to go back to sleep." I hear her bedroom door snick shut behind her and the murmur of another voice in the background. "I want you to just take it slow, but don't completely close yourself off. You deserve love more than anyone I know, Lan."

Tears unexpectedly prick the backs of my eyes and I squeeze them shut to try and keep them in. Ever since my breakup with Brad I have focused on being independent and excelling at my job. I vowed to myself that I would work up in my career and find what makes me happy. I've done the work part, but I haven't checked the happiness box quite yet.

Until Alex, I was perfectly content being single, but now I'm thinking that might not be what I want. The question is, do I feel like this is the right person to open myself back up to?

I know the answer, even if I don't want to admit it to myself.

Loving someone is terrifying. Loving someone means letting them in and letting them in means showing them your weaknesses. Weaknesses that they could exploit and use against you. I showed Brad all of my weak spots, and when it benefitted him he used them to his advantage.

"I'll try."

"Good. I love you."

"Love you, too, Cam. Thanks for picking up."

"Always."

She hangs up and I check the time on my phone, realizing I need to get up and get moving if I'm going to have time to eat anything before work. Just as I'm sitting up, a soft knock sounds at my door.

"Lanie, you awake?" Alex asks through the door, not opening it.

"Yep, I'm up. Come in."

He cracks open the door and peeks his head through it. I smile at his warm eyes and the way a swath of curly hair falls on his forehead. He is full of boyish charm and charisma right now and I want to run right to him, but I hold back.

"Just checking on you, didn't want you to sleep in on your first day."

"Thanks for setting my alarm for me, I'm sorry I wiped out last night." His cheeks blush and I know for certain now that I asked him to stay with me.

"It's no problem. I'll make breakfast, should be ready in about fifteen or twenty minutes."

"You don't have to do that."

"I know."

I hear his footsteps descend down the hallway and I sigh, getting up to get ready for my day. Alex is one of the kindest and most respectful men I know. I can't think of a world in which he would act like Brad did. If there were any man I would open myself back up to, it would be him.

CHAPTER 31

Alex

I SMELL STRAWBERRIES AND VANILLA BEFORE SHE EVEN enters the kitchen. I turn so my back is facing the entrance, wanting to give the illusion that I'm not at all affected by her, even though I absolutely am. It's like my body has been made aware of her and now we're connected by some invisible string. It tugs me towards her and I can feel when she's near, sense when she's around.

Last night was so perfect. It was everything I wanted it to be and the way her eyes sparkled when I brought out the cookies and cocoa will be burned into my memory forever. If that's how she reacts, I'll bake her cookies and make hot cocoa every day for the rest of her life.

"Morning," she murmurs as she enters the room. Her bare feet shuffle across the floor and she steps up next to me at the counter top to grab a mug. I reach out to stop her, instead placing a hot latte in her hands.

"Thanks." She looks up at me through her thick lashes and smiles.

I give her a small nod and walk over to the bar, pulling out a chair for her. The plate of eggs, bacon, and toast is placed on the table with another setting right next to it.

She walks over and sits down, sipping her latte and humming in approval before she sets it down and picks up her fork.

"You didn't have to make breakfast."

"You already said that," I tease.

"Well I just don't want you thinking I expect you to cook for me every morning that we're here. I can always eat a granola bar or something."

I know she tends to forget to eat when she's stressed. After a year of observing her during tight deadlines and stressful meetings with higher ups, I've seen her skip a meal or three. She doesn't need to know it, but I will be making sure she is properly fed—my protective instincts are taking over and I don't plan on reining them in.

"I'm counting on you paying me back with those Christmas morning cinnamon rolls."

She gives me an apprehensive smile and picks up her fork. As we start eating, the room grows awkwardly quiet. I wondered how much of last night she would remember, and it's seeming like she's remembered a good bit if she's this awkward now.

"Look I'm sorry I asked—"

"This doesn't have to be awkward—"

We both start at the same time, then pause for a second before we start laughing.

"It's really fine, Alana. No need to discuss it, really."

"Okay, fine. Onto other big topics then. How nervous are you for today on a scale from one to ten? Because right now I am at about a nine."

"Ah, I'm a cool three."

"A three? Well that's just unfair. Men always have it easier."

"I'm just kidding. I'm probably around a six, but I'm pretty sure we have nothing to worry about. At least for today, we will just be learning the ropes and getting to know the current staff."

"Cheers to that," she says and holds her mug in the air. I tap it with mine and we both take a sip, peering at each other over the rim of our respective mugs.

"Have you heard from *he who shall not be named* again?" I ask as we eat.

"No, thankfully. I'm hoping your phone call keeps him away."

"Me too, but you'll let me know if you hear anything else, right?"

"Yep."

I drop the subject and move on to better topics.

"You and Charlie like doing all of these traditions every year, but I imagine that's pretty tough with his NHL schedule."

"Yeah it totally can be. Usually we just work around his schedule and plan things for when he's home. I wish I could go to more of his away games, but it is what it is."

"Is he usually home on Christmas Day? I don't know much about the NHL."

"He is. They don't schedule games on Christmas, thankfully. We need to get you to a game when we get back."

"I would love that."

My phone buzzes—it's Marco letting me know he's here to take us to the office.

"Ready? Marco is downstairs."

"Sure, let me just put my shoes on and we can head out."

Alana is wearing a tan turtleneck tucked into a black skirt that rests a few inches above her knees. She's got on black sheer tights underneath and is zipping up a pair of knee high black boots. She looks sophisticated and sexy all at the same time, and it's torture.

Not only are we not there, yet, but we have a job to do. That's the whole reason why we came here and I need to remember that. Getting distracted and doing a less than stellar job would disappoint Heather, and Alana and I respect her too much to let that happen.

We walk to the foyer and she pulls on a long tan coat that

matches the shade of her turtleneck. I pull mine on, too, and open the door for her.

We step into the lift and I get distracted when she reaches into her purse and pulls out a pink tube of lip gloss. She squeezes a bit out, swiping it over her lips, and I feel like I can't breathe. The gentle back and forth motion puts me into a trance and I desperately want to lean in and kiss her.

The ding of the lift arriving at the bottom floor saves me from myself, and I reluctantly pull my gaze away from her. We head out the door of the building and Marco ushers us into the back seat of the town car.

The heater has been on, so it's toasty inside but not so warm that I need to remove my coat. The drive to the office is short, only about five minutes, so I buckle up quickly and we are on our way. We haven't actually visited the office yet, so I am shocked when we pull up to a small building. It's a cream color with four different pastel colored doorways lining the front.

"It's that one there," Marco says as he nods his head towards the pistachio green door on the left. "They're expecting you."

Alana takes a deep breath next to me and squares her shoulders. I can visibly see her gearing up to exit the car and face our new project for the next few weeks. I sit quietly, waiting for her to be ready. Finally, she reaches out to grab the door handle, but I place my hand on her wrist to stop her.

"Don't. I'll get it. You ready?"

"Why do you insist on getting my door every time?"

It's apparent every time I try to do something nice for her, that Brad didn't give her the attention and care that she needed, but I'm determined to show her what a real man taking care of his girl looks like.

"Because if I'm around there's no need for you to get your own door."

She doesn't respond, so I get out and round the car to her side, opening the door and holding out a hand for her. She takes it and I watch as she steps out and smooths down her skirt.

"You look stunning."

"Well you're not so bad yourself, Ashford."

I bump my shoulder against hers and we continue forward to the front door of the office.

"Do we knock or just walk in?" she asks, hesitating as we approach.

"I think we should just go in."

"Are you sure? What if—"

Alana is cut off by the door to the office opening and Amélie greeting us with a warm smile.

"Hello," she says in an almost comically bright voice. "We have been waiting for you. Come in, come in, it's freezing out there."

We follow her inside and hang our coats on a rack to the left of the door. This office looks more like a home than an office. There are small rooms on either side of the hallway we walk down. Inside are islands of desks with large desktop computers sitting on top of them. The desks are huddled together, so that each person is facing one another.

As we walk past, people look up from their work and smile and wave at us. It makes me feel ten times less anxious about the dynamic in the office and I can tell Alana is feeling lighter as well.

Amélie leads us down to the end of the hallway and into a larger room where she says we will be doing most of our work. It's clear that this is the biggest room in the space and the desks are grouped in fours and scattered throughout the room. The only ones occupied, however, are two desks in the back left corner.

"This is where our editors work. As you can see, and as you know, we are down a few." Amélie smiles sheepishly. "You can place your things down in here and I will go ahead and give you the tour. Genevieve and Luis, meet Alana and Alex."

Alana makes her way to the back corner of the room where the only two remaining editors sit, and I follow. She holds out her hand for them to shake. "You can call me Lana," she says with a sweet smile.

Genevieve looks at her hand suspended in the air and hesitates. For a second I'm afraid she won't shake it all, but finally after a long awkward pause, she places her hand in Lana's.

"C'est un plaisir de vous rencontrer. Nous allons beaucoup nous amuser ensemble," Genevieve says as she shakes her hand. Luis snorts a laugh from her left and Amélie sighs behind us. I know she said 'It's a pleasure to meet you', but I'm not fast enough to understand the second sentence, and with the way the others in the room reacted I'm not sure I want to.

Lana laughs uncomfortably and holds her hand out to Luis next, who shakes it with zero emotion on his face. After the warm smiles and waves from the rest of the staff, it's jarring how ice cold it feels in here.

Amélie leads us back out of the room after we say our hellos to our new office besties and we head back to the front. She takes us through each room, introducing us to the staff members inside and telling us what each of them do. We don't run into any other cold greetings like the first ones we received, thankfully.

She shows us the kitchen, which is just a small narrow room with a refrigerator, sink and coffee machine. I make each of us a cup before returning to the editor room. We sit down at a few desks towards the front of the room and Amélie joins us.

"Alright then, are you two ready to get started?"

I nod and glance over at Alana. She hasn't said much throughout the half hour that we've been here and I find myself wanting to know what she thinks of all of this, and if she's anxious or excited or nervous.

"I have planned for you both to meet with Genevieve and Luis this morning in order to get a better picture of how you can be helpful with completing their tasks. Once you all meet, I think you'll have a good plan for moving forward. Then this afternoon we have two interviews. Alex, I'll have you sit in on those and we can discuss after what your thoughts are."

Despite my very basic understanding of French, I am concerned about understanding the interviews. I couldn't even pick up what Genevieve said a few minutes ago, I don't know how an interview will be any better.

"We will conduct the interview in English if the candidate speaks it, that way you can follow the conversation. About half tend to, so we should be okay for the most part," Amélie says, practically reading my mind. "If they do speak English, you are welcome to sit in as well, Alana. The two candidates today do, so we will have you both in there."

"That sounds great," Alana replies with a smile. "We will start out with Luis and Genevieve, and I look forward to the interviews this afternoon."

Amélie lets us know she will be in her office and we are welcome to check in any time, and then leaves us to our new team. They are huddled in their corner, whispering to each other in French and snickering every so often. I look over at Alana with a look that hopefully communicates *I already hate these two*. I'm pretty sure her eyes say *Me too* back to me.

We both take a collective breath, then stand and head back to the duo.

Alana

THE ROOM FEELS COLD—NOT BECAUSE OF THE temperature, but the environment of the two editors. It's exactly what I expected from what we heard about Luis and Genevieve before we arrived. We sit down at the island of desks that they currently inhabit and I flip open my notebook to a new page.

I knew that whatever Genevieve had said to me when I first met her couldn't have been kind. I can tell when someone is being sarcastic, even if I can't understand the language. That, plus Luis's snickering after she said it told me all I needed to know about her welcome.

The chaos and anxiety in my brain quiets as I get out my variety of colored highlighters and line them up in a neat row. I grab my pink gel pen and write the date at the top of the page, then switch to a black one and move down to begin to take notes.

"So, what does the current workload look like for you two?" Alex asks as they finally look up from whatever they were looking at on Genevieve's phone.

"We don't want you here," Luis says. I hope the shock on my face at his words isn't obvious, but I don't have a great poker face so I'm sure it shows. I'm shocked he chooses these words as the first ones he speaks to us and I'm taken aback at how straightforward he is with his hatred. I anticipated it would be difficult to fit in here, but I did not expect outright dismissal.

"We have things under control and we don't need *Americans*," he spits the word, "coming in to show us how it's done."

Alex looks over at me, concern and annoyance obvious in his green eyes. I take a deep breath and try again.

"I can acknowledge it probably is frustrating having people here that don't understand or know the way your office works, but we're just here to help."

He rolls his eyes at my cautious smile and looks back to his computer, done with the conversation. Amélie intended for this meeting to take most of the morning, but that is looking less and less likely.

"Look," Genevieve says, "Neither of us are happy you're here. But if we're honest, we are buried in work." The flash of betrayal in Luis's eyes tells me all I need to know in regards to how he feels about needing our help. "I think if we can each take on a section or two and split it up that way, it should work. Then we're each taking on the work of two or three editors and not a whole team."

My pen starts flying across the page and with each scribble, my shoulders drop. Making plans and a well organized page of notes acts as a balm to the anxious feelings I experience. For some people it's the gym, for me it's an organized page of color coordinated notes.

"That sounds doable," Alex says. "Which ones would you like us to take over?"

We spend the next hour deciding how we are going to divide up the sections and Genevieve gives us a status update on the tasks left for the ones we're responsible for. Luis sits to the side and doesn't say a word, clearly not willing to warm up to us in the slightest.

After the meeting concludes, Alex and I move to the other side of the room and begin working. I start by making a to-do list and tackling each item one by one. Alex works in a less organized way, but he always gets his things done.

I open my laptop and pull up the program *Impress* uses for project management and editing. I notice Alex looking over at me every few minutes as we work. Eventually, I can't take it any longer and I turn fully toward him.

"What?" I ask, almost irritated but not quite there yet.

"What do you mean what?"

"You know what. You've been looking over at me every few minutes for the last hour. Do I have something on my face?" I ask, reaching up to touch my cheeks and forehead.

"No, Lanie. Your face is perfect."

I look down in an effort to hide the blush that I am certain is showing, but I'm startled by the gentle hand under my chin forcing my gaze back up and into Alex's eyes.

"Don't hide from me."

The effect those words have on me should be studied by doctors, because there is no way it's a healthy response. Butterflies take flight in my stomach and my toes curl in my shoes.

How am I supposed to respond to that?

Well, definitely not by giggling, which I am currently doing. I'm laughing and for some reason I can't stop. It must be contagious, because after a few seconds of staring at me in confusion, Alex joins in. I don't have any idea why we're laughing, but I guess I'm glad I'm not doing it alone.

Genevieve and Luis glare at us with utter disapproval, but I can't seem to make myself care. I'm not able to focus on anything but the full and beautiful sound coming from Alex's lips. After a while, the laughter dies down and I realize we've gradually been leaning in, gravity or whatever else pulling us towards one another.

We are so close I can feel his breath as he sighs against my lips. He must be thinking the same thing I am, because I notice his eyes dart down to my lips for the smallest second before he reaches up and softly tucks a strand of hair behind my ear.

I expect him to pull his hand away, but instead he lets it float down to my cup my cheek and *oh my gosh* I think he's going to kiss me. And I'm going to let him.

"Did you two just come here to flirt?" Luis's voice breaks the moment and I shoot back, suddenly aware of our surroundings, almost toppling my chair back and tipping over. "Good to know you're both so dedicated. That might be something Amélie would want to know."

Way to hit the mark there, Luis. It's like he knows exactly what to say to get under my skin, and it works.

I mentally berate myself for getting swept up like that. Kissing your coworker while at work is definitely *not* the way to earn a promotion, and now Luis is threatening to report us to Amélie which means word would absolutely get back to Heather.

Alex whispers a soft sorry to me before he settles back into his work. I try to do the same, but I'm not very productive. I can't stop thinking about his breath on my lips, his hand on my cheek, the way I could feel his racing pulse through his touch, and that leads me to thinking about how we're going to get reported to the boss and I'll probably get fired. Then everything I've worked so hard for will go straight down the drain.

This is why I didn't want to get involved with anyone. I've been trying to work on myself and my career and climb the ladder. I know all a relationship will do is distract me from what's important.

But what if you can have both? What if climbing the ladder isn't the only thing that's important?

I turn back to my notes and my pens, but it's not helping. I can't stop my racing thoughts. Normally this is when I would get up and go for a run, interrupt my thought train, but obviously that isn't an option.

"I'm going to step outside and get some air."

"It's freezing outside, Alana."

Okay, full name. Got it. Drawing a line.

"I'm aware, Ashford. I'll be fine."

He looks a little wounded at my dismissal, but I desperately need to breathe air that doesn't smell like cedar and sandalwood. I head down the hall and completely forget my coat. My breathing turns heavy the closer I get to the door and I can tell I'm nearing an anxiety attack.

I push through the front door and stumble to the side of the building, putting my hands on the back of my head to try and open up my chest. I feel like I can't breathe, and even though I know it's just the panic, I can't seem to get a hold of it. It's frustrating that I let these things affect me, but if I was honest I know it's not Alex's fault. He's acted as a remedy to my anxiety lately. In fact I wish I had asked him to come outside with me, even though his almost kiss is what started all of this.

This has nothing to do with him specifically, and everything to do with me placing too much pressure on myself and being terrified to let someone in again.

As I try to get control of my breathing, I remember the technique he taught me when we were back at home. I breathe in for four counts, hold it for seven and then breathe out for eight. After a few rounds I finally get control of my breathing and close my eyes, leaning up against the wall.

I feel an intense burst of pride shoot through me at the realization that I just got myself through that on my own, and it gives me the confidence and energy I need to push my way back into the office.

"You okay?" Alex whispers when I sit back down next to him.

"All good."

Alana

THE RIDE HOME THAT AFTERNOON IS QUIET, BOTH OF US lost in thought. After my *moment* outside, I went back in and worked at my desk with Alex for the rest of the morning. Neither of us brought up the almost kiss and after lunch we sat in on the two interviews Amélie told us about and they both went well.

I'm thankful the first two spoke English, because it allowed me to feel like I contributed somehow. After the morning's events, it was a good reminder that I'm here for a reason and Heather believes in me to do this job well.

As we pull up to the building, Alex looks over at me and narrows his eyes, glancing at the door handle.

"Don't worry Ashford, I know the drill. I'll let you hold on to your fragile masculinity."

He scoffs and exits his side of the car. I sigh, thankful we're back to our light banter at least for now, and wait for him to open my door. When he does, I take his hand and step out of the car.

We make our way in and up to our flat, bypassing Maura thankfully, and as we step inside the sight of our newly decorated tree lifts my spirits.

"I have something planned for us tonight," Alex says.

"Nothing that has any specific timeline, but I figured we could grab some dinner and then walk around and look at the different Christmas window displays. Cross another thing off your list." He shrugs like it's no big deal and doesn't meet my eyes when he says it.

He's downplaying how genuinely sincere and thoughtful his mission to help me feel the Christmas magic is, and I'm going to let him. It's easier than thinking about what his thoughtfulness really means.

"That sounds like fun. I just need a bit to freshen up and then we can head out."

Before I go to my room, I make my way into the kitchen to grab a glass of water, and spot a crystal bowl on the counter full of the different chocolates Alex usually gives me each day.

"You're giving me free access?"

"I figured then you could pick which ones you want."

"What if I want two a day instead of one?"

"We could arrange that, with proper payment of course," he says with a smirk.

"And what would proper payment be?"

"I'll think about it, sunshine."

He turns and walks out of the kitchen, leaving me to overthink that interaction, much like I've been doing for all of our interactions lately.

I fill my glass, grab a dark chocolate peppermint bark square and head down the hallway. I flop down on the bed and fall backward, closing my eyes and breathing deep. Today has been a lot, but I'm proud of myself for getting through it and not letting my anxiety win. I make a note to share this win with Dr. Rodriguez during our next session. She's been gracious enough to find times that align to meet, even with the time difference.

Sometimes my panic attacks are bad enough that I'm so wiped I need to leave work early, and on those days I honor that and go home, but I can't say it isn't frustrating when that happens. It causes me to be behind on my work and even though Heather is an understanding and compassionate boss, she can only allow so much.

I grab my phone to text Cami and Charlie and update them about the day and after a few back and forth updates on their end and mine, I get up to get ready for the evening. I still can't believe Alex is setting out to complete all of the items on my list, but then again I guess I can. I shouldn't be surprised anymore, these past few weeks he's shown how thoughtful and caring he can be. That's the kind of guy he is.

I touch up my makeup and slip into a comfier, but still cute, outfit—matching light gray sweats, a long dark gray coat and green Sambas. Since we'll be walking I make sure to dress warm, and then I head out to the living room with my book to read for a bit in front of the tree.

Alex must have lit the fireplace, because it's crackling and glowing, and the scene is almost magical. I curl up on the velvet couch, grab a blanket and open my book. When the days are stressful, reading always helps.

Before long, I hear him make his way down the hall and I glance up from my book to take him in as he enters the room. He's wearing black jeans and a black hoodie with a brown coat overtop, the hood hanging on the outside of the jacket. He looks effortlessly handsome and I'm irrationally angry that I can't claim him as mine in this moment. I want to go to him and finish what we started in the office today, but I know I can't.

He clears his throat, which must mean I've been looking a little too long, and I snap my eyes up his body to his eyes.

"Take a picture. It'll last longer," he says with a cocky smirk. I grab the throw pillow nestled behind my back and toss it at his head. Unfortunately, he catches it before it makes contact and I frown, unhappy that it didn't hit its intended target. "Come on, grumpy. Let's get you some food."

"Don't patronize me," I say with an eye roll, then stand before putting the blanket back and setting my book on the coffee table. I'm thankful the mood is light after the heaviness of the day. We bundle up and head out to Marco who takes us around to see a few different larger stores with elaborate displays.

First, we stop by Galeries Lafayette's where they have a large Christmas tree each year that brings many visitors. They also transform the inside of the store each year along with all of the window displays. This year, the store has become a beehive. Inside, the alcoves have become honeycombs and the dome ceiling portrays a night sky. All around the store the bees are depicted preparing for Christmas. They're picking out toys, gathering food, setting the table, and decorating the window displays.

Next, we head next door to Printemps Haussmann. Their windows tell a story of children taking different transportation to collect their gifts. The attention to detail is astonishing and we spend a long time just pointing out all the small things the artists took the time to add.

We stop at a nice restaurant for dinner and then Marco takes us back to the area around our flat, where we take off on foot to look at a few more.

As we walk, we stop and look at the windows of the small shops that line the streets, making comments about funny looking characters or beautifully decorated scenes. From nearly a block away, the pinks and reds in one of the windows catches my eye and something in me is drawn to it. My steps speed up as we approach, my body anxious to get to the shiny ribbons and bursts of color.

I stop in front of the window of Nouveau Visage, what seems to be a skincare store, and take in their display. The windows are lined with stacks and stacks of various sizes and shapes of gift boxes, each wrapped with pink, gold and red paper. The little girl in me squeals at the ribbons tied on top of each present. The velvet bows are tied perfectly with just the right size loops and tails. The red ones have pink stitching down the sides, and the pink ones have red stitching.

"These are beautiful," I say. My hand floats up and my fingertips lightly touch the window. I gaze longingly at the bows, wishing I could have one for myself. "When I was little my mom got me a bow like this that I used to clip in my hair each day." I'm not sure why I'm sharing, but this memory has surfaced and I have to get it out. "She loved it the first time I wore it, and I kept trying to get her attention by wearing it over and over again. It never really worked, but I loved that bow. I don't know where it is now." I can feel Alex standing beside me, his hand on the small of my back, but I'm not here with him. I'm back in my childhood home, struggling to get the bow in just the right spot in my hair.

He speaks softly, bringing me out of my trance gently. "Why don't we go inside?" He guides me into the shop and tells me to look around and pick something out. The more I walk, the easier it is to shake off the memories and the more I come back to myself. I'm feeling much better by the time I find Alex again. I spot him standing awfully close to the back drop that separates the store from the window display.

"You look like trouble."

"The best kind of trouble, Lanie. You up for being my lookout girl?"

"I've already done this once with the tree. What do you need a lookout for this time?"

"Just trust me, it's for you." There's those words again, *just trust me.* I want to. "Turn around and if you see anyone headed this way just say the code word."

"What is the code word?"

"Soleil." The French word rolls off his tongue with ease.

"What does that even mean?"

"Not important, now turn around." He places his hands gently on my shoulders and spins me so my back is to him. I do as I'm told and keep watch, but the woman working in the store stays at the register at the back, so Alex is in the clear the entire time.

About two minutes later I feel his hand on my lower back begin to steer me out the front doors.

"Bonsoir!" I hear the woman in the back shout at us.

"Bonsoir," we say in unison.

I try looking back at whatever Alex has procured for me, but I'm pushed forward and not able to see what he has behind his back. Once we get out onto the sidewalk, I spin to face him.

"What is it?"

"Hold out your hands and close your eyes." I roll my eyes.

"Oh, come on. I'm not five." But as I say it I close my eyes, an excited grin on my face. I couldn't tell you the last time someone took the time to surprise me with something. Before this week, I hadn't experienced anything like this. Sure, Cami might grab me a coffee without me having to ask and Charlie has randomly sent me five bucks for a treat, but I haven't had someone curate a surprise specifically for me. That's changing, though.

I feel the soft fabric land in my upturned palms and I know what it is before I open my eyes. The beautiful pink and red bow rests in my hands and I look down at it in awe.

"You took this for me?" I ask in a quiet voice. He nods and I feel the first tears slide down my face. He shifts from easy confidence to worry.

"What's wrong, Lanie?"

"Nothing," I say, smiling up at him. "These are happy tears."

"You're sure?" He reaches up and swipes the tears from my cheeks. I close my eyes and take in the feeling of someone caring for me.

"I'm sure."

"Here," he takes it from my hands. "Turn around."

I turn, and he gently pulls all of my hair behind my back. I already had the top half pulled back away from my face, and I feel him tie the bow gently into the elastic I have there.

"There," he says. "Now we're tied together."

"What do you mean?"

"Well, now you have something to remember this trip. I like having something tying us together. I don't commit crimes for just anyone," he says with a wink. I sniffle and dry my tears, shaking off the nostalgia and sadness and focusing on the way he makes me feel.

"I won't report you this time." I slip my hand into his, why I'm not sure, but I don't question it tonight. It feels like the right thing to do and my heart can't help but acknowledge the way our hands fit perfectly together.

I'm afraid I am tied to Alex in more ways than one. I'm slowly beginning to become used to the way he cares and looks out for me, and I am really enjoying our conversations and time together. After waking up to his lattes each morning and enjoying dinner with him each night, going back to reality is going to be difficult.

I put those things out of my mind tonight, though, and enjoy our walk back. I don't even feel the cold wind whipping around my face. Not with Alex next to me.

Alana

I'M DAYDREAMING AS I WALK BEHIND ALEX INTO OUR flat. This whole evening was straight out of a fairytale and I'm having a hard time believing that I'm not dreaming.

"Something came for you while we were out. I had Albert put it on the table," Alex says.

"What?" I say, still so distracted by our evening and the bow in my hair.

"On the table." He nods his head in the direction of the dining room.

I walk over to the table to find a large box with Charlie's return address on the shipping label. I have a sudden wave of homesickness seeing his name, missing him and the comfort of my sibling.

I begin opening the package, eager to see what he sent me, and I feel Alex step up behind me. There's tissue paper hiding what is inside the package, and a note sits on top of it. My name is written in Charlie's handwriting and I brush my fingers over it.

"I miss him."

"I know," Alex says behind me. His hands are on my shoulders and he rubs my arms up and down in a comforting way. "Open the letter, Lan."

I do as he says and begin reading.

> Lana,
> Alex let me know that you needed a little
> Christmas spirit, and of course I had to assist.
> Making advent calendars is one of my favorite
> things we do each year, and I wasn't about to let
> 3,500 miles stop me.
> Love you

I don't notice I'm silently crying until a tear drops onto the page and makes the ink bleed. I miss Charlie more than I realized. We haven't been in Paris for very long, but for some reason just knowing how far away we are from one another and the added fact that I'm missing my favorite time of the year with him has me feeling especially emotional.

I tear at the tissue paper, not able to get to the gift fast enough. Sitting in the box, surrounded by foam packing pieces for safety, is my very own advent calendar.

I look over my shoulder at the man standing behind me in astonishment. "How'd you know?"

"It was on the list."

"How did you know we made them for each other?"

"I called Charlie and asked. I called him about the whole list, actually. I just wanted to make sure I didn't miss anything. He told me about how you make them for each other every year, so I asked him to send you one."

"But I only just gave you the list a few days ago. How did you get it here so quickly?"

"Express shipping," he answers with a nonchalant shrug.

That must have cost a fortune. I stare at him in disbelief. It had to have been a fortune to ship, because it's heavy and we're in Paris.

I'm sure Charlie would have covered the cost of shipping, but something tells me this is all Alex.

I gave my brother his calendar early this year, and I had made peace with the fact that I wouldn't have one.

The calendar is in the shape of a large gingerbread house. He decorated it with fake white icing all around and swirls of pink and green. I set it up on the table in front of me and open the first few days that I've missed so far. Each one is filled with a short and sweet handwritten encouragement and a small chocolate.

I pop one in my mouth, then unwrap the next one and hold it over my shoulder for the man who is still hovering there. He leans forward and wraps his lips around it, taking the chocolate from my fingers. I shiver at the contact and he laughs.

I turn around, facing Alex.

"Thank you."

"For what? Charlie did all the work."

"He put the advent calendar together, but I know you're on *mission-complete-all-traditions* so I know you made it happen. Thank you."

He just shrugs and pulls me in for a quick hug. He presses a kiss to the top of my head and I practically melt.

"What's the story behind these? Charlie didn't give me much background."

"Our mom used to do it." I smile at the memories. "Every year on the last day of November, she would give us our own advent calendars. They were different each year and sometimes they'd have a random theme, other times she'd pick something we had really been into that year, but they were always over the top in detail."

"That must have taken her a long time."

"You have no idea. Not only were the calendars themselves detailed, but she would make our gifts each day a mini scavenger hunt. There would be a tiny rolled up piece of paper in each day's window, and when we opened it there was a riddle to a place around our house. We'd find all kinds of things. Sometimes it was small, like a chocolate, but other times she'd give us little gifts."

"When did you and Charlie start doing them for each other?"

My smile falls, but I quickly try to recover it. It's sad because it makes me miss my childhood with my mom, but they're also happy memories because I wouldn't trade Charlie and I's relationship for anything.

"It was more of a gradual change. Every few years it felt like she did less and less until eventually it was all gone. She had stopped everything by the time we went to college."

Alex nods his head in understanding and I can tell he's contemplating saying something. He only hesitates for a second before speaking. "When was the last time you talked to your mom?"

I have to think about it. "Right after Heather told us about coming here. I told her I was going on a business trip. We didn't actually speak though, I left her a voicemail because she didn't answer my call. She texted me later and told me she was excited for me, but we haven't spoken since then."

"Have you ever told your parents how their actions affect you and Charlie?"

"No, I haven't ever brought it up. My therapist has suggested it a few times, but I haven't worked up the courage. I know it would be good to talk about it though."

"If you want your relationship with them to get better, it might be a good idea to bring it up. I won't pretend to be the expert on parent relationships though."

I smile sadly at him.

"Do you have any information on your dad?"

"I know his name, but I haven't looked him up. I think I'm a little nervous about what I might find."

"What do you mean?"

"I had this nightmare a while back. I found his address somehow and went to his house. He had a wife and they had this huge house with a pool and a room specifically for watching movies. It got worse when his three sons showed up with their wives and kids. He had this whole other life." He shakes his head in dejection. "It made me think, what about my mom and I wasn't enough for him to do that with us? It scared me so much that I never wanted to attempt to actually find him."

"That's understandable, but if for some reason he did go out and create this whole other life, you have to know that it had nothing to do with you. His decisions are entirely his own. Plus, you have no idea if that dream is a reality. What if you meet him and he's great? You've created this story in your mind and haven't even given your dad a chance to prove you wrong."

"I know you're right, but it feels like this impossible wall to climb."

"What do you think it is that keeps you from reaching out?"

Alex has helped me talk through my fears and worries so much in the last few weeks and I want him to feel just as much support from me as I do from him.

"I don't really love talking about this stuff." He's fidgeting nervously with the strands of hair hanging around my shoulders. We're locked in this embrace, his arms slung over my shoulders and mine wrapped around his waist. It feels as though he's clinging to me like a life raft, like he'll float away if he doesn't hold on. "But I want to."

"I want to listen if you want to share."

"My mom has always built me up, ever since I was small she has always been an extraordinary encourager, but my dad leaving without an explanation left me with a lot of questions. I've wondered for a long time if it was because of me, if I wasn't good enough for him or if he wasn't proud of me as a son. My therapist has helped me realize he and my mom had been struggling for a while, they always fought and I was always mediating their arguments, but I still can't help but feel like I wasn't enough to keep him around."

I stay silent, letting him have the space to share what's on his heart and mind. I am on the edge of my seat, starving for any information I can gather to understand him better, but this is for him not for me.

"I'm scared that if I wasn't enough for him, if he went and started this other family with people who were enough for him to deem worthy, then is whatever family I create one day going to leave me too? Am I just defective, unable to be a part of a cohesive family unit?"

My heart breaks as his eyes look somewhere over the top of my head. I can tell he isn't here with me anymore, he's gone somewhere else. Somewhere where he believes lies about himself.

"Alex," I say softly, reaching up to cup his cheek with my palm and bringing his eyes back to mine. "Stay here with me." He nods. "Would you say you and your mom are a cohesive family unit? Does the absence of your dad mean that you two aren't a family?"

He looks into my eyes for so long, I think he isn't going to reply. But a few seconds later I hear his soft, "No."

"And even though my parents are still together, they don't even treat me like their child. I wouldn't call that cohesive and I know you wouldn't either. Does that mean I won't be capable of being a part of a family someday?"

His response to this is quicker. "Absolutely not, Alana."

"So if you believe that about me, why don't you believe it about yourself? You've learned so much throughout the years since your dad left. You've learned how to be the man of the household, how to take care of the people you love and how to lead a family. That *has* been your role for the last nineteen years. Not to mention, you don't actually know why your dad left. You've been assuming the worst because you don't have any closure."

He's quietly contemplative for a few moments before he speaks again. The environment is heavy, the emotion high. His next words catch me off guard, the adoration in them so clear.

"Where did you come from?"

I don't know what to say, so I just smile up at him, still locked in his embrace. It feels like the perfect moment for a kiss, but we don't. Eventually he pulls away and pours us two glasses of wine.

We spend a few more hours together watching Christmas movies in the living room before we part ways for the night.

Back in my room, I've just settled into bed for the night when I decide to give Charlie a call and thank him for my gift.

"I was wondering when I'd get a call from you," Charlie says by way of greeting. He sounds tired, but clearly happy to be on the phone. Just hearing his voice makes my chest squeeze. Even though it's only been less than a week since I left, it hurts knowing we have weeks ahead of us before I get to see him again.

"Thank you. I miss you." I'm sure he doesn't miss the wobble in my voice, but he graciously chooses not to bring attention to it.

"Miss you too, Lan. How'd you like the advent calendar?"

"It's perfect. The gingerbread house was a nice touch. You sure you didn't get any help from Cami?"

"Oh whatever, you know I can be a creative when I want to be."

"Of course, my apologies."

"How are things going there?" he asks.

"It's going well. We had our first day in the office today."

"How was that?"

"Well, I'm pretty sure the other two section editors are plotting our deaths, but other than that it wasn't bad. I'm exhausted though."

"I bet, working at a new place with new people and then coming home to Alex playing your own personal elf."

I smile at the thought. "I know. He's something."

The silence on the line is comfortable, but I know Charlie is debating whether or not he wants to press further into this topic of conversation. It seems as though he's decided when he asks, "So, anything going on there?"

"I'm not sure. We're getting closer, having deeper conversations, and he touches me like we're something more than friends, but I can't get past the mental block."

"Brad still bothering you?" I love this about my brother. I don't have to tell him much, but he almost always knows what's going on inside my head.

"It isn't so much him as it is the affects of our relationship. Ever since I ran into him, it's been worse. The reminder of how he treated me and what happened makes me more afraid to open up to Alex."

"That would make sense. It ended really badly and he was extremely disrespectful to you. Has Alex done anything to show you that he'd treat you in a similar way?"

"No, he's been better than I could have ever expected. I know logically that he wouldn't do or say the things Brad did."

"So how do you move forward and let him in if your fear is telling you one thing, but your heart is telling you something different?"

I pause and think about the question for a few moments. He doesn't push me, he just allows me to sit in the moment and think.

"I think I just do it scared."

"Do it scared?"

"Yeah, some of the best things that I've done I was terrified to do. If I had let my fear stop me from even trying I would have missed out on so much. I think I need to just give this a try, even if I'm terrified."

"I think that's a great decision."

"It might take me a little while to make that first move, but I know there's something going on with Alex and I don't want to miss it."

"Good. That's good, Lan."

"Hey, I know this is a little random, but have you talked to Mom in a while?"

"It's been a few months. I've been ignoring the post-game calls. Why?"

"Alex was asking me about our relationship with them tonight."

"You weren't kidding when you said you were having deeper conversations."

An uncomfortable laugh falls from my lips. "I think I want to try talking to them about everything."

He scoffs. I wince.

"Good luck even getting them on the phone." His tone makes me sad. I know what he's saying is probably true, it is impossible to even get them to answer sometimes, but I want his approval I guess.

He must notice my silence and correctly take it for sadness, because he backpedals.

"I'm sorry, I'm not trying to be a cynic. If you need to talk to them and you think that will help you then I think that's great. I'm not ready for that though."

"I get that."

We talk for a little longer and he updates me on hockey and Cami and how things are going at home. He tells me they are planning to go see *The Nutcracker* ballet and that makes me a little sad, but I hope he can't tell.

"I miss you," I say after an hour.

"You already said that."

"Still true."

"I'll see you soon, Lan."

"Goodnight."

"Night."

Alana

THE FIRST WEEK OF WORK HAS BEEN FULL OF UPS AND downs. We've met at least four new candidates for the editor positions that we feel would be a good fit for the office, so I'm grateful we're fulfilling that part of our role here. Working with Genevieve and Luis, however, has been a different story. They are the most challenging people I have ever had to work with.

Any time Alex or I have a question about their process or something we're working on, their answers include the least amount of details possible. It's like they give just enough information so that it doesn't seem as though they aren't cooperating at all, but what they give has maybe about 10 percent of what we actually need to know. It's infuriating.

Alex and I are at dinner, seated at a table tucked away in a corner talking quietly. Over the last week, our relationship has taken a turn in a direction I'm not sure I fully understand. Any time we aren't working, we make excuses to spend time together and the small but intimate touches we exchange cause my blood to heat. I know there's something going on, but neither of us has ventured into the danger zone and spoken about it. I have a feeling that's about to change.

Even though this *whatever* has been really nice between the two of us, and having his support in this way feels nice, I still feel the pull to focus on work and I'm nervous about the balance of it all.

"I think we should talk about this," I say.

"About..."

"This." My hand gestures between us in a back and forth motion.

"Ah, okay." Alex takes his napkin and delicately wipes the corners of his mouth before placing the napkin in his lap and clearing his throat. "I've been waiting for this."

"I think we need to stop." There. Band-Aid ripped. Done. Alex nods and takes a long pull of his wine. "At least for right now."

"And why is that, Alana?" Full name. Okay, ouch.

"I like you."

"And I like you."

I am startled at how good it feels to hear those words. I had suspected as much, but having it confirmed is a whole new ballgame.

"I just think it might be best to put it on hold for right now," I say, hesitantly.

"What does that mean?" The question is serious, but not unkind. Gone is the calm, cool, collected Alex. In his place is a straightforward man who is clearly going after what he wants. Which apparently, is me. I'm flattered, and if I let myself think about the fact that he seems to be fighting for me I might just decide to give in, but I can't.

"We're here for work," I state.

"Are we really?" he teases.

"Stop it, I'm trying to be serious. Whatever this is between us would be a distraction that neither of us can afford."

His eyes pierce me over the rim of his wine glass as he takes another drink. The seconds stretch as we sit in silence, staring at one another over the flame on the table.

"So you think you wouldn't be able to do the work if we were also exploring our relationship?" he asks, even though it sounds more like a statement. One he doesn't entirely buy.

"I just think it would be hard to give both things the amount of time needed. We committed to helping *Impress Europe* and I want to be sure I'm doing that."

"Does this have anything to do with the promotion?" he asks, and I tense.

We haven't discussed this elephant in the room since Ian announced his departure, and I really don't want to talk about it now, but I know we need to. Alex is just as good of a candidate for it as I am, which is a fact I've been ignoring.

"It's a factor."

He nods and takes another bite of his food. His eyes feel like they hold secrets, like they know something about me that I don't know.

"I'll bow out," he says and I begin to choke on my salad. His eyes are wide when he looks up at me, but I take a drink of my water and get my coughing under control.

"What did you just say?"

"I'm serious, Lanie, this promotion would be great but I'm happy where I am. I don't need it. I'll just tell them I'm not interested and then it'll be yours."

Why does that make my stomach sink? I don't want to get the promotion by default, then I'll never know if I truly earned it. I can see what he's doing, trying to make room for an *us* somewhere in the mess we're currently in, but this isn't how to do that.

"I don't want you to do that, Alex. You deserve a shot at it, and I would feel weird if I just got it by default. I've already told you, you can't do everything for me. I want to earn this."

"I get that." He pauses. "Do you not feel like you're worthy of it? Even if I wasn't in the running?"

I shrug. He's hitting a sore spot.

"Sunshine, Heather knows your work ethic. I'm not trying to talk you into trying something with me because I know you're going to make your own decisions and I want that, but I do want you to recognize that you're a dedicated member of the staff and that shows itself in your work."

I wish I could believe the words he's saying. I do, somewhat, but not fully. I know, logically, that the work I've done over the last year at *Impress* has shown how dedicated I am, but I still feel the need to prove myself worthy.

"I know I work hard, but if I'm going to get this, I really need to make sure my work here is exceptional. We're already pulling teeth with Luis and Genevieve and I just don't know that I have the emotional capacity for anything else."

That is a true statement. I feel like I'm already struggling so much with keeping it all straight and the emotions of everything lately can get really overwhelming. Facing my fears of flying, pushing through anxiety attacks, missing Cami and Charlie, trying to make my own Christmas magic away from them, proving myself to my boss and now two coworkers who seem to hate us for absolutely no reason.

I'm not sure I can add anything else to that list. I know that if I get involved with Alex, he might ease some of that for a little while, but what happens when we hit a snag and have a disagreement? Will he stick around to work through that? I'm not even sure I have the emotional capacity to survive if he didn't.

"I'm scared," I blurt out.

His beautiful green eyes soften and the affection in his gaze is startling.

"I know." He reaches across the table and places his hand over mine and squeezes it once, twice, three times. I look down at our joined hands and something inside me breaks a little. I want this so badly for myself and it's frustrating that I can't let myself have it.

"Lanie, I think you are an incredible editor. You work insanely hard and give yourself fully to your job and your relationships. You're selfless and funny and beautiful and absolutely everything a guy could want in a partner. I know that the things Brad did and said really messed with your head and caused you to internalize a lot, but I want you to know that I am certain he is the biggest idiot ever for treating someone like you the way he did and letting you go. The most stupid man on earth." He takes a breath before continuing, clearly annoyed to even mention my ex's name. "I know you aren't ready, and that's okay, I'll wait, but I want you to know that if you were mine, you would be cherished. You would be seen as an equal, you would be told how worthy and good and incredible you are. You deserve someone who treats you like the prize you are and I am prepared to do that, I just need you to get to a place where you're ready for it too."

The stinging behind my eyes burns and no matter how hard I work to force it to stay inside, a hot tear slides down my face. Alex reaches up and cups my cheek with his hand, then uses his thumb to swipe across my cheekbone and catch the tear as it falls. He doesn't drop his hand though, he keeps it there and continues swiping that thumb across my cheek. Back, and forth. Back, and forth. I close my eyes.

"No one has ever said those things to me," I say in a small voice.

"I thought that might be the case. That's too bad, sunshine, because I plan to keep saying them to you."

I take a deep breath and on my exhale, I breathe out the tension and stress and just melt into the moment, into his hands on me. He is such an incredible guy and maybe I will eventually get there. I think I'm way closer to giving in than I'd like to admit to myself, but I'm not there right now.

When I open my eyes again, I'm startled at how close we are. Our faces are inches apart and it's just like back in the office when we almost kissed. I can feel his warm breath tickling my lips and it would be so easy to just lean in a few inches and...

Alex pulls back and I immediately miss his touch and the heat of his hand. I take a second to recover before speaking again. I find myself feeling sad that he didn't close the distance between us, but I understand why. I just finished telling him I wasn't ready yet.

"Thank you, Alex. For saying that and for supporting me not just these past few weeks, but for a while now. I know we haven't spent a lot of time together until recently, but the small things you've done to help me over the last year haven't gone unnoticed."

His blush is so cute it makes me want to go sit in his lap and bury my face in his neck, but I stay seated and smile at him. He smiles back and we continue on like we didn't just have an incredibly emotional conversation in the back corner of this restaurant.

"So you started watching *The Office*," he says.

"I did. I'm in season four right now." I'm grateful for the change in topic, especially to this one. I can't believe I hadn't seen the show before now. It's probably one of the funniest ones I've watched.

"What episode has been your favorite so far?"

"I just watched the one where Jan and Michael throw a dinner party. I was doubled over laughing."

"Ah, that's a really good one. There's one in a later season where they meet the founder of *Famous Amos* cookies that kills me every time. Let me know when you get there."

"Will do."

We eat and we drink and we talk about work and his mom and my brother and it feels warm and cozy and safe. *I feel safe with him.* I don't think I've ever felt this kind of safety with anyone other than Cami and Charlie.

At the end of our meal, we head back to our flat and as we walk inside Alex grabs my hand to stop me. I turn back and he smiles at me. What is he up to?

"There's a surprise for you in the living room, but you can't look yet so I need you to close your eyes and I'll guide you to your room to change."

"Change? Into what?"

"Come on, just close your eyes and cover them with your hands." I obey and he turns me around, his hands softly on my shoulders, and begins to walk me towards my room. After a few steps he stops me and reaches around, placing his hands over mine.

The hard lines of his body are pressed against my back and with his arms up and around me, it feels like I'm resting in the warmest embrace. I would be happy if this was the surprise.

"What are you doing?" I ask timidly.

"Making sure you aren't peeking." I giggle and we continue our quest towards my room. Once we're there, he pulls away from me and I turn to face him. "Now go put on your comfiest PJs and wait like thirty minutes, then yell when you're heading out."

"Sir, yes sir," I say with a mock salute. He rolls his eyes and I make my way into my room to change.

After pulling out a light pink set of lounge pants and a buttery soft T-shirt, I undress and pull them on, sighing as the fabric brushes against my skin. I slip on a pair of white fuzzy socks, then sit on my bed and scroll social media, glancing at the time on my phone every two minutes. After the longest thirty minutes of my life, I stand and make my way to my door, cracking it and sticking my head out to yell.

"Okay, I'm coming."

"I'm ready for you," he shouts back.

I walk down the hallway and as I turn to enter the living room I'm completely in awe at what I see. The entire room has been transformed into the biggest adult sized fort anyone could have ever dreamed up.

He has covered the entire floor in more blankets than I've ever seen in my life and there are even more hanging from the ceiling and draping over the couches and chair. He has created a little cocoon around the far wall of the room and there's a small opening that I assume leads to the man himself.

I walk towards it and peel back one side of the blanket door, only to be stunned to silence once again as I open it and step inside. He's sitting on the floor, a smug look about his face which is definitely earned, and he's enclosed the tree in our fort so the lights are glowing in the dark space.

There's a projector set up and the menu of the movie *Barbie in The Nutcracker* is lit up on the wall. He knew I wouldn't get to see *The Nutcracker* ballet, so he brought it to me. He must mistake the shock on my face for alarm, because he abruptly stands and comes to me. He's crouching a little because he's too tall to stand up fully in here, but it makes me giggle a little so it helps.

"Sunshine, what's wrong?" His eyes are frantically moving all over my face to try and figure out what is happening in my head, good luck because I barely know, and he takes my face in his big hands and brings my gaze to his.

"Nothing. Absolutely nothing is wrong, Alex. This is incredible."

His shoulders drop a little, but not fully, and his hands don't leave my face. He lets out a nervous laugh. "Could've fooled me."

"I promise, I'm better than ever. I just wasn't expecting this. No one has ever done anything like this for me before." He pulls me into him and I wrap my arms around his large frame. He tucks my head into his chest and places his chin on top of it, and I feel like I'm wrapped in a weighted blanket. I feel so small wrapped up in his arms and it's the best feeling.

"Come on, let's watch the movie. I made popcorn and I figured if you couldn't go see the ballet, we could watch the next best version," he says with a wink.

"I have to say, the fact that you know this movie exists is a bit of a shock."

"I may have gotten a little help from Cami." His smile is shy. It warms my heart to know he is reaching out to my friends to talk to them about me.

"Oh, I see. You cheated. Have you watched it before?"

"This will be the first time."

"Well, you're in for a treat."

We're still standing in the same embrace, although he's pulled back a little so he can see my face. I look over to see the pile of pillows and blankets on the ground make up a small palette that looks just big enough for both of us. My palms start to sweat thinking about us laying side by side.

"I can see you overthinking. I heard you loud and clear, Lanie. I know you're unsure, but let me take care of you tonight. Let me show you how safe and cared for you are with me. Let me take all of the stress from work and show you both things can happen together, work and me. I think you could have both, if you let yourself."

I know I'm blushing, but I nod and move to sit down. He comes to sit next to me and lays down, then pulls me down on top of him. My head rests on his chest and his arm drapes over my back, his hand resting gently on my hip. He presses play and we watch the movie together, laughing at all the cheesy parts and getting quiet at the dramatic ones.

Yes, there are dramatic moments in Barbie movies.

And as we do his hand never stops moving. He's got it resting on my hip and his thumb swoops back and forth, he's got it tangled in my hair playing with the strands, he lets it drape over my body and takes my hand in his.

He's showing me, in all the small ways, what a life with him would look like and even though I told him just hours ago that I wasn't ready, I know this is what I want—to feel cherished and loved, to know someone out there in the world is thinking about me and looking after me and thinking about what I might want, and what might feel special to me. Better yet, I want to be that person for them.

I want to be known in all the small ways and I want to know someone else in all the small ways. I want someone to know what would make me happy after a hard day. What my favorite flower is and what my biggest fears are. I want them to know what drink to order for me at a restaurant and how I like my coffee. I want them to know I love Taylor Swift and the color pink, and I want them to celebrate that and not belittle me for it. I want them to know all the tiny pieces of me and still choose me. That's what I want, and Alex is showing me that that's exactly what he plans to give me.

CHAPTER 36

Alana

THE PAST FEW DAYS HAVE BEEN SUCH A WHIRLWIND AND I feel like I haven't had a chance to take a breath. Even Alex and I haven't had a lot of time together this past week, and I'm finding myself missing him even though we're living in the same apartment.

After the movie night last week, he walked me to my room and kissed my forehead and sent me on my way. Nothing else happened, just like he promised, and I've been thinking about how it felt to lay in his arms ever since.

I'm terrified, but after realizing how empty I've felt without him around this week, I'm ready for the next step. I finally have a grasp on work here, even though I am pretty sure I'm running myself into the ground, and I've come to the conclusion that, despite my fears, I'm pretty sure my heart is in good hands with Alex.

I haven't had a chance to talk to him about any of that, though, because...work. Things at the office are moving smoothly, albeit no thanks to Luis or Genevieve, but it feels like I'm barely keeping my head above water. Two weeks in and we're still only just making it.

It's almost midnight and I know that this project I'm working on is going to keep me up for most, if not all of the night. I'm trying to pick up the slack from the few weeks that *Impress Europe* went without an editing team and it's proving to be more work than I anticipated.

Alex has been taking on the interviewing and hiring with Amélie, which is also a ton of work, but that has mostly happened during the workday and during a few dinners this week. Because he's putting all of his focus there, I've been taking the brunt of the catch up work for the section editors. I know he'd help me if I asked him to, but I don't want him to have to.

Most nights I work in the office in our flat until dinner time and I either take a break and eat a quick dinner with him or— what's been happening lately—I take it into my room to work while I eat. Usually I forget the food is even there. It's an unhealthy habit, one that I've been doing way too often, but as soon as I get caught up I can rest.

I last saw him a few hours ago when he brought me dinner. He's been cooking every night and I know If he wasn't feeding me, I would be eating less than I am now which is already not a lot. This is how I get when I get focused on a job. I put my head down and don't pick it back up until it's done, which is good for productivity but bad for my overall health.

I notice the signs that my body is shutting down around four in the morning on Friday, but I brush it off as needing to wake myself up. It's almost the weekend and then I can rest.

A good run and an electrolyte drink will do the trick, I think, so after another hour or so of work I make a drink and down it quickly before throwing on my running clothes. I leave Alex a note so he doesn't worry and head out on my run.

It's early and the sun isn't even close to rising, so the cold is biting. At first, it's nice. The temperature wakes me up and invigorates me, which is exactly what I was looking for. But the longer I go, the more that feeling wears off.

I can feel myself getting fatigued and I start to slow down. About twenty minutes in I realize I probably should head home and start jogging back in the direction of the flat. The jog quickly turns into a walk and instinctively I know something is wrong.

The walk back takes significantly longer than the first twenty minutes of the run out and I'm starting to realize I have made a mistake. I'm freezing cold, but my whole body is hot. It's like I'm hot from the inside, and my palms and forehead feel clammy and itchy.

My vision feels a little funny, but I somehow make it to the front door of our building. I stumble up the steps and through the door, passing Albert who reaches out to steady me. He speaks, but I can't understand. I press the button for the lift and stand there, waiting for it to arrive. I notice I'm swaying, as if I'm standing on a boat, and I reach out to steady myself.

That's the last thing I remember before everything goes dark.

ALEX

I press the lift button for the hundredth time in the last thirty seconds and curse it for taking so long. Albert called around five thirty, right after I woke up, saying Alana was acting strange on her way in from her run and I was immediately unsettled. She has been working way too hard the last few days and I know she hasn't slept much, but I've been trying not to overstep. She asked me not to do everything for her, so I've been cautious of that.

When I saw her note that she had gone on a run I resisted the urge to go after her, not wanting her to think I was being an over-protective *whatever I am to her*, but I should have gone.

The lift doors slide open painfully slowly and the scene in front of my eyes will be featured in my nightmares for nights to come. Albert has Alana cradled in his arms and she is just barely conscious. Her head is rested on his shoulder and her eyes flutter open and closed. I instinctively reach for her and Albert passes her to me. He moves around us and goes to open the door to the flat for me.

"Can you grab me a wet washcloth please?" I say as I rush us inside.

I probably should just lay her down on the couch, but I feel like if I let her go I'll go insane, so instead I sit down with her in my lap and cradle her head in the crook of my arm. I brush her hair back from her face and flinch at how warm her head is.

"Alex?" she whimpers. "I was running. How did I get here?"

"Shhh you're okay, Lanie, I got you."

She closes her eyes and turns to burrow herself into my chest. "I don't feel very good."

"I know you don't. You've been working a little too hard lately. Do you remember the last time you slept?" I gently ask. She pulls her head away from my chest and seems to be thinking, which automatically worries me. If she can't remember the last time she slept, she hasn't had nearly enough sleep or something is seriously wrong.

"I think I slept on Monday night."

Monday night? It's Friday. I automatically begin beating myself up for not noticing this. She lives in the same damn apartment as me and I didn't realize she was working herself into exhaustion.

Things have been really busy for me at the office this week, too, and I have been trying to help her bridge the gap from the last few weeks, but I've mostly left her to it. I didn't realize how much she was working after hours to get it done.

"Alright, Lanie. We're going to get some fluids in you and some sleep. How's that sound?"

Whatever I said must have startled her, because she shoots up from my lap with wide and crazed eyes. "Sleep? But we have work. It's Friday morning, we can't sleep right now. I have to go to work." My relief at her knowing what day it is quickly fades as she frantically tries to get out of my grip.

"Hey, hey. It's okay, Lanie, we don't need to go into work today." I gently move her to lay back down in my lap and draw slow circles on her back with my hand. "You've done enough, they've got it all handled."

"Do you promise?"

"Yes, I promise." I lean down and kiss her forehead, something I've been doing a lot lately to keep from kissing her lips.

"I feel funny. I shouldn't have moved so quickly. Is the room spinning? Can you make it stop?"

"Yeah, sunshine, I can make it stop. All you have to do is close your eyes."

"Oh, okay." Alana closes her eyes and a deep sigh leaves her lips. Mine follows as I realize I think I've finally gotten her to calm down. I press the damp washcloth on her forehead and Albert checks that we're okay. I am pretty certain all she needs is a good rest, but I ask him to give me the number of a few doctors so I can call if I need them.

"Alex, you're so smart. The room stopped spinning and I feel so much better. Why do you have to be so smart? And beautiful? And why are your hands so perfect and soft?"

I chuckle softly at her barely conscious babbling. She won't remember any of this once she's back to normal.

"Okay as much as I would love to hear all the things you like about me, I think it's time we take a little nap." I stand with Alana in my arms and begin to carry her down the hall. She curls into me and even though I hate that she's sick, I can't hate the way she feels in my arms.

I stop in the hallway at her door and debate taking her in there, but think better of it and cross the hall to my room instead. I would rather be able to monitor her and there's a couch in my room I can lay on.

I push the door open with my foot and gently place her on the left side of the bed. I pull her running shoes, mittens and jacket off before tucking her into the bed. I start to pull away, thinking she's already fast asleep, but she stops me with a hand on my wrist.

"Stay," she says, blue eyes watering with unshed tears. "Please."

It's just like the night we decorated the Christmas tree, but this time I don't make the same decision. Instead, I wordlessly slip into the bed next to her. She curls her body into mine and I let her snuggle closer. She dozes off to sleep and I pull my phone out to let Amélie know we won't be in today, then I decide it would be best to go ahead and call the doctor. Better safe than sorry.

I'm not tired, so I turn on the television to a Christmas movie and turn the volume down really low. Alana breathes a deep, contented sigh and buries herself further down into the covers. I take my first deep breath of the last hour, too, now that I can see she's here and safe in my arms.

I'm overwhelmed with all the same feelings I felt the last time I held her close. It was torture to lay with her and watch that movie and not be able to kiss her and tell her how I'm feeling, but I don't want to spook her. She told me she wasn't ready and I told her I'd wait. I think we're a lot closer after that night, but we haven't had a chance to have another conversation about it since then.

I can't help but feel guilty that I didn't realize what was going on and put a stop to it, or help her manage her workload better. I'm thankful I know now, despite the intense fear I felt upon seeing her passed out in Albert's arms.

I look down at her sleeping peacefully and reach out to brush a strand of chocolate brown hair out of her face. As I watch her sleeping form rise and fall with each breath, my thoughts wander to my dad. I wonder if he's out there some-where settling down in bed with his wife after having a warm meal where they talked about their day and he laughed about something she said. I wonder if maybe it's the opposite. Maybe he's alone tonight, eating a frozen meal he warmed up in the microwave. I wonder if I'm just like him, if I'll never be able to be the husband and father someone might need. Someone like Alana.

I try to push those unhelpful thoughts aside and remind myself that, despite my fears, I don't have to be like him. I can learn from his mistakes.

Leaning down, I place a gentle kiss to the top of Lanie's head and settle back in to watch the rest of the movie.

Alana

My body feels like it was hit by a truck.

That's the first thing I register when my eyes peel open. The second thing is the warm, hard body I'm using as a pillow. His cedar and sandalwood scent surrounds me and I breathe it in deep, instantly feeling comforted despite my uncertainty about why Alex is in bed with me.

Wait.

Alex is in bed with me.

"What's going on?" My voice is groggy and hoarse and I instantly start coughing from how scratchy and dry it feels.

"Here, drink this." Alex grabs a glass of water off of the table by his bed and holds it up to my lips. I sip the cold liquid and instantly feel relief.

"There's my girl. How are you feeling, sleeping beauty?"

My body is draped across his, although now my head is lifted from his chest. His arm is slung low on my waist and protectively he pulls me closer into him.

"I feel awful. What happened?"

"You haven't been sleeping. You went on a run and had a spill when you got back, gave Albert and I quite the scare."

I knew the lack of sleep would catch up with me at some point, but I figured I would just sleep through the weekend. The run I took was definitely pushing it. That, on top of the few meals I skipped, was stupid.

"How did I get here? In your bed?" I know the blush in my cheeks is giving away my thoughts, but I can't help it. Being cuddled up with Alex in bed is doing things to me.

"I wanted to keep an eye on you. I tried taking the couch, but you insisted I stay."

"Um, I'm sorry," I stammer. "I didn't mean to force you into bed with me." I start to sit up and move off of him, but that arm around my waist tightens and he halts my escape.

"Stay, Lanie. I wouldn't have done it if I wasn't comfortable with it. I wanted to make sure you were okay and sitting right next to you was the perfect spot to do that."

He reaches up and brushes the hair from my neck, then touches the back of his hand to my forehead. A look of concern flashes in his eyes.

"I think you still have a little fever. The doctor should—"

Alex is cut off by a strong knock on our front door and I jump, startled. He swipes his hand back and forth on my hip in comfort.

"That's him now, I'll go get the door." He presses a kiss to my hair and climbs out of bed. It's so gentle and caring that it has me holding back emotional tears.

A few moments later he walks back in with the doctor. He takes my temperature and asks me something, but I'm distracted by the effortless way Alex commands my attention. He's dressed down in a pair of red and green flannel pajama pants and a plain white T-shirt. I don't know how he can make such a plain outfit look so enticing, but he does.

"Lanie?" he prompts softly, a knowing smile on his face.

"Sorry," I say, hoping my feverish flush hides my blush. "I think I just got too tired and wasn't drinking enough water."

The doctor gives me an IV of fluids to help with the dehydration and reminds me of the importance of getting proper rest. I feel better after just a few minutes and I sigh happily.

After the treatment, Alex leads the doctor out into the hallway and I snuggle into the plush white comforter, the cool fabric feeling refreshing on my fever flushed skin, and glance at the quiet television on the left of the room. One of my favorite movies, *The Holiday*, is playing and Amanda is bursting through the cottage door to tell Graham she's changed her mind and is going to stay. A tearful Graham embraces her and the love in both of their eyes warms my heart.

"Do you think you feel up to eating? I can make you some soup."

"That sounds nice, but you really don't have to keep taking care of me. I can manage, I'm sure. I know you've got a lot going on and—"

Alex moves across the room to stand next to the bed and reaches out to touch my shoulder gently in protest.

"Lanie, I am right where I want to be." His mouth curves upward with tenderness and he squeezes my shoulder three times before pulling away. "I'm going to make that soup, you stay here and rest and be sure to drink that whole glass of water. The remote is on the table if you want to watch something."

He turns and walks out of the room, leaving me to the end scene of *The Holiday* and my own swirling thoughts. The happiness on the couples' faces on the screen create a deep longing within me for someone to look at me like that, and the ability to return their loving gaze. It feels more possible now than it did a week ago, and I'm beginning to realize that protecting my heart by keeping it to myself might not be the best.

I reach over to grab my phone from the table and send Charlie a quick text to check in. I know I haven't reached out at all this week in my work focused state and he must be worried. Before I hit send, I decide to just call instead, thinking it would be nice to hear his voice.

"Hey, Bug, it's nice to know you're alive." The childhood nickname makes me smile and his warm voice instantly soothes something in me. It makes missing him even more intense.

"I'm sorry, I know. It's been a crazy week and I just got distracted."

"Distracted? Too distracted to let your own brother, the most important person in your life, know that you're still breathing?"

"Ugh, I know. I'm sorry."

"I'm just messing with you. Alex called a few hours ago and let me know what was going on. No sleep since Monday?" Alex reaching out to my family to let them know I'm okay makes me smile.

"I know." I groan, rubbing my eyes. "Work has been so stressful. I feel this intense need to prove myself and I guess I just let that need drive me to work myself into the ground."

"Why do you feel like you have to prove yourself? They chose you for this job specifically. They trust in your abilities and talent. Why don't you trust yourself?"

"I don't know." Tears of frustration line my eyes and roll down my cheeks as I blink.

"You used to do this in college too." He hesitates before he continues and I tense, knowing whatever he's about to say won't be easy to hear. "Do you think it has something to do with Mom and Dad? Feeling like you have to prove yourself to them?"

"Probably." I sniffle, unsuccessful at keeping the tears at bay, and I know he hears it because he sighs, clearly not happy I'm upset.

"I know Mom and Dad are important to you, but they don't get to dictate what you think about yourself. You get to decide that. In your opinion, are you putting your all into your work? Working hard?"

"Yes. Sometimes too hard, clearly."

"Then that's all you need, Lan. The only person you need to prove yourself to, is you. No one else matters."

I know he's right. I've worked on my self confidence a lot, but work has been extremely stressful and I'm realizing now that I've let the demand force me back into my old habits. I'm thankful he knows me well enough to draw me back to myself and remind me I'm enough in the moments when I need it.

"Thanks. You always know what to say."

"Anytime. I love you. Get some rest and let that man take care of you."

"Love you too."

We hang up and a deep sigh leaves my lips. I already feel lighter having spoken with Charlie, and I resolve to really work out my thoughts about myself and what I deserve. I type out a quick text to Cami, knowing that Alex likely filled her in as well, and hit send.

ME

I'm alive. Sorry I've been MIA but I promise to make it up to you.

BESTIE FRIEND

How do you plan to do that, hmm?

ME

Well, there are cookies on the way to the office as we speak with your name on them and why don't we watch a movie together soon? Maybe sometime this weekend?

Cami and I watch movies together occasionally, even from our separate apartments, by FaceTiming and pushing play at the exact same time. It makes me feel like I'm near her even when I can't be and the thought of doing that right now is extremely comforting.

BESTIE FRIEND

It's a date. Text me once you've recouped and send me a picture of your hot nurse.

ME

<<eye roll emoji>>

A little while later he comes back with soup and sits with me while I eat it. After the IV and now the soup, I'm finally feeling more like myself. We sit together in his bed and watch movies and talk about work and life, and eventually I fall asleep snuggled up in his warm embrace.

Alex

It's Sunday afternoon and Alana and I are lounging in the living room. By some miracle, I've been able to convince her to take it easy and rest this weekend. I think the incident on Friday scared her enough to listen to me, so we've been holed up inside most of the weekend.

After we spent the entire day in bed on Friday, I asked her to stay in my room to sleep. I can't explain the stress I felt when I thought about not being able to see her and make sure she was okay, so having her near was a comfort.

We've played countless games of chess and watched so many movies, including *Wonka*, despite my initial chagrin. I was proven incorrect, it was a great movie.

Now, she's curled up on the couch reading a book and I'm scrolling through emails on my computer. The quiet is interrupted by a loud knock at our door. I'm not expecting anyone, and it seems like Alana isn't either considering the confused look on her face.

"Who is that?" she asks.

"No idea."

I stand and make my way to the front door, then open it to

find a tall man standing in the opening in dark gray coveralls with the building's logo on them.

"I am sorry to bother you, sir." As he speaks I notice Alana has come to stand behind me, curious as to who our guest is. "We are having a bit of a maintenance issue."

"What kind of maintenance issue?" she asks from behind me, then wraps her small hand around my forearm. I try not to get distracted by the physical contact, but it's difficult.

"Someone in the unit next to yours hit a pipe while drilling into the wall. It is a minor issue, however we will need to use your unit to gain access and fix the problem."

"Okay, no problem," I say. "How long will you be? An hour?"

The man reaches behind his head and rubs his neck nervously. I can tell by the apprehension on his face that this is going to be more of an inconvenience than I was thinking.

"Unfortunately, this will likely take longer than that."

"How long is longer?" Alana asks.

"We will need to gain access today in order to properly stop the leak, but one of the parts we need to permanently fix it is having to be shipped. We aren't sure when it will arrive."

Well, that's incredibly unhelpful.

"So, you're saying we are going to have maintenance people in and out for a while?"

The man hesitates again and I brace myself for more bad news.

"In order to fix the issue, we need to open up the wall. The building would like to move you to a different vacant unit for the remainder of your stay because we are unsure of the timeline of the repair." He must see the stress on my face, because he quickly continues. "But not to worry, this new unit is fully furnished and will be stocked and ready for your arrival. It's still in this building, just on the other side."

Alana perks up a bit at that, I assume because she's hoping that means we'll have a view of the Eiffel Tower, and takes a deep breath.

"Alright," she says. "How soon do you need us to be out?"

"As soon as possible, ma'am. No need to rush, but sometime within the next few hours if possible."

He lets us know to meet Maura in the lobby with our things when we're ready and she will get us settled in the new unit.

"Well, who can say they got to stay in two different luxurious flats while in Paris for a month?" Alana asks as we make our way back into the living room.

"Probably a lot of people," I chuckle and say.

"Hey," she nudges me on the shoulder. "I'm trying to find the bright side. I'm surprised they're moving us for the rest of our time here, but I guess it isn't that much longer at this point. I can't believe we only have a couple of weeks left. When we got here it felt like we had forever in front of us, but the time is going by so quickly."

"You're not wrong about that. How are you feeling?" I reach out and place the back of my hand on her forehead to check her temperature. I let out a sigh of relief when it feels normal.

"Not bad, thanks to the on-call nurse living with me. I'm pretty sure you fixed me right up."

"You still need to rest, especially if you want to go back to work tomorrow," I say as we head down the hallway to our rooms.

"I have to go back tomorrow, Alex. There's too much to do to stay home another day."

"You can go back as long as you promise to sleep a full eight hours every night and eat enough throughout the day."

"Scout's honor," she says and holds her pointer, middle and ring fingers up in the air. "Are you going to call Heather or should I? We probably need to let her know what's going on so she can tell her friend."

"I'll give her a call." She nods and heads into her room to pack up her things. I do the same, but before beginning to pack I dial Heather's number. She answers after one ring.

"Hello," she says.

"Hi, Heather, how are you?"

"Doing well. Is everything okay? You reaching out on a Sunday has me a bit worried."

"Everything's fine. We're having a bit of a maintenance issue here at the apartment. It's nothing major, but it is going to displace us for the next couple weeks."

"Oh no," she gasps.

"Yeah, not the best news. But the building has another unit they're going to allow us to stay in that is furnished and ready to go for us, so I think we're all set. I just wanted to let you know so you could update the owners of this flat."

"What a pain. Thank you for letting me know, I'll reach out to her. Are you two doing okay?"

I almost tell her about the situation this weekend with Alana, but decide against it.

"We're doing great. Things here are a bit hectic at the office, but we're figuring out how to manage it."

"Good. Well you two take care of yourselves and let me know if you need anything."

"Will do, have a good day."

"You do the same."

I hang up the phone and stare at all of my belongings strewn about the room. I'm not a messy person, but I wouldn't say I'm extremely organized. Not nearly as organized as Alana. I walk around the room, gathering items as I go. I dump them all into my suitcase and then head to the bathroom to do the same.

Once everything is in the suitcase, I squeeze it together and wrestle with the zipper a bit before sighing in relief once it's fully closed. Next, I head into the office to grab my work items and the few books I've collected while here.

Alana is doing the same, walking in and out of her room to grab random belongings that have taken residence throughout the unit. Maintenance let us know they would transfer our groceries from the kitchen, so thankfully we don't have to worry about grabbing all of that right now. We meet back in the living room, surrounded by suitcases, backpacks and bags. I notice her staring at the tree sort of longingly, and make a mental note to make sure I can somehow get that tree to wherever we're staying next.

After doing one more walk through to be sure we have everything, we pile all of our things into the lift and head down to the lobby.

When we get off we are greeted by an unhappy looking Maura, which isn't all that surprising considering she always looks unhappy.

"Hello. Your new unit will be 14B, on this side of the building," she says and motions to the opposite lift from the one we usually take.

Typical Maura, giving only the exact amount of information needed and not a bit more.

"Thank you," I say. I take the keys from her outstretched hand and we head up to our new home.

CHAPTER 39

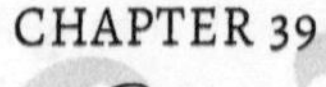

Alana

This has been the craziest weekend.

Friday I fainted and Alex put me in his bed and took care of me. Saturday I spent all day there, cuddled up next to him. Now, here we are on Sunday standing in our new flat for the next couple weeks.

Our new flat with an incredible view of the Eiffel Tower.

And only one bed.

That shouldn't seem like an issue, considering Alex and I just slept in his bed together, but that was different. I was sick and there was no possibility of anyone making any moves. I was simply there so he could keep an eye on me. Nothing romantic in the slightest. Plus he sent me back to my bedroom on Saturday night, so it was very clear that the purpose was nothing more than safety.

Now? I've decided I'm going to face my fears and tell him I'm ready, if that's still something he wants, and if what he's been saying the last few days is still true then I'm sure this one bed is just as tempting to him as it is to me. My original plan was to wait until we got back from our trip, but I don't think that's very realistic if I'm being honest.

Neither of us have said anything, we're both just kind of

staring at it. There was a small entryway that led us into the living room. There is one couch and a television in the corner, a fireplace off to the side. The kitchen is just on the other side of this main room, no walls separating it from the living room, and there's a window in the kitchen that boasts a gorgeous Eiffel Tower view. I move to check it out and open the window to find a small ledge, just big enough to sit on, and a railing for safety. This window and view is straight out of a movie.

Right off of the main kitchen and living room is the bedroom. I glance over at Alex and notice his eyes have stopped there. It's beautiful, really. The king sized bed is pushed up against the wall on the right and has at least six pillows on it. The cream colored comforter looks like a cloud. A blue velvet bench sits at the foot of the bed, reminding me of the couches in our last flat.

This one is much, much smaller, but I appreciate the coziness of it. It feels warm and homey inside, while still being elegant and upscale like the rest of the building. The walls are a tan color with that same gold trim around the ceiling and floor, and there's beautiful artwork on the walls.

There's a window in this room too, just like the one in the kitchen. I'm dreaming of laying in this bed, maybe wrapped up in my roommate, and gazing out the window at the glittering tower. It sort of feels like a dream and although the close quarters is stressing me out a little bit, I can't help but thank whoever decided to drill into a pipe this morning.

I feel his warmth behind me before his hands come up and touch my shoulders. He squeezes down my arms once, twice, three times and then lightly takes a hold of my hands.

"It really is so beautiful," I say quietly, still gazing out the window.

"You really are," he says into my ear. He presses a kiss on my temple and turns away. "I'll take the couch, you take the bed."

I roll my eyes even though he can't see them. Ever the gentleman.

"Don't be silly, we can share. We just shared your bed on Friday night," I say, following him into the living room and sitting down next to him on the small couch.

"I don't know if I can be trusted to sleep in a bed with you again and not touch you."

I'm staring at him and I can feel the blush on my cheeks. I can't figure out how to articulate what's happening in my brain, but as always Alex understands anyways.

"I know you probably don't believe me, but you should." He lets out a laugh that sounds almost frustrated and runs his hand through his hair. "Come on, let's go get dinner and we can handle this when we get back."

We have dinner at a nearby restaurant that doesn't require any driving, both too exhausted to venture out to find somewhere in the city, and head back up to our flat. I am desperate to put on my pajamas and climb into the cold sheets on that gorgeous bed.

When we walk in, I notice our Christmas tree immediately. It has magically appeared in the living room of our new flat and I stand frozen to the spot, staring at it.

"How did you get that here? It looks perfect."

"Asked the maintenance guys to bring it over instead of tossing it."

My eyes sting and I squeeze them shut, willing my happy tears away. I don't want to cry right now. I was so sad when I realized we wouldn't have a tree on Christmas morning because of this stupid maintenance situation, so seeing it here makes me feel all the things.

I turn, wrap my arms around his middle and squeeze. He's surprised for a moment, but quickly eases into the embrace and rests his chin atop my head. After a few seconds we separate and I move on to another topic, one I thought about all through dinner.

"Am I going to have to fight you on the bed, Ashford?" I ask as we walk into the bedroom.

He chuckles. "I just don't want to make you uncomfortable. You've told me you aren't ready to start anything and I want to respect that."

"What's the difference between Friday and now?"

"I wasn't going to make a move on you the same day you fainted. You were in my bed because I was terrified you weren't okay, not because I was trying to start something."

I roll my eyes, grab my pajamas and the things I need to wash my face, and head into the bathroom, shutting the door behind me. It's just as beautiful in here as it is in the rest of the flat. There's a standing clawfoot bath tub in the corner and a large shower in the other. There are gold accents all throughout that make it feel luxurious and royal.

I change and realize that the pajamas I chose show a bit more skin that I normally would around Alex, but I can't find it in me to care. I splash warm water on my face and lather face wash into my hands. I realize, as I reach up to start rubbing it into my skin, that I didn't tie my hair up. I pause for a few seconds and stare into the mirror, trying to problem solve.

My long wavy hair will fall over my shoulders and into the sink if I don't somehow tie it back, but I hate to waste the product on my hands. I let out a groan of frustration as I stare at my reflection.

"What's wrong?" Alex asks, his voice close to the door.

"Oh, I'm fine. I just forgot to tie my hair back and I already have face wash all over my hands."

There's a moment of silence before I hear his voice again.

"Can I come in?" I glance down at myself in my silk tank and shorts set. It's a pale pink and hangs low on my chest showing a bit more cleavage than normal. Oh well, he's going to see it when I step out of the bathroom..

"Um, sure."

The door pushes open and his eyes meet mine. I laugh a little at myself, at the picture he's seeing. I'm standing here with sudsy hands staring at myself in the mirror. His eyes light up and then flare as they quickly glance down my body then bounce back up to my face and he steps towards me.

"Here, let me help." He stands behind me and, with the most gentle touch, begins moving my dark hair. He pulls it all behind my shoulders and then gathers it in his hands in a low ponytail.

"Do you want to tie it up? I probably have a hair tie somewhere around here." I trail off as I glance around the counter top looking for one.

"I'll just hold it, do your thing, sunshine." Our eyes meet in the mirror and I smile at him. I begin washing my face and after a minute or two of scrubbing, I lean forward to splash water onto my face and wash it off.

As I lean forward, my backside presses into him and I feel him jerk back quickly, not letting go of my hair. My cheeks heat at the accidental contact, but I recover by the time I stand back up and grab a towel, patting my face dry.

As I stare into the mirror at the two of us standing together, I am overwhelmed with thoughts of gratitude for this man. The way he takes care of me is unlike anyone else in my life and he has proven time and time again that he isn't leaving. He is there for me in the big things and in the small, and he believes in me with a ferocity that I don't even know that I have for myself.

Suddenly I've made my decision, to hell with waiting. I need his mouth on mine. I need to feel his skin on mine and even though I'm scared, I know I want this. I take a steadying breath, willing myself to tell him this without my voice shaking. I'm about to say the words, I want to try this with him, and then he lets go of my hair and pulls away and I lose my nerve.

He smiles at me in the mirror and walks back into the bedroom, closing the bathroom door behind him. I let out a quiet groan and bang my head on the wall in frustration. This is my fault. I told him I wasn't ready and now he's pulling away, because he thinks I want that. I don't.

I finish brushing my teeth and getting ready for bed, then I slip out of the bathroom and find the bedroom empty. The sheets on the bed are pulled back and waiting for me. I resist the urge to jump right in, and walk to the doorway to see what Alex is doing. I find him piling pillows and blankets onto the couch, then he sits and notices me standing there.

"You don't have to do that. Just come in here with me, you barely fit on that thing." He proves me right when he lays back and his feet hang off the edge. There is no way he's getting sleep if he stays out here, but he seems persistent.

"I'm good. Go to sleep, sunshine." I stand there for a few more seconds just staring at the kind, stubborn and beautiful man in front of me. Eventually, I admit defeat and turn to climb into bed.

I burrow down into the sheets and close my eyes, trying desperately to fall asleep, but the want I experienced earlier in the evening has come back tenfold. My skin itches with desire.

"Alex," I call softly. "Are you awake?"

"You okay?" His scratchy and sleepy voice sends a chill down my spine.

"I'm fine but..." I hesitate.

"Yes?"

"Will you—" I take a deep breath and the fact that he isn't right in front of me allows me to be brave. "Will you kiss me?"

It sounds so juvenile when I say it out loud, like I'm a teenage girl asking for her first kiss, but I know Alex appreciates honesty and I also know there's no way he would make a move until I give him the all clear. He's too good to make assumptions.

For a second, I don't hear anything. It's completely silent aside from my breathing and I think I might have pushed him too far and he's changed his mind.

"Come here," he says, voice assertive and dominant.

"What?" I whisper into the darkness.

"Come here, Alana." Why is him using my full name in this situation so sexy? I slowly get out of the bed and tiptoe across the room and to the living room. I don't know why I'm being quiet, it's only us here, but it feels like if I make any sudden movements I might break whatever is happening between us right now.

I walk over to him where he's sitting up on the couch. I'm about a foot away when I stop and he reaches out and takes hold of my hips, tugging me forward. I go easily, drunk on the way his skin on mine feels.

"Are you sure?" He reaches up and cups my cheek with his warm hand, forcing me to look him in the eye. Not that I want to look anywhere else right now.

"I'm terrified, but I'm sure."

"I'm not going anywhere. I'm right here."

"I know. I trust you." That seems to be all he needs in confirmation. He stands and his hand moves to cup my jaw and tilt it upward, allowing him better access. Before I can second guess a thing, his lips are on mine. His kisses are firm and hungry in the best way. He coaxes my mouth open with his tongue and it's unlike anything I've ever experienced before.

As the kiss heats up, my hands snake up his chest and around his neck, playing with the hair on his nape and pulling him further into me. He moans into my mouth and it's the best sound I have ever heard.

A kiss has *never* felt like this before.

After a few minutes, he slows us down and separates from me, pulling back and looking intensely into my eyes.

I can tell he's doing a temperature check, making sure I'm okay.

"You with me?" I nod. "Let me hear you, sunshine."

I shiver. "I'm with you."

He kisses me again, this time slower, like his life depends on it. With every brush of his lips, he's slowly working me up. He reaches down and places his hands on the backs of my upper thighs and I jump, my legs instinctively wrapping around him.

"So are we doing this?" he asks when he pulls back for air.

"Yes. Bed," I demand, clinging to him tighter and kissing his neck.

"Not that, Lanie," he says with a chuckle. I pull back and look at him, my brow furrowed in confusion. "I mean, are you ready to try this with me? A relationship? I don't just want you in my bed, I want you outside of it too."

My heart melts at his words.

"I'm ready. You protect my heart better than anyone I know. I have some stuff I might have to work through, but I'm done letting my past relationship dictate my current happiness."

He kisses me again, almost like he can't help it, before saying anything else. "I'm so proud of you, you have no idea. I'll help you work on whatever you need to work on and I'll respect the need for professionalism when it comes to work. I know that's important to you and I wouldn't want to take that from you."

I stare into his eyes and reach over and pinch myself on my arm, wincing when it hurts.

"What was that?" he asks, chuckling at me.

"Are you real?"

He laughs and places small sweet kisses all over my face. On my cheeks, my temples, my forehead and chin, on my eyelids and nose. He slowly works his way down my jaw and begins kissing my neck. I lean my head back and let out a happy sound.

"Tell me you're mine," he says, his voice firm.

"I'm yours," I breathe.

"Hell yeah you are." He moves me away from the couch and carries me into the bedroom, setting me down on the bed with such gentleness, as if he was handling glass.

"As much as I would love to take full advantage of the fact that we only have one bed, I don't want to move too fast. It's late and I know you're still recovering from this week. How about we save that for another night? I don't plan on letting you go, so we've got all the time in the world."

"That sounds good," I say, smiling up at him. "But you'll sleep with me in here, right?"

"You couldn't pay me to sleep anywhere else."

We cuddle up in the bed and don't say much else, just listen to the sound of each other breathing. A few minutes after we settle, he says my name softly. "Lanie, look."

I open my eyes and look out at the Eiffel Tower as it shimmers and shines in the night sky. It's a metaphor for the feelings bubbling up inside me, glittery and bright and shiny. Everything feels like it's glowing.

We watch it for a little longer and eventually I fall into the deepest sleep I've had in forever, surrounded by cedar and sandalwood and *him*.

CHAPTER 40

Alex

I WAKE UP TO ALANA'S SOFT BREATHING NEXT TO ME and for a moment I'm startled, confused why she's in bed next to me. Then last night starts to come back to me and I stare up at the ceiling in awe. I expected her to eventually be ready to give this thing between us a try, but I didn't expect it anytime soon.

Hearing her soft voice call my name from the bedroom last night felt like a dream. I made her come to me, just in case I *was* dreaming, and watching her walk towards me was an out of body experience. Kissing her, having my hands on her, is something I've been wanting to do for almost a year now. It felt like coming up for air after being underwater for too long.

She's snuggled up next to me, her hair draped on the pillow behind her in beautiful dark brown waves. The strap on her silk top has slipped down her shoulder a bit and she looks angelic, like a piece of art. I want to stay here with her forever, but I also want to make her breakfast and coffee so I slide out from underneath her as gently as possible and stand. She moves around a little, but eventually settles back in and her breathing returns to a steady, sleepy rhythm.

I pad into the living room and shut the door quietly behind

me. This new flat couldn't have come at a better time, because now this all feels surreal. It's almost as if we've always been together and now we just live together. There's something about sharing a bathroom and a bedroom with someone that feels intimate and I'm already dreading returning to New York.

I texted Banks last night to update him on everything happening here, but that was before the kiss, so I probably should update him again. He let me know my mom was doing well and I told him I'd give her a call soon to check in. I've been so caught up in work and Alana that I haven't taken the time to call her nearly as much as I usually do. She's been great about it though. She's texted a few times to tell me she loves me and she hopes I'm well. I don't deserve her.

I get started on the pancake batter, being sure to add chocolate chips to Lana's because they're her favorite, and put the bacon in the pan.

Before long, the bacon is sizzling and I know that it will wake her up. I'm not sure if it's the sound or the smell, but every time I've made bacon in the last two weeks I hear her making her way into the kitchen shortly after.

This flat has the same coffee machine as the other one, and I make quick work of her latte so it's ready when she joins me. I'm steaming the milk when I hear our door open, but I keep my back turned and give her a minute to make her way into the kitchen.

A few seconds later, I feel her small hands slide up my back and around my middle. She presses her front to my back and turns her head, resting her cheek just below my shoulder blades. I set the coffee down and turn, so I'm facing her. She's wrapped around me, looking up into my eyes so I lean down and kiss her softly.

"Morning, sunshine."

"Morning, handsome." Her cheeks turn pink and she buries her face in my chest to hide her blush. I snicker at her and take her chin in my hand, tilting her head back so I can kiss her again. It's slow and sweet and one hell of a good morning.

"That's one way to start my Monday," I say, staring into her beautiful ocean blue eyes.

She smiles up at me, still a little self-conscious, and raises up to her tiptoes to give me a kiss on the cheek. Before she lowers back down, she moves her mouth to my ear and whispers, "Is that coffee for me?"

I can't help the shiver that overtakes me and she laughs.

"Sure is." I reach behind me and hand her the mug. "Have a seat, breakfast is almost ready." She turns and I watch as she walks to the table. She's put on a long silk robe that is the same pale pink as the set she's wearing. The curve of her chest and hips are accentuated in it and I work hard to keep my eyes on her face and not her body. It looks absolutely gorgeous on her. I'm sure it would be gorgeous *off* of her as well, but it's seven in the morning and we have work to do today so I let the thought pass. I want to do this right with her and that means taking things slow.

"How are you feeling?" I ask, trying to get a pulse on where she is now that she's slept. She seems okay and happy, but I want to be absolutely sure she is. I don't want her to do anything she isn't comfortable with.

"I feel really wonderful." She takes a sip of her coffee then, smiling. "How are you feeling?"

How am I feeling? It's a good question. I've been wanting this for a while now and it feels surreal that she's actually here and she's mine. She told me so yesterday and I can't quite believe it.

"I feel incredible, Lan." I pause and she smiles. "I am a bit scared, though. I can't help but feel like you're going to disappear on me." The hurt and worry on her face make me want to take the words back, but I know if this is going to work we have to be honest with one another.

"I'm not going anywhere, Alex. I want this with you."

"I know you do, but if you get scared, I need you to tell me. We need to talk about it, otherwise it'll drive us apart and I'm not sure I'd do well with losing you."

She nods her head and I bring the breakfast over to her, sitting down in the seat next to hers. I reach over and grab a hold of the bottom of her chair, then pull it towards me so her thigh is almost flush against mine. She doesn't bat an eye and I'm relieved at how comfortable she is with being close to me.

"I trust you. I know you want this, but I also know you're scared. I want you to tell me if you start overthinking. If you have questions or insecurities, ask me about them. Don't sit in it, okay?"

Her eyes get watery and I stare into them, making sure she hears my words and understands. I'm in this for the long haul, and I *need* her to understand that.

She nods and blinks her eyes quickly, trying to hold the tears at bay, but one slips past her long lashes and I lean forward and kiss her cheek where it's spilled over. She gasps and pulls me into her, clinging to me like I'm her only lifeline. The embrace is desperate and needy in all the very best ways. Nothing about it is sensual and it doesn't need to be, this isn't the time for it. I hold her for as long as she needs and eventually she pulls away and begins to eat her breakfast.

"So, are we going to tell Amélie about us? What about Luis and Genevieve? It'll just make their taunting worse, but I don't want to hide."

I contemplate it for a minute. I figured we would need to tell Heather about our relationship so we can fill out any necessary paperwork with HR, but I'm not sure about Amélie.

There's nothing in our contract that says we can't date, I looked it up an embarrassingly long time ago, but there's still a stigma around people dating coworkers. Someone always has something to say.

"I'll call Heather and let her know soon. Maybe we should keep it under wraps a bit here, though. I don't want things to be harder than they already are."

She nods as she takes another bite. "I feel good about that. We won't be here much longer anyways."

We finish up our breakfast and I clean the dishes while she starts getting ready for the day. I head into the bathroom and brush my teeth in the sink next to hers and it all feels incredibly domestic. I could get used to this.

I fix my hair and get dressed quickly, then I sit in the bathroom and watch her as she curls her hair and delicately applies her makeup. She's radiant and it feels surreal that I get the privilege of watching her do something as simple as getting ready in the morning. It's intimate in a way I didn't expect.

When she finishes, I head into the bedroom to let her get dressed, and I put my shoes on, gathering the items I need before we head out. She comes out a few moments later in a gorgeous midi length pink dress that flares out at her hips. She's paired it with nude heels and gold jewelry.

"Would you mind zipping me?" she asks and gives me her back. I clear my throat.

"Not at all." I drape her hair over one shoulder and find the zipper just above the swell of her hips, then slowly pull it up, careful not to catch her skin as I do.

Once I reach the top of the zip, I place a soft kiss on her shoulder and step back, not trusting myself to do much else if we want to get to work on time. It's like now that I have her, I can't keep my hands off of her.

We make our way downstairs and into the car, and before I know it we're at the office.

"One last kiss to last me the day?" she asks, a smile on her face. I lean over the middle of the car and kiss her deeply, hoping she feels the emotion I pour into it even if I can't express them all in words yet. She's breathless when I pull away, and so am I.

CHAPTER 41

Alana

I'M REELING. IT FEELS LIKE I'VE BEEN FLOATING ON A cloud since last night and I never want to come down. I woke up this morning and felt around for Alex, but found his space in the bed empty. For a moment I thought maybe I dreamed it, maybe he slept on the couch and I stayed in the bedroom and nothing happened. But then I heard the sizzle and snap of bacon and smelled the coffee and I knew exactly where he was and what he was doing.

I've come to really enjoy my morning lattes made specifically for me by Alex. I don't have one of these fancy espresso machines at home, but it's at the top of my to-buy list so I can force him to come make me one every morning when we get home.

Home. It's exciting to think about going home, because I miss the city and I miss Charlie and Cami so much, but I also get a nervous pit in my stomach. What will happen when we go home? Will things change once we're no longer in the City of Love, or will we jump right into a serious relationship and move in together? It almost feels like the right step, since that's essentially what we're doing now, but it also feels way too fast. We just got started.

"I can see you overthinking. Relax, Lanie." He reaches out and squeezes my hand three times before letting go. "Whatever it is, we'll work it out together." My blood heats at the pet name and my heart calms at the reassurance. I don't know how he always knows when I'm in my head about something, but he does.

We're walking through the door of *Impress Europe* and I feel my body react to the environment. While Amélie and most of the staff are kind and welcoming, the people we work with day in and day out are not. I've grown to feel quite frustrated while in this building, and I don't think Alex feels the same stress because he spends a lot of his time with Amélie interviewing, while my whole day is spent with Genevieve and Luis.

I say a hello in their direction as I walk to my station and set my things down. Neither of them responds, like always, and I let it roll off my back, like always. I have pretty thick skin, but a person can only take so much. After dealing with their nastiness over and over, I'm almost at my breaking point.

I take a deep breath, trying to calm myself and remember why I'm here. I haven't had a panic attack since our first day in the office and that's progress, because ever since Brad's resurfacing and the changes with work, they were becoming more frequent. Thankfully, I haven't heard from him after his phone call with Alex, and I'm hoping it stays that way.

I'm working on a spread for an upcoming issue when Luis approaches and I brace myself. It's a good day when neither of them speak to me, so it looks like we're off to a bad start.

"Bonjour," he says in the most unenthusiastic tone. Sometimes Alex will be here in the mornings to shield me, but they had an early interview this morning so he went straight back to Amélie's office.

"Bonjour, Luis. How was your weekend?"

"Fine. Do you have the article for the beauty spread on winter makeup trends?" My hands start to shake. I do have the article for the beauty spread, but it's not on winter makeup trends, it's on winter skincare routines. I could have sworn that is what Genevieve told me to write about.

"I have the skincare routines article. I believe that's what Genevieve asked me to write." I glance in her direction and catch the smirk on her face. I immediately feel hot, the anger, frustration and embarrassment rising by the second.

"I'm sure she did not. The section is about winter makeup trends." He has the nerve to look angry with me, which is ridiculous because I know he's in on this little scheme. Neither of them know I worked myself into the ground, literally, these last two weeks for them. I'm trying to help them and pick up their slack and instead of showing appreciation, they make me do twice the work by giving me incorrect information.

I take a cleansing breath and steady my hands, roll my shoulders back, look into the eyes of one of my least favorite people on earth, and smile.

"Absolutely. I was mistaken, she did ask me to write about winter makeup trends. I have the article, it's currently being edited." He startles at my save, but recovers quickly.

"Can I see it?"

"Of course." I reach into my bag and pull out an article on winter makeup trends. The funny thing is, this is something I expected. I obviously couldn't predict what exactly they'd do to trip me up, but I could sense it coming. I figured it wouldn't be a bad idea to have something in my back pocket just in case I needed it. Winter makeup trends is probably the most predictable and easy article to write and do a spread on, so I wrote one up just in case.

I hand the article over to him and I wish I was recording the surprise on his face so I could show it to Alex later. It feels good to beat someone at their own game, and seeing Luis and Genevieve look like they do right now is reward enough. It almost makes the whole passing out thing worth it, except not really because that wasn't smart, but you know what I mean.

"Well, um...thanks." He takes it from me hesitantly and turns to walk back to Genevieve. She looks upset and I would be too if my plans for sabotage blew up in my face. I turn back to what I was working on and ignore them. I have a great job, an incredible brother, best friend, and...boyfriend? Is that what Alex is to me now? I pull out my phone and type up a text, then press send.

ME

Are you my boyfriend?

ASHFORD

Are we really having this conversation over text? I'm in an interview, sunshine.

ME

You told me to ask the questions.

ASHFORD

Okay, then yes. I'm your boyfriend. Are you my girlfriend?

ME

I'd like to be.

ASHFORD

Then it's settled.

I wish I could kiss you right now.

ME

Oh, shut up. I'm working, stop distracting me.

ASHFORD

You texted me!

I giggle to myself and lock my phone, putting it back into my bag. I really do need to focus on this if I want to stop taking work home.

We ordered in from a nearby restaurant and are all gathered in the small sitting area in the office. Luis and Genevieve are off in the corner having their own conversation, as always, and Alex, Amélie, and I are sitting around a table in the center of the room.

"How have the interviews been today?" I ask.

"They've been pretty great. It's one wonderful candidate after another, which makes our job pretty easy. This one over here," she nods in Alex's direction, "is a rockstar. He reads people so well, it's impressive."

I smile over at him in adoration and hope Amélie can't see it on my face that things have changed between us. We chatter on about work and positions being filled, and then I hear Genevieve speak from the corner of the room.

"Alex, Alana, has Amélie told you about the company holiday party?"

I want to say *'why are you asking?'* because I know she would prefer if we weren't there, but maybe she's trying to turn over a new leaf after the incident this morning.

I turn to Alex and he shakes his head. "This is the first I'm hearing of it."

"Ah, oui, how could I forget?" Amélie presses her hand to her head as if to say *what a dummy*. "We have a holiday party each year and of course you're both invited. You can bring a plus one if you like, although I know neither of you have family here so that most likely won't be needed. The party is next Friday."

"We'd love to come," I say with a genuine smile, because I really have enjoyed my time here apart from my two editor buddies in the back.

"Absolutely," Alex agrees and we continue on eating and talking. I don't hear a peep from Genevieve or Luis again, but at least they tried to make an effort.

CHAPTER 42

Alex

We've endured another week of work at *Impress Europe* and it's finally Friday. I couldn't be more thankful to have some time alone with my girl, and I plan to take full advantage. It's been torture not being able to touch and kiss her at work, but it's a lot easier to hold back than it would be to explain it to everyone.

Luis and Genevieve are constantly on her back, so I know that announcing our relationship to people who we don't actually work with and won't see again after we leave just isn't worth it. Our nights have been full of conversations about everything under the sun, some deep and others not.

I'm so eager to check off tonight's list item and I can't wait for Alana to find out what it is. I know she's been excited to complete the last few items on her list, and now that our relationship has changed, this just feels like another opportunity to do something new with her.

We've been home for a few hours, cooked dinner together, and now she's taking a bubble bath. I walk into the bedroom and knock on the bathroom door, careful not to push in even though it's cracked.

"You can come in, the bubbles are covering everything," she

says. I take a steadying breath because just the idea of this woman covered in bubbles is enough to make my blood heat, and walk into the room.

She's got her wavy brown hair piled on top of her head in a messy bun, and short wisps falling down all around. Some of them have touched the water and they cling to her skin, sort of how I wish I was right now.

"We're going to head out for a special activity in about an hour. Think you can be ready?" I ask.

"Oooh what are we doing? Can I guess?"

"Sure you can. There aren't too many items left."

"Ice skating, gingerbread…" She ticks each item off on her fingers and it makes me smile. "PJs aaaand…"

"Cinnamon rolls," I finish for her. She smiles up at me, seemingly happy at my ability to recall her list.

"Is it gingerbread houses?"

"Try again."

"Hmmm…ice skating?" she asks, a giddy smile on her perfect lips.

"You got it." I lean down and kiss her, then turn and head back into the living room. "Be sure to wear something warm," I toss over my shoulder as I go.

I spend some time reading on the bed and gazing out the window at the Eiffel Tower beyond. This flat was made for us, and while I'm a little sad we haven't been here this whole time, I think it came to us at exactly the right moment.

I hear the tub start to drain and minutes later she walks out in a fluffy white towel. She's rifling through her clothes trying to pick out what to wear and I love listening to her commentary as she does it. It's so cute—she'll hum and tsk at different options and talk to them as if they're able to respond to her.

"Hmm I wonder if I paired you with…"

"Wouldn't you look nice with those boots…"

"I just wore you silly, I can't wear you again for at least another week."

It's endearing and it makes me like her even more. I'm well aware that my feelings for her are sailing past like and creeping into the love territory, but it's early and I need to let her catch up. I've been falling for her for a year now, but she's only just started.

Eventually, she lands on black fleece lined leggings, a black sweater, a long white puffy coat and a pink scarf. She grabs her cream mittens and earmuffs that look like they have little puff balls on each end, sets those on the bed for later, and escapes to the bathroom to change.

Fifteen minutes later she emerges looking like every version of perfection.

I stand from the bed and make my way to her, sliding my hand around her waist and holding her close. "You look incredible." I kiss her and she hums into my mouth, taking the kiss deeper within seconds. I pull away and she lets out a sound of unhappiness, which makes me laugh.

"We have to get going or we're going to be too late. Let's go." She grabs her mittens and earmuffs, takes my hand, and follows me out the door and down to the lobby. We get in the car and Marco drives us to the location that I sent him earlier this week. He assured me this was a top place to visit for the holidays in Paris.

We approach the Tuileries Garden Christmas Market, La Magie de Noël, and I am blown away. I can tell Alana is too by the expression on her face. There are people everywhere and booth after booth of different food, drinks, carnival games, and more. There's also a huge Ferris wheel a bit further down and Alana takes my hand in hers and squeezes. "I want to do that," she says.

"Whatever you want, sunshine," I reply, and kiss her temple.

After purchasing a pack of tickets at the booth we begin to make our way through the market. We get cups of hot apple cider and share a churro, stopping to browse at all of the different offerings. We spot bumper cars and some other carnival-type ride where the people on the ride swing back and forth. It doesn't look like one I'd particularly enjoy, so I'm thankful when she doesn't show any interest in it.

Eventually we make our way to the ice skating rink and I hand the woman at the front our tickets. She gives us skates and we sit down at the benches to put them on. Alana starts to untie the tennis shoes she's wearing, but I reach out and stop her.

"Let me," I say and kneel in front of her. I pull off her shoes gently and then slide the skates on, taking time to make sure each of them is safely laced up so they don't wobble or slip off of her feet. As I finish up, I look up to find her staring down at me with watery eyes.

"Hey, what's that for?" I ask, a slight panic in my voice. This is supposed to be fun.

"Nothing, nothing," she says, sniffing her tears away and waving her hand in the air in a gesture of dismissal. "I'm just a big baby. Thank you, Alex." She leans down and kisses me sweetly and I feel better knowing this was likely just a moment for her. One of those ones where she realizes how poorly she was treated before, and how she won't be treated that way ever again.

I put mine on too and stand, then reach out a hand for her to hold on to as she gets her footing in the skates. She wobbles a little at first, but once she gets the hang of it she's walking just fine. We go hand in hand to the edge of the rink and I step out carefully, then hold a hand out for her. She and Charlie do this every year, so she probably has some experience. I don't have much, but hopefully I pick it up fast.

We begin to move together, our hands tightly gripped together, and little by little we both begin to gain some confidence. After a few minutes of hesitantly skating, we start to pick up speed a little. Her death grip has loosened and we're just enjoying each other.

A while later, I turn and skate backwards, pulling her forward by her hand.

"Show off," she says, rolling her eyes. "It's annoying how good you are at everything."

"You love it." I wink at her.

"I do not."

"Sure," I say sarcastically. Just as the word leaves my lips, my skate catches on a patch of ice that isn't as smooth as the others and I'm going down before I can even realize what's happening.

Thankfully, I have enough awareness to let go of her hand so she doesn't tumble down with me, but I fall hard, landing on my butt then my back, and the pain shoots through me.

I know I'm not seriously hurt—it hurts my pride more than anything—but the shock of falling keeps me on the ground for a few seconds before I attempt to stand. My skates are sliding out from underneath me and Alana is dying of laughter, so I have nothing to grab onto.

"Wait, wait. Stop flailing around like a baby deer, here grab hold." She is still shaking with laughter as she puts her arm out, and I can't find it in me to be annoyed that she's laughing at my pain. I *love* her laugh, and I'd fall a million more times if that meant I could keep hearing it.

"I was humbled pretty quickly there."

She wheezes, laughing harder now. "You sure were. Don't worry, I don't think anyone else noticed. I won't tell." She mimes zipping her lips, locking them, and then places the imaginary key in the front pocket of my flannel.

"I'll keep it safe," I say and pat the pocket.

We continue skating, thankfully with no other falls, and it's perfect and magical and everything a date during the holidays should be. I back myself up against the wall of the rink and reach out for her hips, fitting my hands right in the curve where her waist meets her torso, and pull her in towards me. She comes easily, thanks to the skates, and I love the way my hands fit perfectly in the curves of her body, like it was made for me.

I pull her into a passionate kiss and she sighs happily against my lips. We stay like that for a few moments, my hands sliding down to cup her bottom and squeeze, until someone whistles at us and it breaks the moment.

Alana is snickering into my jacket, too embarrassed to show her face for a few moments. I'm lost in thought as I look at her and eventually my eyes move to the people skating around us. There are lots of adults, but so many families.

"Do you think I'll be a good dad someday?" I startle, hearing the question leave my lips. I was thinking it in my head, but didn't intend to ask it out loud. I look down at Alana, seeing the surprise on her face and immediately worry I touched a topic I shouldn't have. Before I can take back my words, she speaks.

"Of course you'll be a phenomenal dad, Alex." She reaches up and brushes back a curl that's fallen in front of my face, then leaves her hand on my cheek. "Where did that come from?"

The care in her eyes warms me from the inside and makes me feel like I can tell her anything.

"I think the fact that I didn't have a father figure growing up caused me to have a lot of fears about ever being one myself. I, um —" I clear my throat, feeling the burn of tears in the backs of my eyes but desperately trying to keep them in. "I think I'm scared that because my dad didn't stick around for me, I won't know how to be a good dad to my kids one day."

My fears sit heavy between us and I wonder if I should have just kept these thoughts to myself, but I know Alana needs to hear this. I've asked her to share her fears with me, it's only right that I do the same in return.

"Alex, you are going to be the best dad, no matter who you parent children with." She looks straight into my eyes, a ferocity burning in hers. "Over the last year you have shown me how caring and intentional you are. You pay attention to every little thing I say and do, you find places where I might need help and gently pick up the slack without making me feel bad about it. You are affectionate in the sweetest ways and you're steady and safe, everything a child needs. Your kids are going to be so lucky to have you as a dad."

I feel a single tear escape and before I can reach up, Alana leans forward and kisses it away. She goes to pull back, but I bring my hand up to the back of her head and direct her back to me instead. I kiss her deeply, audience be damned, and she melts into me.

"Thank you, Lanie." This conversation didn't magically fix the doubts and fears swirling around in my head, but I feel lighter having someone to share my burdens with.

Eventually we make our way out of the rink and back into our street shoes. We wander around the market a bit more, grab a few other treats, and take a ride on the Ferris wheel. On the way home, I clasp her hand in mine and squeeze three times, saying three words silently that I can't quite say out loud yet.

CHAPTER 43

Alana

AFTER ALEX'S MANY SURPRISES FOR ME THESE LAST FEW weeks, I figured it was time I stepped it up. I secretly grabbed two gingerbread house kits at the Christmas market we went to last night, and I plan to set them up for the ultimate competition tonight.

The last week with Alex has been a whirlwind, and I hope it never ends. I would have thought the moments of fear and anxiety would be more frequent, but the truth is it all just feels right. My concerns about it being too fast seem silly now that I'm in it. We've known each other for enough time that this feels so natural.

We've cuddled together on the couch all morning, sipping coffee and reading the day away, stealing kisses here and there. It was a scene straight from a movie, the room bathed in sunlight and the glow from the tree in the corner giving it warmth.

I kicked Alex out of the living room about a half hour ago, and now I'm almost ready for him to come out and see the masterpiece I've put together out here. Usually, these gingerbread decorating competitions get brutal between Charlie and I. We used to do it with just the two of us, but a few years ago Cami started joining us and now we make a whole day out of it.

Typically we'll go shopping for special things to add to the houses and then spend all day decorating. I went ahead and did some of the shopping earlier this week, and now I've pulled out all of the decorating items.

Square cereal pieces, HERSHEY'S KISSES, candy canes, broken up chocolate bars, marshmallows, coconut shavings, M&Ms, cookies, gumdrops, and various sprinkles are all scattered around the table in bowls. We also each have two bags of icing, already loaded into a piping bag with a few different icing tips. I made a special themed cocktail, and I pick Alex's up before heading to the bedroom door.

"Knock, knock," I say as I push open the door to our room. "Ready?"

"Well, what do we have here?" He stands and crosses the room before taking the drink from my hand and placing a sweet kiss on my lips. He takes a sip and hums happily. "This is fantastic, what is it?"

"A Mistletoe Manhattan," I say with a proud smile.

"Cute." He smiles and as I turn to walk him into the kitchen, he reaches out and tugs on the tail of the braid I've thrown my hair into this evening. I turn back to glare at him. He just laughs.

We make our way to the table, where I've set everything up, and he stands looking down in awe.

"You like it?"

"Like it? This looks incredible. I am *so* going to wipe the floor with you."

I scoff. "Yeah right, you've never seen me in action. I've won this the last three years against Charlie."

"Well, I'm about ten times better than Charlie in all aspects of life, so we'll see how this goes."

I giggle at his casual mention of my brother and it warms my heart. Charlie told me the last time we talked that he and Alex had started talking more frequently ever since he enlisted his help with the list. Knowing that they're friendly eases something inside me that I didn't realize was unsettled. Charlie doesn't really have friends and that worries me. He isolates himself too much.

We sit and get started decorating. I teach Alex how to use the boiled sugar to glue the house pieces together, because he hadn't ever used that technique, and I tell him it's the only free tip he's getting from me.

Once the houses are physically assembled, we get to work on the decorating. I use the cinnamon cereal squares and glue them to look like shingles on the top of the roof. I sprinkle coconut shavings on top for the snow, and then get to work decorating around the house. I add icing to all of the edges and use different piping tips to make it look a little more fancy.

I peek over to see Alex intensely focused on getting a peppermint to stick to the door of his, and it keeps falling. Eventually he frowns in frustration and tosses the peppermint somewhere behind him. I giggle.

We work in near silence for a few hours, both concentrating on this more than we have been on anything lately. Finally, I announce I'm finished and look over to see Alex is putting the finishing touches on his as well.

His house looks great for a rookie, but not as good as mine. He's added gumdrops as a path to the front door and made use of the piping tips as well to add icicles to the edges of the roof. His is colorful and fun, but a bit messy, just like us I guess.

"Okay so who judges?" he asks me as he washes his hands.

"I'll take a picture of both of them and post them on my Instagram story. We'll add a poll and let people vote, then check it in a few hours and see who won."

I move the houses carefully to sit on the mantle of the fireplace and take photos of each of them, then add them to my story. We decide to watch *The Holiday* while we wait for the vote and I've nodded off by the time the credits roll.

"Hey, Lanie," Alex whispers softly. He nudges my shoulder a few times and I groan, wanting to stay asleep in the warm position

I'm in. "I want you to sleep and normally I'd just move you to the bed, but I gotta know who won. It's killing me."

I laugh and pat around my lap for my phone before pulling up the app and checking the story, then holding it up for him to see.

"A tie? That's unacceptable."

"I guess we'll never know." I'm pretty sure I hear him mutter something like *A tie is a joke, I absolutely won*, but he picks me up and carries me into our room, setting me on the bed and climbing in behind me. For the first time in many years, I couldn't care less who won.

CHAPTER 44

Alex

WE'RE HALFWAY THROUGH ANOTHER WEEK AND I'M becoming more and more optimistic about us leaving at the end of the month. At first, I was a bit worried we wouldn't get everyone hired and ready to go in time, and our trip would be extended, but we only have one more editor position to fill and Alana has been working with the new hires this week to get them trained and working.

Up until now, she's been picking up all of the slack with little assistance from me, a fact I have been frustrated by, but she's assured me she has it handled. Ever since the scare we had, she's been a lot better about not bringing work home. Our new living situation has also helped me keep an eye on her, not to mention the fact that we share a bed now.

Alana went out for a run, so I decide to check in on my mom and fill her in on everything going on here. I tap her name on my phone and hold it up to my ear, waiting for the call to connect.

"Hi, sweetie." Her voice instantly warms me and I feel a tinge of homesickness come over me.

"Hey, Mom. How are you?"

"Oh you know, just trucking along. Not much is going on

here, Banksy and little Hallie are keeping me company." I snicker at her nickname for him. He hates it, but he loves my mom so he'd never tell her to stop.

"I'm glad they've been around. Why don't you take them to dinner next time they're around, my treat?"

"They eat dinner here often, but sure I'll take them out on the town next week. That would be nice."

"Good. Take 'em somewhere fancy."

"It's a date," she says, and I can tell by her tone of voice that she's smiling. "Now how are things there? How's that girl of yours?"

My mom has suspected there was something going on between Alana and I for a while now. Probably because I speak about her often, even though I never noticed it until Banks pointed it out to me a while back.

"Things are good. We've almost hired all of the editors, so I think we should be good to come back when we're scheduled to. The people at the office here are mostly nice and the editor-in-chief is great. We get along really well."

"That's great sweetie, I'm happy to hear it. I can't wait for you to be back home." She pauses, probably waiting to see if I'll go on, but I don't so she asks, "And Alana? How are things with her?"

"They're really good, Mom," I say, a smile appearing on my face against my will.

"Like...*good*, good? Or just good?"

"Good, good. We're together."

"Oh my goodness, since when?" Her sweet excitement for me squeezes my heart and I wish I was in front of her and sharing this news so I could experience it first hand.

"Not long, it's been a little over a week. We had a maintenance issue at our old apartment and had to move to a much smaller one. It's a one bedroom and I guess it sort of pushed us together." It's true, but it's not the whole truth. Alana did a lot of work to overcome her fears, but that isn't my place to share with my mom.

"And it's going well? I know you've liked her for so long. I just can't believe my baby has a girlfriend!" She's really going for it now. I haven't been in a serious relationship in a while, the last time I was in one was in college and we amicably split ways after a few years.

"Things are going well. I think this one is pretty serious, at least it feels that way, but we'll see when we get back to the States."

"That is just the best news. I can't wait to meet her." I can't wait for my mom to meet Alana, either. She is one of the most welcoming people and was always willing to bring friends into our home and feed them and show them a loving environment. I know Alana is missing that from her parents, and hopefully she'll have the opportunity to mend those eventually, but I'm hopeful that my mom might help ease the sting of those missing relationships in the meantime.

"How's the dynamic between the two of you in regards to that promotion?" This is a great question, and one I don't really know the answer to.

"We've barely discussed it, and I'm a bit worried about it to be honest. She really wants this promotion and I know it would be great for my career, but I don't feel strongly one way or the other. It would feel wrong accepting something when I know I don't really want it. Is that silly, to turn something down that would be an advancement for me?"

"Not if it's not what's best for you, honey. If you'd rather stay in your current position and that's what makes you happiest, *that* would be an advancement just as much as a promotion would be."

She always knows exactly what to say and I'm grateful to have her to lean on and talk through these things with. I take it for granted way too often.

"Thanks for saying that, Mom. I really needed to hear it."

"You're certainly welcome. Just see how it plays out and if you get offered the promotion you can make whatever decision feels right for you."

"I can do that."

"Good. You should get something in the mail pretty soon. I sent something for Alana as well."

"Mom, you didn't have to do that."

"Oh, hush. I can do whatever I want, I'm your mom. Banks helped me take it to the post office and get it sent out."

"Thank you, really," I say, hoping she can feel my sincerity through the phone.

"You're welcome. I'll let you go, I know you have all sorts of things going on there," she says with mischief in her tone. I laugh at her and smile.

"I love you."

"I love you, too, honey."

Alana

It's the night of the company Christmas party and I'm on a video call with Cami, trying to decide what to wear. I've cycled through most of my outfits and I haven't had time to go shopping since we found out about the party, so I don't have many options.

"Are you sure you don't have anything else?" she asks, sounding a bit annoyed by my lack of preparation. "I told you to bring more formal wear."

I glare into the tiny screen propped up on the bathroom counter. Alex is in the living room working on a few things while I get ready. He's wearing a pair of black trousers with a ribbed and collared back sweater. He looks delicious and I'd love nothing more than to skip this party and spend the whole night here with him, but we need to make an appearance at least.

"Yes, I'm sure. I wasn't expecting a party like this."

"Wait!" she yells into the phone. "What about that red Valentino mini dress?"

"Oh my gosh you're right." Instant relief floods me as I go sifting through the closet and find the garment bag hanging in the very back. It's the same color as the closet itself, so when I looked before I totally missed it. "This is perfect. Thank you for convincing me to bring it."

I unzip the bag and look down at the beautiful dress. The bows on the shoulders make me smile, because it seems like bows are Alex and I's thing, and I pull it out of the bag and hang it on the back of the door.

We have this invisible connection, and when I think back to the last year of my life working with him I think that's been true the whole time. Obviously not always in a romantic way, but it's always felt like we were connected. What started as a friendship has slowly grown into more, and now I feel like he knows me better than I know myself and vice versa.

I go back to curling my hair while Cami paints her toes at home. It's around five thirty in the evening here, which means it's lunch time at home. She took the day off today, so it's been nice to be able to video chat with her. Most of the time it's quick texts and phone calls late into the evening for one or both of us.

"Things are still going well with Alex?"

I filled Cami in after the whole *Come here, Alana* moment (I still get chills thinking about it) and I've been keeping her updated since then. She, of course, boasted about how she was right and she knew he was into me and *blah blah blah.* It's been nice to have someone to talk to about all of it.

"Things are really good, Cam. I think I'm starting to fall for him."

Her answering smile is ear to ear and I can't help but return it with one of my own.

"I'm really so proud of you, Lan. I know it was hard easing back into something after he who shall not be named, but you did it. You're thriving and you deserve every single good thing that man is going to give you."

"I love you," I respond, wishing desperately that I could be with her physically right now.

"I love you, bestie friend. Now go get ready and send me a picture of the two of you later."

"Will do, talk to you later."

"Bye."

After I finish my hair and makeup I slip on my dress and start to leave the room, I see the pink and red bow on the counter out of the corner of my eye. I hold it up to the dress, realizing the colors match perfectly. I reach back and fasten it into my hair, smiling at the way it makes me feel to wear something he got for me.

I head to the living room in search of my assistant to zip me up. Upon entering the room, his jaw is slack and his eyes wide as he stares at me.

"You've got to be joking, Alana. You're stunning."

I blush and turn my back to him.

"Zip me up?" He stands quickly and comes straight to me. I turn and I feel his fingertips touching my hair and the bow almost reverently. He presses kisses up my back and slowly drags the zipper up, leaving goosebumps in his wake. "You keep that up and we won't make it to the party," I whisper through giggles.

He chuckles darkly and buries his head in the spot where my neck meets my shoulder, kissing me there. "I don't think that's the threat you think it is, sunshine. You smell incredible, is this a new perfume?"

I hum something like *mmhmm* and tip my head back to give him better access. Eventually he pulls away and saves us both by stepping back and gathering my purse for me. I take it in a daze and sigh happily, taking his arm and following him out of the flat.

The party is being held at a nearby hotel in one of their ballrooms, and it's more extravagant than I anticipated so I'm thankful Alex and I dressed more formally, because we would stick out like a sore thumb if we hadn't.

He's been by my side all night, which I'm thankful for, and we've been introduced to more people than I can count. There's no way I'll remember even half of these names, but I don't think I even need to.

We're gathered around a small cocktail table with Amélie and a few other staff members from the magazine, sipping our drinks and having casual conversation. I spend some time gazing around the room and taking in the various decorations. It's beautiful here. There are real spruce trees scattered all throughout the space, giving it a natural holiday scent, and each tree is decorated with warm white lights and gold ornaments.

There are presents under each tree, covered in beautiful gold and white wrapping paper and topped with bows. It makes me want to sit near one and shake them to see if I can guess what, if anything, is inside. I'm reminded of years with my brother doing that exact thing.

"Right, Lan?" Alex asks and I snap my head towards him, trying to remember what was just asked. "We're eager to get home and get back to work?" he helps.

"Oh, yes absolutely. We've loved our time here, but I'm certainly missing home," I say with a diplomatic smile.

"We will be sad to see the two of you go, I have to say," Amélie chimes in. "Especially you, Alex." He blushes at the attention and tips his head at her in a thank you.

I place my hand on Alex's bicep and he looks down at me with such sincere love in his eyes. I know he hasn't told me yet, but I'm pretty sure I know he feels how special what we have is. We haven't gone public with our relationship yet, but I'm sure the people around us can tell by the way we're practically joined at the hip.

"I'm going to use the ladies' room."

"Let me walk you there," he says and starts to turn away from the table.

"No, I'm alright. It's just right out in the hallway, you stay here. I'll be right back."

"You sure?"

"Positive."

"Come right back."

"Yes, sir, Mr. Ashford." I wink at him and don't miss the way his eyes heat. I head out of the ballroom and into the bathroom, releasing a sigh of relief when it's empty. I need a second to breathe and not be forced to plaster on a smile.

I stand at the mirror for a few minutes and touch up my makeup. Reaching for my phone, I realize I left it at the table with Alex, so I turn and head into one of the stalls. A few moments later I hear the door open and decide I shouldn't hide out in here too much longer.

I'm getting ready to leave the stall when I hear someone who sounds very much like Genevieve. She's speaking in English to whoever else is out there, and at first I don't question that, but a few moments later it becomes clear to me why.

"You should have seen the last article she gave us," she laughs bitterly. "First, she lies and says I told her to write about winter skincare routines. Why would I ever tell her to do that? That is *so* last year."

I roll my eyes at the stall door, bracing myself for whatever else she's about to say. I'm determined to not let her get to me. All she wants is to make me second guess myself, and I have been working so hard these last few weeks to stop doing that very thing.

"Then, she hands in the correct article and it's a disaster. There are countless errors and her writing is *une catastrophe.*" Don't have to know French to understand that one. "I don't even know how she got this job. She clearly has no idea how to do it well."

Ouch. It seems she knows exactly where to hit. I feel the familiar sting of tears welling up in my eyes and my breathing starts to pick up. I notice the early signs of a panic attack, and I'm reminded of the moment with Alex in the office.

"Come on, trust me. I'll count, you breathe."
I take a breath, 1-2-3-4.
"That's my girl, now hold it for seven seconds." I count in my
head. "Now slowly let it out for eight seconds. Okay, good. Let's do it
again, breathe in."

I practice the breathing exercises and it allows me to force the panic and the tears back. *I will not let her get to me.*

"And to think she has that stupid boy wrapped around her finger. Give me five minutes and I bet you I can get him to go home with me."

At that, I decide I've heard enough. She knows I'm in here and I'm done playing her game. She doesn't get to speak about Alex like that. I take a deep breath, then push out of the stall, letting the door slam closed behind me. I walk up to the mirror, pull out my lip gloss, and begin touching up my lips.

"Hello ladies." I say it nonchalantly, like I had no idea they were even there. I can tell Genevieve is annoyed that she didn't get the reaction that she wanted out of me. Too bad. I refuse to fall prey to her schemes. I'm too strong for that.

They don't reply, but I don't need them to. I've made my point. I turn and head out of the bathroom and back into the party. My eyes find the back of Alex as soon as I enter the room, and I smile to myself at the amount of comfort his presence brings. I feel a little off after the whole bathroom situation, but I'm hoping I can keep it under wraps.

I suddenly want everyone here to know that Alex is mine. Maybe it was Genevieve's snarky comments, or maybe I just want to be publicly affectionate, but for whatever reason I walk up to him and plant a kiss right on his cheek.

He startles for a second before he realizes it's me, and then he smiles like I just told him he won the lottery. He slips his hand over my lower back, then drapes it lazily over my hip and pulls me close to him.

Amélie smiles at us from across the table and I try to join in on whatever conversation is taking place, but my mind keeps wandering. I can't get those words out of my head no matter how hard I try. No matter how much I know they aren't true.

I don't even know how she got this job.

She clearly has no idea how to do it well.

Her writing is une catastrophe.

Alex squeezes my hip and the pressure brings me back to the present. "What's wrong?"

"Nothing," I smile up at him, but I know he can tell it isn't real. The longer I look up into his eyes, the longer I wonder why we're even still here. We've come, we've made an appearance, and I didn't run as soon as Genevieve made moves to sabotage my night. I could choose to be done now. "Actually, I just want to go home. Will you take me home?"

"I'll take you anywhere you want to go."

Alex

WE'RE IN THE CAR WITH MARCO AND ON OUR WAY BACK home. My girl is quiet, but I have her pulled close to me and I'm having trouble not asking if she's okay every five seconds. I know she isn't, but she hasn't told me what happened when she left for the bathroom and came back different. Timid and unlike herself.

We get home and I run her a bubble bath. She undresses without much emotion and overall just seems extremely in her head. I stay in the bedroom and allow her privacy as she gets settled in the tub. After a few moments, I hear her voice. It's small and quiet, but she's calling for me.

"Can you come in here?"

I can't say no to the woman, not that I'd want to, so I stand and enter the bathroom. She looks beautiful. Her hair is piled on top of her head, a few tendrils falling out of the messy bun and framing her face, and the bubbles cover her completely. It looks like she's sitting in a cloud.

"I want to tell you about what happened tonight. I know you know something happened." I shake my head in affirmation and make my way to the stool sitting by the clawfoot tub. She pulls her hand out of the water and reaches for mine. "It's really not a big deal," she says.

"I want to know."

"Well, I was in the bathroom and I heard two women walk in. After a few seconds I realized one of them was Genevieve." I tense, knowing this story doesn't have a happy ending. "She was speaking in English so I knew immediately that this was likely some sort of scheme. She just said some hurtful things to try to get to me."

"What did she say?"

"That really isn't important, I don't even want to repeat it. She basically just attacked my ability to do my job, and to be with you."

"To be with me? How did she even know we were together?"

She laughs and raises her eyebrows, giving me a look that says *'It's not that hard to tell.'*

"Okay, fair enough, she figured it out. Why does she think we can't be together?" I can feel the anger building and I try desperately to tamp it down because it isn't helpful in this moment.

Her eyes close and she releases a heavy sigh. "She just thought she could get you to take her home instead of me."

Alana stares at me in shock when I start to laugh hysterically. It's an uncontrollable kind of laughter. After a few seconds, once I finally tame it, I shake my head. "There is absolutely no way I would ever go home with that woman. Most certainly not when given you as a choice over her. Not in a million years, Lanie."

"I know that. It was just hard to hear. It threw me."

I stand now and make my way behind the tub, positioning myself directly behind her upper body. I place my hands on her shoulders and begin to knead them. "I understand, that would be difficult for anyone. How do you feel now?"

"Better now that we're away from her and I'm in this bath. And you're rubbing my shoulders."

"We don't have to go back. We can tell Amélie that we're going to work the rest of the days from home. There aren't that many left."

"No, I don't want to let her win like that. I want to go back in and face her every day and show her how little she affects me."

"That's my girl. I'm proud of you." I rub her shoulders a little longer, then place a kiss on her temple before leaving her to the rest of her relaxation time.

While she finishes up, I head into the living room to make her some chamomile tea. I add a bit of honey and stir, then take it over to the couch. She comes out and sits down next to me, reaching out for the mug that I offer.

She brings it to her lips and breathes, the steam floating around her beautiful face.

We lay there on the couch and she cuddles close. After a few minutes, she asks me to turn on *13 Going on 30* and I do, because I would do anything she asks. We stay out in the living room until the early hours of the morning, and when she's finally fallen asleep in my arms, I carry her to our bed.

CHAPTER 47

Alana

THE LAST TWENTY-FOUR HOURS HAVE BEEN INSANE, AND I'm thankful to not have to worry about anything else between now and Christmas. These are supposed to be my favorite days of the year, so I'm working hard to push back the emotions from yesterday.

This morning we went out and had breakfast at a cute little cafe near our building. Alex ordered for both of us and I sat back and took it all in. It has been a crazy few weeks, but we did it. We came to Paris, took on a huge job and an unfamiliar city, and ended up in each other's arms. If that isn't a success I'm not sure what is. It was a surreal feeling of accomplishment and joy.

Despite my overall happiness, I was still a little off emotionally. I worked really hard to just be okay, but when people get to you it's sometimes difficult to just shake it off. There is one thing I remember Cami doing with me when something similar happened at work a while back.

It had been an awful week and Ian had thrown out every idea we took to him. The pressure was on to get the issue just right and I was really feeling it from all sides. One of the editors under me made a snarky comment about how I clearly wasn't fit for the job if all of our ideas kept getting rejected, and I took it to heart.

Cami followed me inside my apartment that day and shuffled the *Reputation* album, then told me to dance it off. I just stood there in my kitchen, staring at her as she jumped around and flailed her arms. After a few seconds I started to laugh, and after a few more seconds I started to sway side to side, and eventually I began dancing and singing with her.

The dancing didn't magically make all of my problems disappear, but it did help reset my nervous system. The tension in my shoulders eased, it felt easier to smile and joke, and that person's voice stopped echoing in my head.

I was remembering this technique just as we arrived back home, and before I could think much about what I was doing I pulled Alex by the hand into the kitchen and hit play on the same album on my phone.

"This is Why We Can't Have Nice Things" starts playing through my phone's speaker, and I begin dancing and singing along. Alex does the same routine as I did with Cami. First he laughs, then he sways, and finally he dances.

We jump around and scream the lyrics (yes, Alex knows them and yes, I am impressed) and it feels like the most therapeutic thing I've done in a really long time. It feels good to release all of my emotions this way.

After a few songs, *"New Year's Day"* begins to play and he pulls me to him, swaying us back and forth as we listen to the lyrics. He's pressed my body to his firmly and I don't think there's one inch of me that isn't touching him. My head is tucked under his chin and I get an overwhelming feeling of safety. I smile into his chest as the lyrics talk about not wanting to just be around for the fun times, but for all of the messy times as well. It feels like an exact mirror of my feelings. We dance for a while longer in our tiny kitchen with the Eiffel Tower just outside our window, and I feel immense happiness.

Eventually, I drag him to the bedroom and collapse on the bed, pulling him down next to me. I take the longest nap of my life cuddled close to him, and when I wake up, he's still laying next to me. His eyes are open already and fixed on my face, and he reaches over and brushes the hair away from my eyes.

"Do you think we can come back here someday?" I ask, my voice scratchy from sleep. "I feel like we missed out on so much because we were working."

Alex smiles down at me. "We can come back whenever you want." He places a soft kiss on my nose and continues. "Maybe we can make it a tradition. Add it to that list of yours."

"I wouldn't mind a yearly December trip." It feels good to make plans for the future. I notice how different it feels with Alex. He doesn't scoff at my ideas or push them off like I'm being clingy or too much, he listens and he cares. I love him. I want to tell him, but I'm not sure when the right moment is.

"We're going to need to start packing things up soon. We've got stuff everywhere around here," he says as we both stare at our bedroom. There are various items strewn about and he's right, we need to start getting ready to go home.

"I don't want to think about that yet."

"Fair enough," he says before pushing back the covers and sitting up on the side of the bed. "Are you hungry? I can make us some lunch." As soon as he says it, my stomach growls. "Well, I guess there's my answer."

We make our way out into the living room, but I pull him to a stop before we make it to the kitchen.

"I have a question."

"What is it, sunshine?"

"Is that for me?" My eyes move to the present under the tree and his follow.

"It is."

"Is it my pajamas?"

"It is."

"Can I open it?"

He smiles a handsome, crooked smile at me. It's a smile that lights up my insides.

"Sure, but only if that one," he gestures to the gift I wrapped, "is mine."

I reach under the tree and take both presents out, handing his to him and holding mine in my lap.

"You go first," I say.

He begins unwrapping the box and takes his time pulling on the edges of the paper, being careful not to rip it to shreds. He's too delicate with it, to be honest. Usually when I open presents, I dive right in.

He takes the tissue paper out and sets it to the side, then pulls out the pair of pajamas I got him. They're a flannel set of pants and a button up long sleeve shirt, and they're covered in vintage baseball cards. Different baseball legends are littered all across the chest, arms and legs. Players like Babe Ruth, Willie Mays, Hank Aaron, and Jackie Robinson. He turns them over and over in his hands, not speaking for a full minute and making me second guess my decision to honor this part of him.

This is something he shared with his dad and maybe it wasn't the right call to bring this back up in this way.

"Lanie." He swallows and his eyes are glassy. I want to run and hide, I'm so embarrassed. "These are incredible. Where did you get these?"

Thank you sweet baby Jesus.

"I scoured the internet until I found them. You really like them?"

"Like them? Sunshine, I love them. Thank you so much." He leans forward and places a sweet kiss against my lips. "Okay, your turn."

I do the complete opposite of him, and rip into the package like a feral cat. There's shreds of paper all around me, but I don't care. Every other area of my life is organized and neat, but this is the fun part about opening gifts.

I gasp when I pull the silk set he chose out of the box. It's a button up shirt and pants, and they're a vibrant red. The best part, though, is that they're covered in pink bows. The silk is cool to the touch, like a cold pair of sheets you're sliding into after a long day, and I love that he knows I enjoy sleeping in silk. I love that he knows me.

"They look just like my bow," I say as I stare down at them.

"I can't look at bows now without thinking of you."

"They're beautiful, Alex. Thank you. I can't wait to wear them tomorrow."

"I can't wait to see you in them," he says with a wink.

Later that evening, Alex makes dinner and we play a board game. Around midnight, he makes ice cream sundaes, topped with whipped cream, caramel sauce, sprinkles, and a cherry. We sit criss-cross on the couch, facing each other, eating ice cream and laughing about embarrassing stories from our childhood.

I never thought I'd have this. I thought I had it once, and then I lost in a way that made me believe it didn't exist for me. I believed that lie for so long, but all it took was the right man with incredible patience and love to waltz into my life and shake it up for the better.

CHAPTER 48

Alex

It's Christmas Eve and Alana is so giddy. It's adorable.

She has this bounce in her step everywhere she goes and a smile plastered on her face that I don't think could be wiped off even if I tried. Not that I ever would.

She's out shopping right now, and she told me I had to stay here because she might find something that I can't see. We didn't discuss getting gifts for each other this year, but I got her one anyway.

I'm working on packing up a few of my things when my phone rings. Heather is calling, and seeing her name reminds me that I need to let her know I'd like to remove myself from the running for the promotion. Now's as good a time as any.

"Heather, how are you?"

"Hi, Alex," she says, her voice chipper and light. "I'm doing quite well, how about yourself?"

"Things are pretty good here."

"I'm glad to hear it. How's our girl doing?"

"She's doing well. Excited for the upcoming holiday."

"Good, that's good to hear." The line goes quiet for a minute before she speaks again. "Listen, Alex, are you alone?"

My stomach sinks. That can't be good.

"Yeah, I am. What's going on?"

"Well, I have some exciting news for you." *No, no, no.* "We'd like to offer you a promotion, but probably not the one you're thinking of."

Oh.

"Amélie has thoroughly enjoyed working with you and has been singing your praises to Ian and I, and she asked us a few weeks ago if we'd be open to sharing you with her. At first I was an absolute no, but Ian spoke with me and explained that this might be a really great career move for you."

I'm speechless, but it's okay because she keeps going.

"I know you were hoping for a promotion here in New York, but we're planning on offering that to Alana. I'd appreciate it if you let me share that good news with her, though."

"Wow, Heather. That's an honor that Amélie would want me here. I really appreciate the offer."

My heart rate is running a mile a minute, but I think back on the words she just said and realize that Alana is getting the promotion she wants. I can't wait for her to find out; she's going to be so excited. Her hard work really paid off.

"Absolutely, you earned it. I know it would be a big change, but it would come with a raise in salary and more responsibilities. Plus you'd get to live in Paris, which is a total dream. You'd of course get a relocation package so you can get settled and be comfortable, but I'm getting ahead of myself. You think about it, I'll send you an email with the offer later today so you can look it over, and then get back to me sometime next week."

"Okay, that sounds good. Thank you again for checking in and for the news."

"Of course, merry Christmas."

"Merry Christmas, Heather."

The line goes silent, and I'm frozen in place trying to process everything I just heard.

They want me to move to Paris.

They want Alana in New York.

No. Absolutely not that is not happening. I just got her and there is no way I'm losing her now. Plus, I have loved my time in Paris and with Amélie these last few weeks, but my home is in New York. I'd be way too far from my mom and from Banks, and I know no one here. It just doesn't make sense to even consider it.

Decision made, I stand and continue packing my clothes. I decide I'll go ahead and let Heather send the offer over and then respond to her sometime next week officially declining and asking to remain in my current role.

An hour later, Alana comes waltzing into the flat with bags lining her arms. She looks so happy, and I realize that Heather must have called her while she was out.

"Have fun?" I ask as she sets all of her bags down on our bed.

"I did, and I have some really great news."

"Oh really, what's that?"

"Heather called..."

"Really dragging it out there, Lanie."

"She just had some news for me." The humor in her eyes makes me smile.

"Any day now."

"I got the promotion! You're looking at the new managing director of *Impress*." She drops the bags at her feet and runs towards me, jumping into my arms with an excited squeal. It's adorable and I realize there is no way I can ruin this moment for her and bring my Paris promotion into it.

"Lanie, that is incredible. I knew you'd get it. I am so proud of you." I set her feet back on the ground and kiss her. I am so excited for her, she deserves this opportunity more than anyone.

It feels wrong to not tell her about my promotion, but I don't want to steal any of her joy and I know I'll have an opportunity to tell her about it soon. I plan to turn it down anyways, so it can wait.

We have plans tonight to cook dinner together and then watch a few holiday movies to ring in the special day.

Before it gets too late, I decide to head out and grab one more gift I had my eye on for my mom, and she decides to get to work on the prep for the cinnamon rolls we're going to bake tomorrow. Apparently there is some mixing of dough and things to do the day before so it can rise properly overnight.

I walk out into the kitchen and see her standing there with her dark brown hair piled on top of her head and the cutest pink apron tied around her curvy hips. I imagine a world in which this happens every year and then I imagine her in a few years with little feet running around in the flour and small hands helping her knead the dough.

I smile at the thought.

"I'm going to run out and grab that gift for my mom."

"That's sweet of you. I'd kiss you but I think I have flour all over me." She laughs and a cloud of white pillows around her, which causes her to laugh more. I lean in for a kiss anyways and then head out the door.

Alana

I SMILE AS I POUR THE YEAST INTO A BOWL OF WARM water and wait, watching it bubble. After everything that happened at the holiday party, I wasn't sure I would be able to muster up enough Christmas magic to make these days as special as I wanted them to be. My phone call with Heather did the trick, though. Plus the kitchen dancing last night.

Despite all of the good news, every so often my mind likes to remind me of the things Genevieve said, and every time I tell it to shut up. It's getting exhausting, but I know eventually it'll get easier.

I've decided to put all of that out of my head, though, because today is Christmas Eve and I couldn't be more excited. I have tried calling Charlie a few times today to wish him a happy Christmas Eve and just spend some time with him, albeit virtually, but he isn't answering any of my calls. He's probably holed up with some girl he took home, and it's annoying. I try to put that out of my mind too and stay in the present moment. I'll talk to him eventually.

My pink and red pajamas are sitting on my bed waiting for me and I plan to slip them on and cozy up by the fireplace as soon as I get these cinnamon rolls prepped.

It's important to mix all the ingredients for the dough the night before, that way it has enough time to rise. Sometimes I do that two days before and then I go ahead and add the filling, roll and cut them ahead of time, that way I can just place them in the oven Christmas morning. This year though, I thought it would be fun for Alex and I to do that part together, so I'm just getting the dough done.

Before long, I've got everything mixed up and the bowl greased. I place the dough into the bowl and grab a kitchen towel to cover it. As I'm placing the bowl into the fridge to rise overnight, I hear my phone chime. Turning back around, I pick it up and glance at the screen but realize it isn't my phone, it's Alex's. He must have left his here by accident.

I never snoop on his phone, I've never felt the need, but my eyes have already seen the email notification that's come through. It's from Heather and the subject line says Promotion Offer. The preview of the email shocks me further.

To: alex@impress.com
  From: heather@impress.com
  Subject: Paris Relocation Promotion Offer
  Email: Alex, Thank you for the phone call today. I am excited about...

I can't see the rest, because his phone is still locked and I don't even want to read it. I drop the phone like it's a hot poker and take a few steps back, trying to rationalize this in my head. No matter what way I turn it over and over, I can't make it fit.

Alex wouldn't keep this from me...*would he?* My initial sadness is because of the word 'Paris' in that email, but after a few seconds I realize I'm more crushed that he's keeping secrets from me. This relationship is new, but I never thought this is something he would do.

I look at the clock and realize he's probably going to be home any minute. I can't process this information here, and I need to think before I confront him with a conversation. I need to figure out my feelings about this before I'm forced into that.

I rush into the bedroom and pull out a bag, then throw random items inside. I'm not even sure what I'm grabbing, all I know is I need to get out before he gets home and convinces me to stay. I don't even realize there are tears streaming down my face until they land in splashes on the bathroom counter as I'm gathering my toiletries. I ignore them and continue packing. I need to go somewhere where I can breathe, where I won't see him everywhere I turn. I am certain I'm in love with him at this point, but if he's going to keep secrets from me, I don't know if we're going to work.

I spot the pajamas he got me and pause before grabbing them and throwing them in too. Even though I need space to think, it'll be nice to have him with me in one small way.

I quickly look up the nearest hotel on my phone and call them. I'm aware that it's Christmas Eve, so finding a hotel room might be difficult, but I need to try. After three different no's, I get a yes and book the room without thinking twice about it.

Before I leave, I scribble out a note for him and leave his phone right by it, then I shut the door behind me and climb into the car with Marco. I give him the address to the hotel and he only flashes me a look of concern before climbing into the front seat and driving me there.

CHAPTER 50

Alex

It's too quiet and still when I enter the flat. I set the shopping bag to the side and walk a bit further in, trying to figure out what's going on.

"Alana?" I call out. Nothing.

I rush into the bedroom, but she's not there either. Suddenly an image flashes before my eyes of her passed out on the bathroom floor, but I don't find her there either. What is going on? I reach for my phone to call her, but it isn't in my pocket. I haven't had a need for it the entire time I've been out, so I didn't realize it wasn't with me.

I walk into the living room to see if it's in there, but nope.

I head into the kitchen and that's when I see it. My phone, and a note sitting next to it. Her handwriting is sloppy, like she was in a hurry, and my heart drops when I notice the ink is smudged from what looks like water. Was she crying?

I pick the note up, dread growing with every word I read.

Alex,

I went to a hotel for the night to think. I saw

the email on your phone, I promise I wasn't snooping I just thought it was mine, and I got scared. I need time to process before we talk. This isn't me giving up. This isn't me breaking up with you. I will be back, I promise, I just need a minute to think.

The name and address of the hotel is on the back of this note, and I have my phone with me. Please don't reach out unless it's urgent. I need a little time.

Lanie

Her use of the nickname I gave her at the end helps me breathe a little easier, but I'm still freaking out. I pick my phone up to try and figure out what could have upset her and cringe the moment I see the email from Heather. I curse under my breath. She probably thinks I'm planning on leaving her and my heart breaks at the realization. Everyone in her life has left, and I can't bear the thought of her thinking I would. It's not what she thinks it is, but regardless it is a secret I kept from her. This looks really, really bad and I want to respect her request for alone time, but I also really want to explain this to her.

I do the next best thing and click Charlie's name, then bring it to my ear to wait for him to pick up. His flight should be landing right around now and I need him to come to my rescue.

"Hey man, I just landed. I'm grabbing my luggage and then I'll go look for your fancy driver guy."

"Hey Charlie, I'm glad you landed safe, that sounds good. I need you to do me a favor though."

"What's going on? You sound weird."

"Alana left."

There's silence on the phone for a good ten seconds before he speaks again.

"What do you mean she left? What did you do?"

I explain the situation to him, but I leave out the news about her promotion. I want her to be able to share that with him herself.

The idea of her choosing to end our relationship when it only just started makes my skin crawl, but I cling to the words she wrote in her letter. *This isn't me giving up. This isn't me breaking up with you. I will be back, I promise.*

I give Charlie the address of the hotel and tell him I'll give Marco a call and let him know as well. He doesn't say much about the whole situation, which leaves me feeling uneasy. At this point, he's my only in with Alana right now. I'm hoping he understands my situation and at least explains the whole thing to her, so she can have all of the information needed to make whatever choice she needs to make.

I walk into the bedroom after hanging up the phone and notice her pajamas are gone. Longing clenches my chest as I realize she must not be too mad at me, if she chose to bring those. I wish I could see her in them and pull her close. I already miss her and she hasn't been gone for more than an hour or so.

I'm wandering aimlessly around the flat, too restless to sit still and mind running too fast to let me rest. Moving into the kitchen, I realize that she's measured out all of the ingredients for the cinnamon rolls tomorrow and left me detailed instructions. My heart squeezes at her thoughtfulness and my eyes grow misty at the ghost of her floating around this space.

I finally sit down in the living room and turn on the television to a random Hallmark movie. I try to pay attention but I can't. I'm counting on Charlie to comfort his sister and hopefully help me out in the process.

CHAPTER 51
Alana

The first thing I did when I walked into this extremely lavish hotel room was cry. After writing my note to Alex, measuring out the ingredients for him—because I couldn't not—and leaving the flat, I dried up my tears. I didn't want to startle Marco and I also wanted to keep the tears at bay, but for some reason walking through the door to this room was like removing a dam and the tears haven't stopped since.

I slipped on my pajamas a little while ago and that made me cry harder. I washed my face and my tears mixed with the warm water I splashed all over my face. Then I decided I would get in the shower, because crying in the shower doesn't count, but that didn't help much. Now I just look a bit like a drowned rat. My hair has somewhat dried and my face is splotchy and I know if someone saw me right now they'd be terrified.

That is why the apology is already on my lips when I open the door to my room for my chocolate cake I ordered from room service, except I don't find chocolate cake, I find my brother.

My brother is standing in front of me, in Paris, holding onto a suitcase and a backpack and the tears start falling faster. I'm sobbing uncontrollably now, big ugly gasping sobs and Charlie finally steps forward and wraps me in his arms.

I am immediately soothed feeling his arms around me and I let all of the emotions from the last few days out. He walks me back into the room and we sit on the bed together. He lets me cry into him for who knows how long, and eventually when my sobs have quieted into small hiccups, I speak.

"How are you here?"

"There's this thing, it's really cool. You get inside and it flies you anywhere you want to go."

I swat at him with the back of my hand, but a small smile slips past my lips and I think that was what he was going for.

"Your boyfriend flew me here," he says, and the words shock me. I'm just staring at him, and then I'm staring just past him as I try to reconcile this truth with what I learned about Alex a few hours ago.

"What do you mean he flew you here? All of this only just happened."

"The trip has been planned for a few weeks. He wanted to complete the last thing on your list."

The last thing on my list. Bake homemade cinnamon rolls *with Charlie* on Christmas morning. He knew I was sad about not being with Charlie for the holidays, so he spent his own money to fly him here for me, even though we're going to be home in six days.

I squeeze Charlie around his middle again, burying my face in his shoulder.

"I can't believe you're here. I missed you so much."

"I missed you too, Lan. It's really good to see you." He hesitates. "You gonna tell me what's got you looking like that?" His eyes sweep up and down my body in a judgmental way and I scoff.

"I saw something on Alex's phone and got scared." He shakes his head in understanding. "Did he tell you?"

"He did."

"What did he say?"

"Well I think you might have a few things twisted up since you don't have the full story, but I want to hear what's going on in that head of yours. Then we can talk about what he said if you want. I'm here for you, not him. If you decide you want to talk to him about the situation, he needs to be the one to explain it to you."

"I'm just scared. I don't want to have to come back from heartbreak again. I'm worried about him taking this promotion and staying here while I'm in New York. It would be awful. Plus he didn't tell me about it."

Charlie strokes my hair and smiles at me sympathetically.

"Lan, I think you're maybe getting ahead of yourself here. Did he keep information from you? Yes. Should he have told you when he found out? Maybe. I also think he deserves a little time to download that information before sharing it. It's not like he kept it a secret for months."

"I guess you're right. I just don't want to jump into something if he's not fully in it either."

"I think you and I both know Alex is in this."

I nod my head, he's right. Alex is fully in this, he has been since before I even was, and that fact is what helped me feel secure enough to take the leap initially.

"It's so frustrating. I just want to stop being scared and throw caution to the wind, but then when I try, something like this happens."

Charlie chuckles at me. "You can stop being scared, while still being cautious. Those two things are not synonymous. I admire the way you look out for yourself and think before you make moves, it keeps you safe. Sometimes the right decision is the scary one, and you can step into that while still being aware of what is going on around you."

"I hadn't ever thought about it that way before. I was committed to just doing it even though I was afraid, but part of my fear was because it felt reckless."

"I think that's a common misunderstanding, but think about how much you'd get to experience if you stopped being scared. Or you let yourself be scared, but you did it anyway. You didn't let the fear win."

You let yourself be scared, but you did it anyway. That is what I want. That's what I'm trying to do.

"How do you do that?"

"I'm not totally sure. I think it looks different in every situation. What do you think it looks like in this one?"

I think over that for a second, trying to decipher what exactly it is I'm scared of.

"I think it would be giving this relationship my all, even though I know I might lose it one day. Diving in head first, even though I know it might end up hurting in the end."

Charlie nods his head and narrows his eyes, something he does when he's thinking.

"What would happen if you ended up hurting in the end?" he asks a few moments later. I tense. I haven't let myself think this far, I've just pushed it away and put it somewhere I don't have to acknowledge it. But for the first time, I let myself go there.

"If I ended up hurt, it would probably suck for a while."

"Uh huh, and what else?"

"I might have to find a place to live if we moved in together and that would be weird."

"Sure, anything else?"

"Work might be weird for a while, but Alex and I are mature so it would probably be okay."

"Good. Then after all that, what would happen to you?"

"I'd be okay."

He smiles at me. I sit on those words. I'd be okay, I know I would be. Would it be a crushing weight for a while and would I have nights where I cry myself to sleep? Probably. But I'd come out on the other side.

"I'd be okay and I would have had an incredible experience with an incredible person and we would have great memories."

"You would."

"I think I need to go home."

He chuckles and throws a pillow at me. "I think you do too. But first let's hang out for a little bit. I stopped downstairs and asked them to send a pizza up."

"Oh, and I ordered chocolate cake."

CHAPTER 52
Alana

ALEX DID WHAT I ASKED AND HASN'T TEXTED OR called. While I appreciate him being respectful, I also miss him. It hasn't even been more than a few hours and I miss him.

Charlie and I watched a movie and ate dinner. It lifted my spirits, and I was feeling so much better by the time I left. He told me he'd stay in the hotel room tonight and come meet us in the morning, that way we'd have some time to talk.

I'm sitting in the back of the car now, and I'm sure Marco is just itching for all of the juicy details of what went down tonight, considering he's been carting all of us all around town today. We arrive at the building and butterflies are swarming in my stomach. I don't know why I'm nervous.

I make my way up to our door and push inside. Alex stands abruptly from the couch and rushes to me, wrapping me in his arms and kissing all over my face. It's like he's trying to prove to himself that I'm real, that I'm actually here and this isn't a figment of his imagination.

I'm wearing my pajamas, something Maura pointed out as I passed her desk on my way in, and he notices a few seconds later.

"What are you doing here? I missed you. These look great on

you. Can we talk?" He's frantic and I feel bad. I know my leaving might not have been the best reaction, but it felt like the only thing I could do in the moment and I know he'll understand that.

"I'm sorry I left."

"No, don't be sorry. I'm the one who's sorry."

He leads me into the living room where he mutes the TV and we sit down side by side on the couch. He immediately changes our position, pulling me to sit on his lap and face him. It's like he can't get me close enough. The feeling is mutual.

"Can you tell me about that email?" I ask in a voice smaller than I'd like.

"Absolutely. I'm so sorry you saw that and I wasn't here to explain it to you." He hesitates, playing with the hem of my pajama shirt and not meeting my eyes. "They offered me the managing editor position here, at *Impress Europe*. Heather just called me about it, probably around the same time she called you."

I let that sink in. My instinct is to think he's going to leave me, but I rein that in and make an effort to stay present. Even if he decided to take the promotion, I know I want what's best for him, so if he did leave we could make it work if we had to,

"Are you going to take it? I wouldn't stop you if you wanted to. That would be an incredible career move for you." Even as I say the words, tears threaten to fall. I am so excited for him, but I'm also incredibly sad. Long distance would be extremely tough and I'm not even sure I'd want to do that, but if he wanted to try, I would do it.

"No, Lanie, I don't want to take it."

"Are you sure? I would support you, you know I would."

He brings my hands to his mouth and kisses them, a sweet gesture full of appreciation. "I absolutely know you would, but I like my job. I don't want it to change, even if that means a better title and a higher salary. Plus there's no way I'm leaving you now that I've got you."

"If you're sure."

"Can't get rid of me that easily. Plus, I have to be around to watch your rise to power. Managing Director Alana Cade has a nice ring to it."

I feel heat rise to my cheeks and lean forward, burying my face in his neck and snuggling into him.

"I'm sorry I kept it from you," he whispers into my hair. "You were so happy about your promotion when you got home and it didn't feel like the right time to say something. I didn't want to ruin the moment."

"I understand why you waited, but I also wish you would've told me."

"I know. I'm sorry."

"Apology accepted."

I pull back and he kisses me. It's so passionate, like he's pouring all of his emotion into it. I can feel his gratitude, his love, his pride. It warms me up from the inside out and I hope we never lose this feeling.

He pulls back and stares lovingly into my eyes, and I can see our entire future right there in those beautiful green eyes. A home we'll share, walks to work together, cooking dinner on a weeknight, little babies running around, Christmas morning cinnamon rolls, the whole nine yards. I can picture it all with this man.

"I love you." I don't think, I just say it. I don't give it a ton of thought or work out the ways he might respond. I don't fret over whether he'll reject me or if he won't return the sentiment. I know he will because I know him. I know every bit of his heart and he's taken the time to know mine.

"Say it again," he demands before kissing me passionately.

"I love you." I kiss him again. "I love you." And again. "I love you."

He smiles at me, his eyes warm and his face soft.

"I love you, Lanie. I've loved you for longer than I think I even realized. I'm all tied up in you," he says as he reaches back and tugs on the ribbon in my hair.

"I wouldn't have it any other way."

CHAPTER 53

Alex

Six Months Later

We've been back home for a few months now, and I don't know how life could get better at this point. After Alana came back to the flat and we talked things out, we had a wonderful Christmas morning with Charlie full of presents, movie watching, and of course, cinnamon rolls.

We dated for a few months after we got home before we decided to move in together. It felt weird going from essentially living together, to being apart, and neither one of us liked it. We found an apartment near the office that has enough space for the both of us and we have a guest room in case Banks or my mom ever comes into town.

When we got home, we discovered that Brad wasn't doing as great as he claimed in the money department, despite his fancy job, and had attempted to commit insurance fraud. He's living it up in a six by eight foot cold room, so I don't think I'll have to worry much about him anymore.

Alana was able to reach out to her parents and speak with them about how their traveling has affected her. I don't know if it was the best conversation they could've had, but I was proud of her for trying and opening the door.

I decided to get in contact with my dad and try to get some closure. It took a few calls, but I was finally able to get a hold of him. It was relieving and terrifying all at the same time. We're planning to meet up sometime within the next couple months.

Alana has been killing it in her new role. She took Ian's spot when he left and everyone has been so proud of the transition she's made. I always knew she'd do an incredible job, I think she just needed to prove it to herself.

We're about halfway through the year, and she's already planning out the activities for this holiday season. We have a trip back to Paris planned for early December, and we somehow convinced Maura to let us stay in our small flat there in the building. It was still empty, by some miracle, and the timing just worked out.

I've been speaking with the building owner about possibly purchasing that particular unit, but nothing has been finalized yet. I think it would make for a great Christmas present this year though.

We're discussing getting a dog and of all the things we've done together in the last six months, I think that is what Alana is most excited about. We're planning on heading to the local shelter later this week to pick one out.

It's been busy at work since we got home, but it's felt great to be back in the swing of things. I missed my team and the routines I have here. I'm on my way into a meeting with Heather and Alana, but I stop by the break room first to grab her Diet Coke.

I enter the meeting room where they are discussing our latest issue, her first one as managing editor. The response was incredible and Heather has been singing Alana's praises ever since.

I crack open the Diet Coke and set it on the table in front of her, then place a chocolate square next to it.

"Thanks, honey." She leans over for a kiss, and I oblige. She's become way more comfortable showing affection in the office, and I love it.

Heather was extremely receptive when we told her about our relationship. She seemed to have even been expecting that we might be delivering that news, and I wonder how much she picked up on before we left. Perhaps the selection of the two of us was intentional in more ways than one, not that she's ever said that to me outright. I'm thankful regardless.

We start the meeting and I get lost in thought as I watch Alana run it seamlessly. She is so incredible and I find myself in awe of her daily. Her strength, bravery, and beauty are astounding, and I will keep telling her that every day of her life.

On our way out, we stop by Cami's desk and make dinner plans with her and Charlie. I've also become a regular at *Angel's* and I'm honored to be included in the weekly dinners now.

I follow her into her office and shut the door behind me. She gives me a scolding look before I've even made a move to kiss her and I laugh.

"What? I haven't even done anything."

"You don't have to. I can see it in your eyes."

I take a step forward and she takes one back. I take two, she backs up two. Eventually I rush her and catch her around her waist, pulling her into me and kissing her deeply.

"Stop," she says halfheartedly. "I have so much work to get done. You can't distract me. Plus *you've* got work to do too," she says, and gives me her best *I'm your boss and you do what I say* look.

"Okay, boss. Whatever you say." I kiss her one more time for good measure and start to head out.

"Alex."

I turn back towards her. "Yeah, sunshine?"

"I love you." She smiles.

"I love you too."

Epilogue

ALANA

SEVEN YEARS LATER

The house is in total chaos, and I've been trying extremely hard to get us out of here on time. It seems like we're always late these days, and I attribute it to the little monster running around here somewhere. Motherhood took away the last of my control freak tendencies, and now I'm just accustomed to the chaos.

I'm curling my hair in our bathroom and Alex is taking the dog on a walk before we leave. It's Christmas Eve, and we always tend to be away at his mom's house until late in the evening on holidays. We moved to Texas a few years ago to be closer to her and it's been a great shift for us. Alex's best friend Banks always brings his family, Charlie and Cami of course attend, and the crowd has grown through the years. There's usually a gift exchange, card games, Christmas carols, and movie watching plus whatever his mom added to the lineup this year. She tends to find new things for us to do each year.

"Mom!" Charlotte, our five year old, yells and I hear her feet pitter patter down the hall to our room. "Where's Santa now?"

About a year after we got married, we were surprised with little

321

Charlotte, named after my brother—a fact he never lets us forget. She's asked me about Santa's whereabouts no less than fifteen times today, but I wouldn't dull her excitement for anything. It heals something in me to see her so giddy about the holidays, and I love experiencing it all through her eyes.

"Let me finish curling my hair first and then I'll check, okay?"

"Okay," she says with a firm nod and then salutes me before walking out of the room and back to wherever she was before. I'm not sure when the saluting started or who taught it to her, but it's adorable and makes me laugh every time she does it.

Kids are funny like that. If they discover something that makes you laugh, they'll do it on repeat just to see you break out in giggles again. It's kind of sweet when you think about it.

Not five minutes later, I hear her coming again. I take my phone out and pull up the Santa tracker, knowing that's what she's going to ask, and get to it right as she enters.

"Mom, did you check?"

"Sure did, it looks like he's in Australia right now."

"Aster-rail-ee-ya. Woooow."

"I know. He's getting closer." I lean down and press a kiss into her chocolate brown hair, my mini-me in every sense of the word. "Why don't you go and get your dress? Bring it here and I'll help you put it on."

"I can put it on all by myself. I'm big now because I'm five."

"Oh goodness, how could I forget. Okay you put it on yourself then and come let me know if you need help."

She salutes me again and runs out of the room and down towards hers.

A few minutes later I hear the front door chime and Alex making his way up the stairs. He stands in the doorway to the bathroom watching me, and I pretend not to notice for a few minutes, letting him look his fill.

"How did I get so lucky?" he eventually asks before walking

over to me and wrapping his arms around my waist, placing kisses on my neck.

"Charlotte is going to be back any minute. No funny business." I squirm a little, trying to move him off of me. After getting a few more kisses in, he pulls away.

"Yes ma'am," he says, then salutes me. Well, that's where that came from I guess.

Just like I said, Charlotte comes running in a minute later. She's in her Christmas dress that she picked out for this year, it's red and has a fluffy skirt that '*swirls when she spins*'. She's got something behind her back, although I can't quite tell what it is.

"Daddy!"

"Hey princess, you look absolutely beautiful." She blushes and rocks back and forth on her feet, glowing under her dad's praise. "Whatcha got there?"

"I found it in Mommy's closet. Can I wear it?"

My eyes are immediately misty when she pulls the bow out from behind her back. It's a little worn now, but it's still in incredible shape. I wore it for a while after Alex and I got together, but eventually wanted to keep it safe, so I put it in my keepsakes box. She must have found it when she was snooping around, as she's been doing more and more often lately.

Alex takes the bow from her hands reverently, turning it over in his hand and inspecting it.

"I think it would be really special if you wore this tonight. What do you think?" he asks me, making sure I'm okay with taking it out of the keepsake box and back into the world.

"I think that's a great idea."

I watch as Charlotte spins and Alex takes his time tying in her hair, like he did for me once upon a time. I'm transported back to a time when my mom tied a bow like this in my hair, and the significance of my daughter wearing one now isn't lost on me. It's surreal and almost an out of body experience, watching this happen.

He finishes tying it and spins her back around.

"You look perfect. Why don't you go and put your shoes on?"

She takes off running for her shoes and he reaches out for me. He wraps me up in his arms and tucks me under his chin.

"I'm lucky to be living this life with you, Lana. I love you so much."

"I love you, Ashford."

Acknowledgments

My first book...done just like that. Insanity. Writing and publishing this book has been a dream come true and some of the most fun I've ever had. If someone told me a year and a half ago that I would someday be a published author, I would've laughed in their face.

In March of 2023, an author I admire posted on her Instagram story giving advice to aspiring authors. I responded to one saying I always wanted to write a book, but never had the courage. It always felt like some far away dream that wouldn't ever be fulfilled. She responded with *everyone should write a book,* and I decided at that moment I was going to make this dream a reality. Without that push I don't know that I ever would have started.

While starting was probably the hardest part, pushing myself to keep going was a completely separate beast. There were many days during that first draft that I felt like this book might not ever see the light of day. After so many times of saying 'if this book ever gets published,' my people kindly called me out and I went from saying *if* to saying *when.*

There are so many people who have helped make this happen, it feels impossible to fit them all into a few paragraphs, but I'll try.

First, thank you to Lex who has stuck by me throughout this entire process. Thank you for listening to my countless voice memos, helping me work out never ending ideas and being the very best hype woman. Your encouragement kept me going when I felt like quitting and you believed in me even when I didn't. I'll love you forever for it. Oh and also for my pink bow blanket.

To my alpha readers: Lex, Robin and Taylor, and my beta readers: Natasha, Alicia, Taylor and Kate, THANK YOU! Thank you for taking the time when my book was a hot mess and helping me sort it out. Thank you for screaming how much you loved Alex and Alana and their besties in your google doc comments. Thank you for supporting me and giving your time. I am forever grateful.

A huge thank you to Kristen for editing this bad boy. Your kindness and willingness to share ideas and help me set timelines and goals as a baby author was so helpful and I can't thank you enough.

To Bailey, the incredible and talented woman who owns Wildflower Fiction, I can't say enough thank yous. Thank you for offering to host my pre-orders and making a dream of mine come true. Thank you for being your authentic self and sharing all of life's ups and downs. Most of all, thank you for your encouragement. If you, the reader, have not explored her bookstore you absolutely need to. You can find her on Instagram at @wildflowerfiction.

To all of my advanced readers who took the time to apply, read and review this book, I am eternally grateful. Thank you for sharing, posting, and talking about my books with your friends. If I could give you all a lifetime supply of Diet Coke I would, but alas we live in an imperfect world.

A huge thank you to Sam at Ink and Laurel for designing my INCREDIBLE cover. You blew my expectations out of the water with your art and brought the characters in my head out into the world, and I will forever be grateful for that. You are so talented and it was a privilege to work with you.

All of my love to my friends and family who listened to me talk and talk about this book—marketing, posting, editing, the cover—so much. Specifically to my momma, dad, sister, brother-in-law and bestie, Starr. Thank you and I love you. You all are invaluable.

Basically, what I'm trying to say is THANK YOU!!! If Alex were here, he would give everyone chocolates and forehead kisses.

So...what do you say we do this all again? *Read on for a Sneak Peek of Cami and Charlie's fake dating romance!*

Chapter One

Charlie

"Bottom line, you're going to get traded if you don't make the people love you. You're a storm cloud of grumpy and mysterious, and while that was intriguing to the public for the first few years, they've forgotten about you now."

Sophie is the best agent money can buy, and trust me there's a lot of money involved, but right now I want to wring her neck. I'm coming up on a contract year with the New York Rangers and she seems to think the only way I'll stay with them through the end of my career is if I brush up my public image.

She isn't wrong, I guess. I would say the state of my image right now is...nonexistent. I don't have one. I don't go out, I don't have friends besides my sister and Cami, I don't join the team for post-game bar crawls, and I don't date. If I can stay out of the tabloids, I'm happy. There's nothing to talk about because I do nothing. It's easier that way.

Except now, if I want to be a part of the elite group of players in the National Hockey League who stay with the same team their entire career I need to step it up. Not being traded at some point within a player's career is not the norm, but when I signed on with the New York Rangers in my senior year of college, I knew I had to defy the odds.

I had found a solid organization with a solid coaching team and from what I experienced, the guys weren't bad. I wanted to get comfortable there, but not too comfortable, and do what I needed to in order to stay under the radar. Not only from the media, but from my team as well. The last time I got close with my teammates, it didn't end well. I promised myself I would never put myself in that position ever again. If I get traded, I might get stuck with teammates like *them*, and that can't happen.

So as much as I wish what Sophie was saying wasn't true, I know it is.

"And how do you suppose I do that, Soph? I don't like *the people*." I use my hands to put quotations around the words and Sophie rolls her eyes, done with my drama.

"Charlie, we both know you aren't this grumpy, surly, mean man that you present to the world. Underneath it all you're just a giant teddy bear." She reaches up and squeezes my arms. I swat her hands away. "To the world you're just another big scary hockey player with a nice face, and we have to change that. We need to make you one of *the* faces of the Rangers, that way there's no way to separate you from them. When people think of the Rangers, they think of you."

She's not wrong, I don't let anyone see the softer side. I used to, but once someone takes advantage of your kindness and vulnerability and uses it against you...it's hard to come back from that.

Sophie is one of the few people who get this version of me, this more open and lively version, and she's earned that place in my life. When I graduated college I had lots of men in their forties and fifties wanting to work with me as my agent, but the barely five foot blonde in a kick ass pantsuit caught my attention immediately. She's young, in her thirties, and beautiful, but that isn't what caught my eye. The way she held herself and spoke about her craft showed confidence and maturity, plus she was a woman in a male dominated field. That in and of itself was impressive.

"I guess you're right."

"My two favorite words," Sophie says with a wink. I scoff.

"So what do I do?"

"You need to start dating someone."

Excuse me?

"*No*. Dating someone? How is that the first solution you jumped to?"

"Charlie, come on." She says the words like it's ridiculous that she needs to explain it to me. "Love sells, I mean look at Taylor and Travis. If the media starts to see you with a girl that's charismatic and spunky on your arm, you are sure to catch their attention. Especially because you never date. It'll be front page news and then, once they're hooked, you can keep showing them the softer side of you. They'll love you."

That is my problem. I don't want anyone else to see the softer side of me. My soft side is reserved for a very small group of people who have earned their way there and the media is nowhere on that list.

"Sophie, I don't think this is the best solution. Plus, you know I don't date. I don't even know where I'd start with trying to find someone to date."

"Okay, so I'll make you a few profiles on dating sites," she says, completely ignoring my first comment. "*Honey Love* apparently is doing really well right now. Their success rate is a solid thirty percent."

"You do hear yourself, right?" She smacks my shoulder with the back of her hand. "*Honey Love*? A success rate of thirty percent?"

"Well, it's better than *Grab n' Go*," she scoffs.

"There's a dating app called *Grab n' Go*?" She nods her head solemnly. "I don't even want to know what that is referring to."

"Don't go to their website. You don't want to know."

"You don't have to tell me twice."

I run my fingers through my hair and swipe my palm down my face, releasing a frustrated groan. It's irritating that this is my current reality, but I can't help but feel grateful. I've been with the Rangers for seven years now, which is really unheard of. Hockey players don't stay in one place for long. There are only around 120 something guys that stay with the same team their whole career and I'm determined to be one of them.

Not only do I want to stay with teammates I've grown comfortable with and somewhat trust not to turn their backs on me, I don't want to leave my sister. Alana and I had an interesting childhood with parents who did the bare minimum when it came to loving us. They showed their love to me far more than they did to my sister, and the more they showed me favor the more I resented them. Now, she's the only close family I have and it's the same for her. If I move away from the Rangers, I'd also be moving away from her.

I groan realizing that, with those things in mind, I know I need to do this. Sophie is the expert and if she thinks a girlfriend will keep me in New York, then I need to do whatever she says.

"Okay. I'll do it." I breathe in deeply and let it out. Sophie starts bouncing up and down on her toes and clapping. "But I'm not dating someone for real, just until I get another contract. And she's going to know it's for show from the start. I don't want to loop someone into this and have them think it's something that it's not. I'm not doing this to get into a long term relationship and I don't want someone expecting that."

"Aww!" She reaches over and playfully pinches my cheeks. I pull my head back and push her hands away with a laugh. Sophie has turned into family in the seven years we've been working together. She's not as close as a sister, but I'd say she's definitely in cousin territory. "You're such a good guy, Charlie. Some woman is going to be very lucky to fake date you."

"Whatever. You're just saying that because you're my agent. You have to."

"Not true, you're a stellar guy. Once you let someone see every side of you and you let them all the way in, they don't have any other choice but to love you."

I smile at her placatingly, but she's wrong. No one knows every side of me, and no one ever will, not even Alana. But I can smile and keep up appearances while I fake date someone. Once I get signed again everything will go back to normal.

"I'll find someone, I don't need to get on a dating app."

"Have you seen the current dating scene, Charlie?" I just stare at her. She knows how long it's been since I've tried to date. "Here look at this."

She shoves her phone at me, a screenshot of a guy's profile lighting it up. The man is in his late thirties and standing in one of the dirtiest bathrooms I've ever seen. There are stains all over part of the countertop and behind him the sheetrock in the wall is completely torn apart, so there is a gaping hole in the wall. The shower curtain is pulled back to reveal a grimy tiled tub and a broken shelf. The guy himself has one arm out of his shirt, leaving that side bunched up around his shoulder. He's flexing his (imaginary) muscle, but really it just looks like he got caught in the middle of taking off his shirt.

His bio says he's married.

"Married? What the hell?"

"I know. If men have anything, it's the audacity. You haven't even seen the worst of it, this was the second photo on his profile."

She scrolls up and shows me a photo of the guy in his bedroom. His disgusting bedroom. He has *Among Us!* sheets on his twin sized bunk bed, let me remind you he's in his thirties, and there's trash everywhere. Without saying anything, Sophie reaches over and zooms in on a box sticking out from the top of the bed. A box that absolutely should have stayed in his side table drawer where no one would have ever seen it. I want to puke.

"Sophie, did this guy like you?" I ask, alarm clear in my voice. I have to cover my mouth to keep from gagging.

"Just one of many. You're sure you don't need any help?"

"I'll figure something out."

"Whatever you say, boss man."

This whole thing is extremely overwhelming and makes me uncomfortable, but I don't have a choice. I have three months to work on my public image and while I don't want to pretend to date someone just for some bogus media stunt, I know I need to. I just need to figure out who.

About the Author

Baleigh Jayne is a Texas native who loved to read and write from a very early age. She found herself immersed in worlds outside of her own and in the lives of characters she'd never met, and longed to create ones of her own. Fast forward a few years, and she decided to make her dreams a reality by becoming an author. Now, Baleigh writes contemporary romance that is full of light-hearted fun, swoony kisses, and deep lessons that just about anyone can learn from.

When Baleigh isn't writing or posting on Instagram, you can find her sipping on a Diet Coke and listening to Taylor Swift, or hanging out with her nephew Elliott. She also loves cozying up with a good book or spending time with her family.

To learn more, visit her website https://authorbaleighjayne.com/ or follow her on Instagram @authorbaleighjayne.